The
Optical Effects
of Lightning

S. J. Kember

A Wild Wolf Publication

Published by Wild Wolf Publishing in 2011

Copyright © 2011 S. J. Kember

ISBN: 978-1-907954-11-5

www.wildwolfpublishing.com

That one can put reality into the past and thus work backwards in time is something I have never claimed. But that one can put the possible there, or rather that the possible may put itself there at any moment, is not to be doubted.

Henri Bergson

Acknowledgements

Cover Art by Mashinc

With thanks to Martin Geupel (www.racoon-artworks.de) for permission to use humming-top

Drawings and Illustrations
Flying buttress – Liz Vasiliou
Gothic house – Liz Vasiliou
Newspaper report – Mashinc
Lightning illustration – Mashinc (based on 'A Lightning Primer
from the GHCC' http://thunder.msfc.nasa.gov/primer)
Cell fusion – Mashinc (based on Kenneth L. White
'Electrofusion of Mammalian Cells' in Jac A. Nickoloff (Ed.)
*Animal Cell Electroporation and Electrofusion Protocols. Methods in
Molecular Biology*, Humana Press, 1995)
Trap door effect – Mashinc
Nose pyramid – Mashinc
Building notice (online) – Mashinc
Web links, online formatting and lightning photo – Eleanor Dare

There are many people to thank for their technical and/or moral support, and for their advice about analogue and digital forms of writing. They include my agent, Laetitia Rutherford of Mulcahy Conway Associates and other patient and encouraging readers: Janis Jefferies, Bryn Musson, Bill Schwarz, Carey Smith, Phil Terry, Liz Vasiliou and Joanna Zylinska. Thanks also to Michèle Allardyce (aka Mashinc), Jan Campbell, Eleanor Dare, Gary Hall, Linda France, Kath James, Bec Hanley, Frances Hubbard, Ann Kember, John Kember, Phil Kember, Lester Mills and Pete Woodbridge.

I'm grateful to Goldsmiths, University of London for granting me a period of leave to write this book. Much of the thinking behind it – about time, change, media, bodies and technologies – is the product of many conversations over many years with my students and colleagues.

One of the things I've learned is that when other writers say that their book would not have existed without the help and support of others, including significant others, they mean it quite literally. Writing was always a collaborative process and in its digital incarnations it is becoming more so. I share this book, if not its faults, with a number of people. I'm very grateful to all of them and most of all to Liz.

Opening Statement

The following alterations to my schedule occurred on the day of my lover's disappearance.

June 9th

6.20am

I got up, showered, dressed and readied myself for work as usual. I didn't immediately notice that Suhail wasn't there because I had slept in my own bed that night. We had not argued, but Suhail had gone to bed early and, since he is a light sleeper, I didn't want to disturb him. It's not unusual, and I heard nothing untoward during the night. I generally sleep well.

7.00am

Suhail's bed was empty and unmade. I straightened the covers, and thought that he must have gone away and forgotten to tell me. This seemed much more likely than me forgetting that he had told me, but I checked my BlackBerry anyway. There was no entry concerning Suhail on that day, or the next. He is not inclined to get up early, or go in for morning exercise. I only wish he was.

In any case, when I checked the bathroom he'd clearly taken some toiletries with him. His overnight bag was missing from the cupboard, and his wardrobe revealed that he had packed a few of his clothes, though not many. This seemed to confirm my assumption. I was just a little put out that he had planned to be away from home without telling me first. I tried his mobile phone, but it was turned off.

7.45am

I was 5 minutes late for work, and when I checked my emails, there was nothing from Suhail.

8.30-9.30am

Spoke with clients and met with colleagues as usual.

9.30am

When I returned to my desk, I quickly checked for any text or answer phone messages on my mobile phone – I keep this for personal use – but there was nothing from Suhail.

11.30am

As well as carrying out my normal activities for this time of the morning, I phoned home. I don't know why I did this, and was clearly not expecting an answer. I got my own voice on the answer machine. Suhail was not there.

12.30pm

I was tempted to phone again, and even to go home at lunch time. I find the reasons for this difficult to explain. Perhaps his sudden absence (I did not yet think of it as a disappearance), had unnerved me more than I thought. I calmed myself, and realised that I couldn't go anyway, as I had a lunch appointment with an outsourced researcher. After lunch, I did try the email and then the mobile again, but was not surprised when it was still switched off. I reasoned that this was because he was with someone. Unlike me, he isn't accustomed to having more than one conversation at a time, and he dislikes being interrupted by his own phone or anyone else's. For me, it is a valuable tool of the trade. Mine is never off.

2.00-5.30pm
A normal afternoon.

5.30pm
No email from Suhail, who was unlikely to be near a computer. I left a message on his mobile, pointing out that he'd forgotten to tell me where he was, and would he please do so at the earliest opportunity.

6.00pm
I travelled straight home, exercised and ate alone. This did not seem particularly strange. Although I prefer us to eat together, Suhail sometimes finishes his day between 6.00 and 8.00pm, so it isn't always possible.

8.00-10.00pm
I did an evening's work, as I always do.

10.00pm
Instead of watching the news, I decided to log on to Suhail's computer to see if he had made any arrangements by email. I only read the subject headings, but as far as I could see, he hadn't. I quickly scanned his desk for any notes, or slips of paper, that might indicate where he was. There was only a scattered pile of books, and his journal. I hesitated to open the journal, but resolved to do so if I didn't hear from him in the next day or so. At that time I was confident that I would.

11.00pm
I slept well.

§

This is the second statement I have made about Suhail's disappearance. I hope, and trust that this time it will be taken more seriously. Previously, you, the authorities, concluded that there was no evidence of any harm or wrongdoing, and that since he was not a minor, you couldn't justify the use of scarce resources in what would undoubtedly be a futile search. You informed me that the majority of people who go missing return within weeks or months, or they do not return at all. I don't doubt your wisdom or professionalism, but I have waited now for exactly twelve months, and I have reason to believe that a search would not be futile and is, in fact, necessary.

Since the day of his disappearance on June 9th, I have amassed various forms of evidence as to the reason for it, if reason is the right word. I also have evidence pertaining to the events that followed. It is still not possible to say precisely where he is, but I will be able to indicate the region, and I want him found for his own sake and mine. As I said in my first statement, Suhail and I have been a couple for more than a decade, and we have lived together for most of that time. This is not easy for me. The last year has been a very difficult period of great uncertainty and upheaval. I want you to understand that. It has affected my work if not my health. At first, as I've already set out in a schedule of the day in question, my routine was barely broken. I assumed that wherever he was, he would soon be back. However, after a day had passed I became concerned, and after 3 days I reported him missing. By then I didn't know what to think, and my confusion must have added to your circumspection.

I recall that questions were asked about the nature and the state of our relationship. I had to expect that. I was equally certain that he hadn't left me, but I couldn't prove it to your satisfaction or, at the time, to mine. Suhail is not the leaving type. Far from it. He finds it hard if not impossible to let things go, and his tenacity, alongside his impetuosity and other characteristics, which I will outline, has made him a danger to himself and others. That is what I intend to demonstrate. That is the purpose of this file. Suhail is dangerous and he needs help. Your help.

A statement alone was clearly not enough to persuade you to seek him and intercept him, so I will compile a case file. I will supply all of the evidence that I have. It will be enough. I do not mean to presume or interfere. I am not trying to do your job for you. I am doing this in order to assist you. I will arrange my evidence clearly and logically. I will be thorough, careful and objective. I trust that you will appreciate my methods. Although I am trained in another profession, I hope that you will find me collegiate. Once I have put the evidence of harm and of wrongdoing before you, then duty and justice must and will prevail. I am certain of this.

The devil, as they say, will be in the detail, but the essence of my case is as follows. Suhail did not leave me. He went to find his brother, who had himself been missing for many years. I will state immediately that this was never going to be a straightforward journey or a simple reunion. Their relationship had been as fraught as it was intense, or at least that is the way in which Suhail judged it. It so dominated his mind that it further unbalanced what was already a quite extreme personality and determined the way in which he felt, thought, and acted in the world. It was all-encompassing. Need I say more? It is not easy to care for a man whose feelings for his brother overwhelm him. I persisted, obviously, but with little doubt that I was the third party to a relationship that pre-existed our own. I learnt to accommodate myself, and to put any feelings of resentment to one side, because Suhail and I were a match. We really were. What happened then, his disappearance, was not unpredictable, but it was still a blow. The sort that drops you heavily to the ground. I may be down then, but I am not defeated.

Although my performance levels have not been as high as usual recently, my job helps, as it always has, in part by providing a routine. I will set this out in more detail. I said I would be thorough, and I am sure you will find it of use.

§

I work in the city, and my role has developed from that of a personal financial advisor. As the title suggests, I worked mainly with individuals, offering not so much financial advice as planning. I'd use my knowledge of tax laws and investments and so on, to give clients a range of options depending on their long or short-term goals. A planner's work always begins with a consultation, where you gain information about the client's current financial state, and their objectives. The plan must be comprehensive and tailor-made, identifying problem areas and selecting investments which are compatible with each individual's expectations, or need for a return, as well as their approach to risk. You can certainly learn a lot about a person through their attitude to money. I've always thought it odd, but conventionally most plans are not written down.

Face-to-face meetings with established clients happen about once a year, in order to supply updated information on potential investments and find out whether they have experienced any career or life changes, which would affect their financial status or their goals. Whether it is through marriage, divorce, a birth or death in the family, disability or sickness, retirement, promotion or relocation, planning is also about managing change.

I've brought a lot of those skills forward to my current job, and they have helped me in other ways too. For example, the submission of all the documents in this case file is a product of them. Some planners buy and sell financial products like mutual funds, assurance, insurance, mortgages etc. But I didn't, preferring to avoid the role of banker and concentrate on people, sometimes taking over responsibility for their entire portfolios. A reputation for client commitment, a good customer base, and a wide network of business and social contacts are still invaluable to me in my present role, which differs in part in that I now have 2 sets of clients to deal with (i.e. individuals on the one hand, and various companies on the other) and my function is to mediate between the two. This is how I would describe my typical day before Suhail left:

6.20am

I am woken by the alarm on my BlackBerry and, after some moderate exercise, I spend the next 25 minutes showering, dressing and getting ready for work. Even though I don't often deal with clients face-to-face, but more by phone and email, I believe it is important to maintain an appropriate image and that there is never any excuse for shabbiness. I wear a dark suit, with a blue shirt and a plain tie. I don't eat breakfast, but I prepare a pot of filter coffee the night before. I drink this with a sweetener and some water while checking the contents of my briefcase, and making sure I am ready for the day.

7.00am

I look in on my partner before leaving. He likes me to try to wake him, but I don't try too hard. Usually I speak his name quietly, or touch him lightly on the shoulder. I don't wait for a response.

7.40am

By the time I arrive at the office, I have already read the paper, and will open my post and then read and respond to emails. I expect between 20 and 30 to have arrived over night, mostly from colleagues and clients overseas.

8.30am

I now generally make one or two phone calls to the clients I need to catch before their day begins, and they become unavailable due to a succession of meetings. I am looking here for information, or what some might call gossip concerning the industry, and specifically any prescribed or required changes in personnel; who is in, who is out and so on.

9.00am

Meet with colleagues to discuss the day's strategy, which I oversee. I delegate research tasks, collate the results of research and networking, and ask each individual to set out their personal objectives for the day. They are assessed in relation to the previous day's objectives, and to the weekly and monthly targets we agreed. The emphasis is on self-evaluation but it is also my job to help them critique their own performance.

9.30am

I return to my desk in order to carry out the paperwork on the client calls I made earlier in the morning, and to make more if necessary. I always prioritise the needs of the various companies who have contacted me in the early part of the day, as this is when they are most likely to discuss their requirements and their problems in a full and open way. Quite simply, I have to get to them before the stresses and demands of their day begin in earnest. I need to get under the skin of any given organisation, and understand how it operates – how it thinks – in order to assist it in filling highly specific roles, and ensuring that it remains true to its identity, its manifesto, and its position in the marketplace.

My commitment is absolute, and I consider myself to be a representative of the client. I must have a complete and total understanding of them in order to act on their behalf. This takes time and a great deal of attention to detail if their goals, and therefore mine, are to be reached. My morning routine also determines my afternoons, since this is when, tired and possibly jaded, individuals looking for change are most receptive to an approach.

11.30am

I review the morning's activities and enter client calls for the following morning and afternoon in to my BlackBerry. More paperwork.

12.30pm

Lunch time. I prefer to go out alone and enjoy a brisk walk or run and a sandwich outside. This helps me to process my thoughts, and provides a refreshing change of scene. However, working lunches are often necessary, and may involve someone from my firm or from either of my client bases. By choice, I don't drink. At most I will have a glass of brandy to help me unwind at the end of the day. Neither do I overeat, as this will impair my performance in the afternoon, and, unlike others in my line of work, I have no intention of becoming bloated or letting myself go. I deplore over-indulgence of any kind. It is too much a feature of city life, of modern life, for that matter.

2.00pm

I now begin the more delicate task of dealing with individual clients. This invariably involves a degree of research and networking. My job is to be highly selective in my approach to these people, and to make contact with them as discreetly as possible. I will draw on my specialist knowledge of the industry, but if their expertise falls outside of this, I will employ in-house or, if needed, outsourced researchers.

There is a fine art to approaching, and having to build a rapport very quickly with a complete stranger. You start with a sensitivity to your environment, an ability to adapt – even your accent and expressions – to your circumstances, and the person you are speaking to. This ability is inherent, but must develop, and become very finely tuned. It is the key to success. An older colleague told me, when I started out, that if my client smoked, I had to smoke. If he drank, I drank – regardless of my own predilections. It is a small sacrifice for what, potentially, is a great reward, which is securing a placement, a perfect fit.

I don't pretend that the reward isn't a financial one. This is how I earn my living. But it is much more than that. It is not only a percentage of a 6 figure salary. It is what I'm all about. Unlike many of my associates who, through a life of ease have weakened their backbones, I relish the challenge of a cold-call and of potential rejection. Without wishing to sound arrogant, I don't think I have ever experienced a complete rejection, an unequivocal no. Hardly ever. At the very least, people are flattered by the approach, and even in the unlikely event that they are happy where they are, they are going to be curious about other options, other possibilities for themselves, as well as any insight they can gain about the movement or otherwise of others.

I am careful to obtain more information than I give out, but also careful to make it appear as if it were the other way round. People like to talk and love to gossip, especially when they should be working. I get a great deal of what we call market intelligence from these afternoon (or evening) exchanges. I build up my client base, and even if there is going to be no fit on this occasion, I have carried out a valuable public relations exercise. I am naturally patient, and am as content to close the deal in a few years when the client finally comes back to me, as in a few days, weeks or months. Planning is vital, as I said. No call is wasted.

5.30pm

I create some order out of the notes I have taken and schedule evening phone calls in my BlackBerry. I do find these new technologies to be such useful instruments. I check emails and ensure that I have my priorities organised for the following day.

6.00pm

I leave the office and travel home, sometimes walking part of the way if my timetable allows it. Again, I like to clear my head ready for the next phase of the day. I try to avoid office based social events more than once a month, which is adequate for basic team building. I exercise for 30 minutes, using the bike and other equipment at home. I like to eat my evening meal at the table with my partner, and hear about what he has done with his day before carrying on with my own.

8.00pm

I receive and make scheduled calls to clients after first checking my emails. I often pick up last minute changes of plan this way. If I'm responding to the client's initiative (rather than cold-calling them), it obviously speeds the process up and indicates the likelihood of success in the short or medium, rather than the long term. It also gives me license to probe them for their strengths and weaknesses, and to channel their own desire for change in the direction I have in mind for them.

Once more, the exchange of information must appear to be, and indeed, is mutual. It is between client and client with me as the go-between. It amuses me that none of the 3 parties involved need meet in person until the deed is already done. It sounds unlikely, but people are a lot more relaxed and off-guard when there is some form of communications screen between myself and them, and they are speaking from the privacy of their own homes or offices. Trust me, the method works. I am at the top of my profession, with a reputation for matchmaking and the rewards that come with it. It's a great job. I enjoy it. I really do.

10.00pm
I usually finish now and watch the evening news to relax.

11.00pm
To bed for my usual minimum of 7 hours and 20 minutes sleep.

§

The morning after the disappearance, I borrowed Suhail's address book from his desk and made a few phone calls after my 9.00am meeting. Unfortunately, I didn't get any leads. I only got answer machines, or dead-end trails. At best I spoke to the occupants of houses once inhabited by friends he had not seen for some time. I tried again from home in the evening, but my efforts were cut short by some demanding client calls. First thing the following day, I accessed his online bank account, which I manage for him anyway, because he is so bad with his finances. A brief scan revealed that there was no activity I was not already aware of.

Wherever Suhail was, he did not appear to have taken a significant amount of money with him. So where was he, and when was he coming back? I didn't know, and I didn't like not knowing. What if something had happened? I was powerless to help. It crossed my mind that he might be trying to worry me, but that didn't make any sense. It wasn't consistent with Suhail's behaviour. All the same, my last night's sleep had been disturbed by a dream I couldn't remember, and I was becoming distracted and less efficient at work. I was going to need to do something, and I decided to visit my local police station the next day if I hadn't heard from him by then.

I felt foolish to be honest because, at that stage, there was so little I could tell the officer that I spoke to. I woke up one morning and my lover had gone. I don't know why or where. I hadn't exactly sold it to the young man, and couldn't blame him for taking little interest. I was so noncommittal that I wouldn't even have blamed him if he'd been slightly suspicious of me, but he was kind. He took down some details, such as age, address, occupation, the last time I'd seen Suhail – which was at about 10pm on the 8th. Was there anything unusual about his behaviour that night, or in the days preceding it? No; nothing out of the ordinary. He'd been working too hard, that's all. So perhaps he was merely enjoying a break, a few days well-earned rest? I had to agree that this was a rational explanation. What else could he say? He was unable to explain why Suhail hadn't told me where he was going. Finally, and with touching delicacy, he asked if, on account of the long hours we were both working, there had been tension between us, and perhaps some harsh words? Was there another close friend he might be staying with? Was there any sign, in recent months of a new relationship? I couldn't suppress what must have sounded like a dismissive exclamation. I hope it did not cause offence.

Suhail's strange preoccupations had more or less confined him to the house, and if there was one thing I was certain of it was his fidelity. There had been promiscuity in the past, but those days were behind him. The interview was inconclusive, frustrating and, to a degree, humiliating. Even though I had expected it, and even though it was not unreasonable, I resented having to discuss my private life with someone so fresh-faced. We were not even in a separate room. Anyone could have heard. It was not his fault, he was doing his job, but I do not discuss such things with anyone under normal circumstances. I do not see the need for it. Others may chatter and brag about what goes on behind closed doors but I believe that there is, and always should be a clear line between the personal and professional. Do not get me wrong. I am not ashamed of who I am. But in my line of work especially, where discretion is so important and I must earn the trust and respect of people of all ages, from different backgrounds, it is better for all concerned if I keep this aspect of my identity under wraps.

As I said, the young officer – he must have been in his early twenties – carried out his assignment competently. Yet as you will see, and as I failed to convey to him at the time, there is a lot more to Suhail's disappearance than a lovers' tiff. Understanding it requires a more worldly and experienced mind. It requires the mind of a detective, such as yourself. As for me, I realised that I needed to provide more information. I needed to do some research. On the morning of June 13th I cancelled all evening calls for two days in order to read the whole of Suhail's journal.

§

I can't exactly say I wish I hadn't. I discovered nothing wholly new or out of character, and yet everything I knew appeared to be distorted almost beyond recognition. This document suggested that something to my mind utterly unthinkable was about to happen. I've said that Suhail has a brother, and that this brother, Saeed, had himself disappeared. In his journal, Suhail implies that he is the cause of Saeed's disappearance. I will allow him to say what he did, but the point is that Saeed subsequently left, leaving Suhail to his guilt. It quickly became apparent, from my reading, that Suhail's sense of guilt was far greater than I could otherwise have known. He spoke of it only the once. It led him to interpret Saeed's disappearance as a form of punishment and indeed, as a harbinger of revenge. It led him, in a way which is clearly disproportionate and irrational, to fear a reunion, and at the same time to desire it above all other things. In short, it affected his mind.

23

Suhail became trapped inside a mind which was preoccupied, almost to the point of insanity, with the prospect of a reunion with his brother. What is more, in order to protect himself from his imaginary fear of revenge, he generated a fantasy in which he could somehow repair his relationship with his brother. He fantasised that he could do this through a single act of transformation which would, in fact, if it were ever to be carried out, endanger them both. It is difficult to clarify such wayward thoughts and imaginings but I will endeavour to do so, to the best of my ability. In order to find Suhail you will first need to understand what drives him, however farfetched and ridiculous it might be. What drives Suhail, and channels his guilt, is his belief in the power of transformation.

This goes beyond what any normal individual might expect or hope for in terms of a change in their lifestyle, career or identity. As I've indicated, my work puts me in daily contact with lifestyle and career changes, and I am of course aware that people can change their identities too. Many people change their image repeatedly in the course of a lifetime. Some even change their names. Most of us strive for self-improvement and the realisation of personal goals, but Suhail was never interested in this. Suhail became interested in a much more radical idea of change. It was an idea he derived from his reading.

It is evident from the material I have examined, and from the books in his study, that Suhail was familiar with the literature of metamorphosis. A cursory inspection of this literature is enough to reveal a formula in which

24

people turn in to animals and insects, or combine with them in order to form disturbing chimeras. In some cases, they are transformed by a bolt of lightning. Suffice it to say that because of its association with a terrible incident in his youth – a violent incident involving himself and his brother – lightning is the key to understanding the nature of the transformation Suhail seeks. From the material that follows you will learn, as I did, the full extent of his preoccupation.

It is all too clear from his journal that Suhail constantly thought, read and wrote about lightning. He generally refrained from talking to me about it, presumably in order to conceal his fixation and protect his fantasy. He became fascinated by the power of it. To an extent, this is understandable, but his fascination became too extreme. Lightning is certainly a significant, to some minds spectacular natural phenomenon. But Suhail began to think of it more as a supernatural, even magical one, the sort that can change one entity into another, or combine the two in one unfortunate hybrid. In other words, he was too inclined to believe in the kind of nonsense he was reading, forgetting, if he ever really knew, that this was mostly myth. It was only a story.

Suhail got his taste for stories, reading and ideas from his university education. He could have studied a useful subject like maths or engineering, but he didn't. He could have chosen something vocational, and it would undoubtedly have been better for him if he had. He would have given himself the chance to acquire a trade, to get a real job, to live in the real world instead of getting stuck inside his own mind where fiction could slide into fact and events that happened long ago could fester and grow out of all proportion. If you ask me, it was a waste.

It is not necessary for me to explain exactly how Suhail's imaginary lightning-based transformation might occur, or what it could result in. He himself addresses the detail in his writing, and if you do not find him and stop him, if it is not already too late, the consequences will be evident soon enough. I fear that whatever the precise nature of his fantasy, his own disappearance signaled his intention to carry it out. This can only portend harm to himself, his brother, and anyone else who might be obliged to deal with the outcome, meaning me. I do not hold literature or learning responsible for this, despite my reservations. I am not an ignorant man but a practical one. I have learnt a lot, if not from books then from people, experience, professionalism and human decency. I know enough about life to realise that only those whose values are already corrupt can be led to transgress the laws of human nature, that only those with weak and desperate minds latch on to fantasies in which they are completely changed in to heaven knows who, or what.

§

There are three principle documents in my case file, discounting my own statements.

Suhail's Journal
This appears to have been written intermittently during the months preceding his disappearance. In my view, it is not a journal, as much as an exaggerated series of reflections and inventions, made by someone

who was preoccupied with his past, and who came to believe that he could free himself of it through a single reckless act. If I have found the reflections difficult to read, I have found the inventions still harder, because they concern me, or a fictional character that represents me.

This character is presented in far from flattering terms, and is clearly an archetype derived from literature. Suhail's engagement with literary themes and figures obscures his reality, but becomes a means by which he can deal with his troubled and deep-rooted feelings about his brother. There is nothing to suggest his present whereabouts in this document, but it does constitute a vital element of my case.

You will doubtless have less difficulty with this material than I did, and once you have read it, you will understand why Suhail left, and for what nefarious purpose. I should make it clear that I typed up these handwritten pages myself, without making any alterations to the content, frustrating as this was at particular times. Instead, I have allowed myself a small number of interventions in order to correct the factual inaccuracies of which I am aware, and where necessary in order to defend myself against the worst excesses of Suhail's fevered imagination.

The contents of this journal are not only injurious to me. They promote values that may be fashionable, but are not necessarily correct. I am not only referring to the circulation of pernicious ideas, but to Suhail's partial and unconvincing renouncement of his so-called alternative and cosmopolitan lifestyle. By cosmopolitan I mean

27

everybody mixing with everybody else. The idea of the melting pot. A nice idea, perhaps, but that is all. Reality is different. Reality brings conflict and confusion. People are what they are in essence. They don't mix. I believe in types. I understand them. It may be possible, even probable that opposites will attract, but one type will never turn into another. Look at me and Suhail.

Unlike him, I never felt the need to explore my social environment or experiment with my identity. I know who I am. I do not need others to define me. I have a strong sense of self, a very strong sense of self because it is built on a moral foundation that I am not ashamed to call traditional. I am talking about the sanctity of human nature, and in particular, the value of the individual.

As I told you, I work closely with people on a one-to-one basis. I learn everything about them. I have to. It's my job. I know much more than what they want to do for a living. I know much more than they want me to, including their fears and desires. I even help to shape them. Nobody could appreciate the fact that people are unique more than I do. Each person requires a specific kind of attention. Each person demands something different of me. No two people are the same, and no two people could or should ever, under any circumstances, be combined.

Email messages June 15th - 24th
I heard from Suhail after I'd read his journal. I slept fitfully on the night of the 14th, and awoke feeling tired. I was not my usual self. Suhail had been gone for a week, and his absence was more, not less troubling as each day passed. My routine was increasingly punctuated by

28

checks on all potential modes of communication, and my days were being stretched at both ends.

The more I understood about Suhail's reasons for leaving, the more concerned I was to make some kind of contact. I was relieved to discover an email at lunchtime on the 15th. My relief was short-lived. It lasted only a couple of days. Then there was a break during which I didn't hear from him for about another week. After that, well, something happened; that much is certain. I have reason to believe he is still out there, and that he needs to be found. I heard nothing after June 24th, and the last message was incomprehensible.

Even though Suhail hinted about his location, he was not willing, or able to be exact, otherwise I would have gone there immediately. I do not like having to say this, but I need your help in order to find him. That is why I have included a full transcript of our email exchanges.

The Newspaper Report
The full meaning of the email transcript was made clear to me when I discovered an online feature article a short while ago. It is called 'Of Murder and Metamorphosis,' by S. J. Kay. It takes as its subject a local news report, about a photograph of a man running on a beach as he is struck by lightning. The photograph was notable both for what it did, and didn't reveal about the victim, and for what happened to it subsequently as it circulated to a wider audience.

I have been unable to trace the original image. It is not reproduced in Kay's article, which consequently remains, in my opinion, purely speculative and of dubious journalistic integrity. Nevertheless I include it here because its subject, if not its conclusion, is directly relevant. There is, I fear, little room to doubt that the timing of the news report coincides with that of the emails.

§

This final principle document brings my case file more or less up to date. I believe that it will provide sufficient evidence for an investigation and, I trust, a search. Without wishing to pre-empt your response, I will simply add, for the moment, that what links these documents together is Suhail's obsession with Saeed. Saeed is everywhere here, and he is the real reason why Suhail was so concerned with lightning and transformation. For Suhail, lightning was to become the means by which he could re-unite with his brother. It was to become the means by which he could transform not only their relationship, but their very beings.

What follows then is the account of a man, offered predominantly in his own words, who comes to believe that he can change everything about himself, and thereby undo a harm committed in the past. This harm is presented at first as an accident, and then as a crime. It can be undone, Suhail believes, by remaking himself. Literally. That is, he believes he can totally recreate, from the beginning and with no real blueprint, not his appearance, but his very flesh, not his image, but every aspect of his identity, including his identity as a human being. No wonder he didn't tell me. Suhail was and is a fantasist, a self-inventor for whom the concept of the self became as malleable and as transient as that

30

of the geneticist's cell. I'll allow him to try and explain how. I am not a literary man myself, but it is clear that his similes and metaphors collapsed, so that things actually were other things, or were in the process of becoming so. I don't know what to say about this. As I've indicated, he wasn't entirely well.

My own views on the subject of Suhail's delusions are clear. I have endeavoured to exclude them from my editorial input, but I will say here, and for the record, that I am vehemently opposed to the attitudes he describes. The idea of a person undergoing any kind of metamorphosis is abhorrent to me, because it undermines what it means to be human. I do not care for myths and stories, still less for current thinking and practice about what can be done in a laboratory test tube. Human nature exists, and nobody has the right to meddle with it. It is the bedrock of our laws, our civil duty and moral responsibility. I do not need to tell you that. In any case, I contend, and you will surely agree, that the journal is, for the most part, a work of fiction not of fact, driven by Suhail's half-crazed obsession with his brother.

The next two documents show something of the consequences of this mental imbalance, if I can call it that without suggesting that he is actually insane. I do not believe that Suhail is really mad, any more than I believe that he is really dead. What I do believe is that the crime to which he ultimately confesses, far from being undone, may well have been mirrored with effects as yet unknown, but about which you will doubtless form your own considered opinion. Perhaps, through pursuing his fantasy of metamorphosis, he has somehow metamorphosed. Or perhaps it is he himself, not his past, that is now undone. Either way, I submit the following as more than just the case of a missing person.

Suhail's Journal

It wasn't just an orphanage rule that forbade me from being in the girls' dormitory, and I didn't mean to break it, but I did. Perhaps that's why the air tasted bittersweet, catching me at the back of my throat. I covered my nose with my arm and looked around. Lonely wide-eyed dolls in shabby dresses stared back, as if they were accusing me of being something I was not. I didn't care about them. I liked the pictures, because they were of pop stars rather than planes, and didn't just cover up cracks in the wall. Then I saw, in a far corner, a collection of mysterious objects that stood out of the gloom, glimmering in the filtered light from the filthy windows. I made my way towards them, treading carefully on the bare floor, trying not to make a sound in the unfamiliar space. It reminded me of being in church for the first and only time, in the days when my brother still held my hand. I had become restless and he led me away, weaving between the pews and columns, making up stories about the saints. I worshipped him then, like a god, like a parent. He protected me from scornful looks, and stood between me and other children although he was only a child himself. He was always there, at my side, an extension of my body. No-one else could get near me.

I examined red bottles with gold-coloured tops, silver trinkets and delicate boxes full of precious things. I handled them all, touching them with my fingertips and putting them back exactly where they belonged. Something in particular caught my eye, a polished string of black beads draped on top of an oval mirror. As I reached for them, the half-light switched to semi-darkness and something like realisation flickered in the face of my reflected image. I was still a boy, a skinny boy with brown skin and ears that needed growing into, but I saw that being myself had a cost that I was only just starting to pay. I knew my brother wouldn't like it, but I had to have the necklace. It was the same colour as my too long, too wavy hair, and matched the bag that I wore, like a satchel across my chest. I was putting it over my head when I heard thunder in the distance and much closer, a bang on the door opposite the dorm I was in.

A few years before, we'd been together all the time. We were inseparable, they said. We only played with each other and never seemed to need or want anyone else. My brother preferred it that way. He was happy, always smiling, always helping me do things that he could hardly have known how to do himself, like tying shoelaces and reading books. We were twins, but I must have been the youngest one, if only by an hour or a minute. The sound of thunder brought a memory of when we were two or three years old, and the orphanage was still new to me, a scary adventure full of unopened doors, strange noises and vast, shadowy rooms. I stuck willingly to my brother's side, but someone, one of the adults, had got hold of me and led me away. He was showing me something, I think it was the storm itself. He was pointing at the window, but I couldn't see what he was pointing at. Then, as if an invisible giant or ghostly monster had stamped his foot right in front of me, as if he had roared and clapped and blotted out the world in a flash, I was thrown off my feet and fell over. I scrambled up as fast as I could and ran, howling towards my brother, whose arms were already out for me, and who lifted me up even though he wasn't really bigger, even though he barely could, and held me tight.

The others were at school, but it was the anniversary of our parents' death, and Saeed and I had the day off. He paused, and then knocked a second, and a third time as if to emphasise that I wasn't where I ought to be. I kept still and waited,

35

feeling the stormy, perfumed air pressing on the sides of my head, making my stomach turn and my eyes bulge. To distract myself I imagined them popping out on large red springs, waving around in front of me like something you'd buy in a joke shop. It didn't work. The minutes passed slowly until I thought he must have gone. Then there was a single, heavy blow that fired splinters of paint and rattled the door in its frame. There would never have been a door between us before. It was as though we'd been glued together. We were our own company, our own sibling and our own parent and child. We were everything to each other for the first four or five years of our life, and then I, or something in me, started to change. I was not even aware of it at first, but Saeed saw it, and I saw it through him. I saw a look of surprise turn into disapproval, and a look of disapproval turn to anger. I had not seen anger in my brother's face before. It hardened it. Even at that age, we are hardwired to detect the slightest sign of difference in others. Even at that age, Saeed knew exactly what the difference was. I think he felt let down by it, insulted, and abandoned.

The hallway between the girls' and boys' dormitories had, like most of the orphanage staff, not been updated since the last century. There were evenly spaced holes in the plaster where paintings of 'our illustrious founders' had hung, and the wallpaper, which turned flowers into witches as you watched, was faded, but still spooky enough to stop anyone from breaking the rule about dawdling. Saeed was already striding away as I stepped into one of the spotlights made by a naked bulb dangling low from the high, cobwebby ceiling. By now, I'd become familiar with the sight of his back and, since he'd caught me holding hands with Jack, I no longer tried to hide the gestures that offended him and the feelings on which they were based. Jack and I were only playing a game, and he'd gone now anyway, back to his alcoholic mother. There was no reason for Saeed to be jealous of him or of anyone, if jealousy is what it was. My brother was all I ever knew of love. Sometimes I think he still is. He had been horrible that morning as I got dressed, snapping at me and throwing my shoes out of reach. He was worse at breakfast, provoking another boy until they started to fight and then swearing at one of the carers. He never did that. He had never behaved that way. It was as though, at seven years of age and on the day that marked the absence of parents from our lives, he had looked at me and decided he had nothing left to lose.

He turned around sharply: 'Come on! We're going to be late and it's your fault as usual. What the hell do you think you were doing in there? You better not have taken anything.'

I followed him at a distance, turning into the corridors that echoed his footsteps as he turned out of them. I followed him past the closed door of the common room, onto the landing, and down the main wooden staircase, which had been stripped of its worn runner, and which was, after so many years of cover, still dark with resin and sticky under foot. As I grabbed the last newel post I heard thunder again and Mr Jackson, the Head Warden, emerged from his office.

'What was that? Who are you? Oh! Sorry, sorry, of course, I apologise. Good day to you – I mean it's not a good day clearly and not because of the weather, but ... I know it's your parents' ... it's not a good day. Well, off you go then, off you go. I'm too busy to stand around and talk,' he said, glancing nervously around him as if he feared the ghosts of wardens past.

I walked out onto the driveway, where the car was waiting close by, its engine already running, and its other passengers already seated.

'About time,' said Saeed, leaning towards the open door and glaring up at me with large brown eyes that used to soften whenever they saw me. 'Get in!'

This was his favourite car – a black, angular old beast. Second-hand cars came and, increasingly, went with our wardens and supervisors, but he'd never taken to any of them the way he had to this one. He was always asking if he could wash and polish it, and despite the occasion, he would have been thrilled to be going out in it. Not that he let it show. It beat the minibus, I'll give him that. But we didn't need the minibus today. The car belonged to the two supervisors who were coming with us. They were husband and wife and everyone knew they didn't get along. Saeed would far rather have been in the front, but he had to sit in the back with me. We were going to the cemetery where our parents are buried. They died in a car crash. I never knew them.

Saeed shook his head in disgust as I slid my bottom over the leather seat he'd been buffing in honour of the event, and placed my bag between us.

'What is that?' he demanded, eyeing it again as we pulled away and the tyres jolted in the rain-filled potholes leading down to the road.

'It was in lost property,' I said. 'I like it.'

'It's a handbag!'

'No it's not!'

Outside, the sky grumbled to itself, but neither of us spoke again until we were in open countryside, about a mile or so from the village.

'So what do *you* call it then?' he continued.

'It's a satchel.'

He laughed. I didn't say anything.

'Let's have a look, shall we,' he went on.

'Get off.'

'Get off! Get off!' he mimicked, adding hand actions.

'Give it back – it's mine!'

'It's mine now. Let's see,' he said, releasing the catch.

I made a grab for it again, but his hand closed on mine and twisted it. I pulled away, rubbing my wrist and trying not to cry.

'That hurt!'

'That hurt!'

'Just leave me alone will you?'

'Shall I kiss it better?' he asked, in as high a pitch as he could, leaning in towards me.

I pushed him away, instinctively.

'Don't touch me, woosy-boy,' he said, anger dropping an octave from his voice.

He got hold of my wrist again, and I tried to fight him off, but he pushed my face against the window as a white light flashed and seared raindrops into my eyes. We had been driving in to the storm and suddenly, almost immediately, the thunder was so close that it felt like we were in it, that we were it, the clashing elements; hot and cold.

'What are you going to do now, then?' he asked, with his hand still firmly pressed against the back of my head. My cheek flushed against the glass, and I twisted my body, brought my leg up, and tried to push him away with my foot.

'It kicks, it bites; it scratches. You fight like a girl. Try harder!'

I did, but it only made him laugh again.

Our supervisors never once turned round. They'd been preoccupied with their own clash, and I saw them, out of the corner of my eye, staring rigidly forwards at the windscreen, their mouths making shapes like crushed metal pastry cutters.

'Woos, woosy-boy, woofter,' Saeed chanted, over and over again, getting louder and closer each time. Then he forced me to his lap in a headlock, and bent right over me, so that his voice penetrated my whole body.

'Woos, woosy, woofter. Woos, woosy, woofter. Woos, woosy, woofter.' I heard myself shout 'get-off-me!' and somehow I got free, propelled myself backwards and kicked him away. I was panting, but he leant casually into his door and stared at me. I thought at last he'd stopped, but he seemed to be thinking, considering something, weighing it up. Out of nowhere his expression changed into one I'd never seen before; worse than resentment, darker than disgust. He was still leaning against the door, but he was shouting back at me, contorting his face, throwing his head from side to side as if he was having a fit, or as if some evil thing had possessed him. The voice that came out of him was neither his or an attempt to make fun of mine. It wasn't even human: 'getoffme! getoffme! getoffme!'

He made as if to lunge at me, and as he did so, my feet made contact with his chest. I kicked him harder than I would have believed possible. The energy that ran through me was instant and totally overpowering. There was nothing I could do to resist it. It was as if lightning had passed through me and blasted him out of the door. For a moment, it held him there, suspended mid-fall. His head was back and his arms were raised, as if he'd tried to grab the roof and stop himself. But he never had time. The lightning only held him for a fraction of a second, and then he was gone.

*

The car door flapped shut and then opened again as we came to a stop, replaying the image of my brother's fall. I couldn't believe what my eyes were seeing. I sat there until the first wave of panic hit me from my left, from the direction of the front seat, and then I started thinking about how proud Saeed was of this car. He boasted about its condition and its solid, powerful form. He took care of its minor defects, rubbing at the chrome bumpers to remove tiny rust-spots that had made pores in the metal and thinned its edges, sharpening and serrating them as they reached around the side. One of these edges had caught him as he landed, but I wasn't thinking about how he fell. My eyes shifted to the seat belt he had not been wearing, and back to the open door. I could no longer see Saeed falling, but the lightning that had held him frozen in its path now held me, silently crackling, and still.

There was a second wave of panic from my right, and further away. But then a sharp sound tore through me like shrapnel, and I flung myself out of the car and ran back towards my brother. I didn't know what I would find, or do, but I knew I needed to reach him. It was as though what had just happened had been erased from my mind and I'd been taken back to when I was a toddler and I needed my brother, now, urgently. Instinct and urgency took over, but there was someone in my way. It was the supervisor. I think her name was Jane. She was standing near him, blocking my path,

41

obscuring my view. She must have screamed when she saw what the treacherous car had done to his face.

Jane and her husband were circling Saeed, trying to help him. I wanted to help him too, but I was panting now, struggling for breath, and I couldn't speak or focus my eyes. The figures that were near me were blurring, shading dark and then bright again in the storm. I lost my balance and fell to the ground. The tarmac was pitted and rough and the weathered smell of bitumen galvanised in the sulphurous pools of water close to my nose. It mixed with a substance that was metallic and sickly. I waited, with my eyes closed, until my head had stopped spinning. Then I looked up.

Saeed was sitting exactly as he'd fallen, too close to the side of the car. There was something formless, unspeakable dangling from the right of his face, which was concave now, and covered in blood. Part of his cheek was hanging off, limp and dripping, but he wasn't making a sound. He was sitting upright, with his legs stretched out in front of him, and I watched as he raised his hand and passed it, with exploring fingers, over the flap of flesh turned inside out, towards the hole in his face. His eyes were rounded in shock and fixed onto mine. The lightning that I imagined had passed through me must actually have done, because it is the only way, young as I was, scrawny as I was, I could have kicked my brother out of that heavy, well-oiled door. As it did so, it divided us for good, and from that point onwards, it was hard to believe we'd ever been joined at all.

Saeed'n'Suhail. Our only inheritance was a compound name that everyone used until the day of the accident, when Saeed was finally taken to hospital in an ambulance, and I returned to the orphanage alone. I had never been alone before. I'd never been without my brother. He was, even in recent years, never more than a few minutes away, never more than a room away. Now we were in separate vehicles, and he was noticeably absent from this one, that had betrayed him, and that crawled back, with blood on its claw, to await its own destruction. They were very quiet in the front, on the journey back. I knew that when we got there, I would not be able to explain Saeed's absence to the others, and they would not be able to talk to me. Belted firmly into my seat, I was already lost and already waiting for the brother who was no longer my brother, and for whom I had ceased to exist, even as an insult.

When I got out of the car and went in the front door, I fought the urge to run to the nearest place that was dark, small and hidden. Instead, I went straight to the room I should have left from that morning. I walked, with my head down, up the main staircase, across the landing, back along the second floor corridors and into the boys' dormitory. I sat on the edge of my bed and faced my brother's. He'd asked permission to move it further away from me, or swap with someone else, but they'd said no. It was tidy, and well-made, with a down-turned sheet and the standard issue grey-green blanket. Unlike me he had not covered this with something crocheted, and although it offered no outward sign of comfort, I'd often, when we were younger, found comfort there, with Saeed's body wrapped around mine, because I'd had a nightmare, and I was scared.

*

I was sitting at the same table, in the same seat where, almost a year earlier, we'd celebrated our sixth birthday. I had not been able to do anything much, least of all sleep, in the weeks that Saeed had remained in hospital. Even here, in the middle of the day, the sound of chairs being pulled back made me hear the squealing tyres, and the sound of a sharply scraped plate was too much like that scream. If I closed my eyes I saw the colour of blood, and when I lay in bed with my eyes wide open I saw, over and over again, my brother falling, flickering, gone. Across the table, through the space where he had sat, scowling at me, I caught a movement in the doorway, a buzz of interference in our daily routine. It was Mr Jackson, who didn't normally venture this far, and one of his deputies. They were with Saeed, who had just returned, and who glanced in the room as his escorts hurried by. His face was swollen and covered in bandages, and his right eye was clogged and weeping. Some of the other children who saw him exclaimed, and turned to me as if they were asking a question, but I was picking dried food from my unused fork and couldn't think of an answer.

When, eventually, I was able to leave the canteen, I went to the dormitory and discovered, as I'd suspected, that Saeed's possessions had been moved. I checked all the other beds, but they weren't his, and when I asked where he was, I was told that he'd been moved 'for a period of time' to one of the sick bay rooms upstairs.

'Which one?' I asked. 'For how long?'

'Never you mind,' said the lady who had been brought in to replace Jane. 'That is not something you need to know. Saeed will require some privacy now, and it is our task to secure it.'

'I want to see him.'

'It is not about what you want, young man, but what your brother needs. If you have any concern for this, and given

44

the circumstances I rather think you should, you will be patient and wait.'

I waited for a long time. Saeed remained upstairs on a corridor that no-one had access to, unless they were really ill, and when he came down, he would have nothing to do with me. He preferred to be with Bruno and Fin, unlikely companions who had previously shunned us, and called us names. As 'half-castes,' Saeed and I had proved too difficult to home, but nobody even tried with those two. As far as anyone knew, Fin couldn't read a word, and Bruno preferred to stalk outside and spit at teachers, rather than listen to them. They had engaged in random acts of terror for as long as I could remember, but now they were more intent, more organised, and showed a cunning and cleverness that was beyond them. Now, they didn't get caught swinging a chain like a helicopter blade, or putting broken glass in the shower. They didn't get caught sneaking up on you and threatening you with a penknife, or bending your fingers back, or holding your arm over a flame. Certainly, no-one noticed when they crept to my bed at night and stood over me, whispering tomorrow's torments while I pretended to be asleep.

I spent as much time as I could in the library, because nobody else did. The orphanage had once incorporated its own school, but not for many years, and most of the shelves were empty, their contents lost, sold or stolen. Now there was only one wall of books with faded spines, and a few ragged arm chairs. Still, in time this became my sanctuary, and probably the best part of my education. I loved reading about the natural world, how things work, where they come from; the way they evolve. Drawings and diagrams and all kinds of textbook fascinated me, but none more than the primer I found – on

45

lightning. It was a thin book, a pamphlet really, that had lost its cover and piggy-backed on *Introductory Physics*. I found it by chance, but I read its sepia pages more than once. The very first page, the preface, was amazing. It said that lightning is five times hotter than the sun, and a thunderstorm has as much power as a nuclear bomb. A single flash travels at one hundred thousand miles per second and there are about one hundred flashes per second across the world, or, to put it another way, eight million chances of being hit on any given day. They don't know how people survive lightning strikes, but they do.

One diagram showed how lightning is formed by the movement of ice particles inside a cloud. The small ones rise to the top and the heavy ones sink to the bottom. The ones at the top have a positive charge and the ones at the bottom have a negative charge. The difference between them is what generates electricity and lightning is electrical, as Benjamin Franklin found out. A flash can jump between clouds as well as striking the ground, but it only travels up to two hundred feet at a time. When it's the same distance from the ground it can see things, detect them. As if it chooses them, like it chose me.

In ancient times, people believed that it wasn't lightning that chose you but the gods – Zeus, Thor and so on. They chose you because you were bad, and they used lightning as punishment. Not all of them though. Some gods, like the Navajo's bird god, made lightning to heal people and help things grow. I liked this, I held on to it like I held on to my other memory of lightning, although it was smaller, like we were, and further away. Saeed had held out his arms to me then, picked me up. Was it too much to hope that if I took my punishment, accepted what I deserved, he might eventually do so again? This hope, otherwise fragile, was boosted by a more physical memory, a massive surge of power that ran through my body and rendered me, for a fraction of a second, superhuman, god-like; omnipotent. I had destroyed, but I had experienced the potential to do otherwise.

I read all the fiction too, every novel in the place, and along with my lightning primer, I still have one or two here, in my current sanctuary, my own private library, because I couldn't bear to be parted from them. Unlike Saeed's new friends, mine never mocked the tremor that had started in my legs, and that some of the girls offered to help me out with, by sitting on my knees. I let them, sometimes, when we were in the playground, or recreation room, and Bobby Grigson was there. I'd had a crush on Bobby for as long as I could remember, and, although I told myself I liked books more, I would have done anything to impress him, to be one of his boys, lucky boys, who could rough and tumble with him, and who had no fear of being found out. I'd already been found out, and not just for being a nerd. This was why I was not in Bobby's gang, and never would be. He always ignored me, but the others would mince and blow kisses whenever they caught me on my own. It would have humiliated my brother, and they would never have got away with it if he was around.

Saeed had been back at the orphanage for many months when I got a message to go and see the doctor, Mr Clough. He was a big, baggy man in a shiny brown suit, and his real passion was astronomy. His surgery was a shrine to the stars and planets. They lined his walls in place of medical charts and anatomical drawings. Instead of a skeleton, he had a model of Saturn, complete with the rings. Normally, if you were having an injection for example, he would distract you with irrelevant

47

facts about the constellations. But today, he had some pictures of my brother's face on his desk.

'Come over here, boy,' he said. 'I'm going to explain something.'

He had spread out four large colour photographs. I had time to glimpse a profile, and other angled shots, before he turned on his lamp and bent it directly over the first, frontal image. The light flared on the glossy print, sparing me for a moment.

'Closer,' he ordered. 'You won't see anything from there.'

I edged towards the injury that Saeed had hidden from me more than from anyone else, and as my fingers touched the end of the table, I realised, with horror, why he had.

'It may not be as bad as it looks,' the doctor tried to assure me as I brought my hands up to my mouth, stifling a scream. 'Your brother broke his cheekbone, and the surgeons have repaired that.'

'But the scar …'

'What? Speak clearly!'

I took my hands away and pointed at the photograph. The scar zigzagged from his temple to the upturned corner of his mouth. I could hear Mr Clough talking, trying to explain why it looked like that, but I already knew. It was a lightning scorch – the one that I had put there. I'd branded him with it – my own brother – and there it was; a livid rebuke. One side of his face was contemplating me with a hideous sneer that I could no longer endure. I searched the other side for something more familiar that might – one day – forgive me.

*

I was fifteen when I thought finally, that day had come. Although he'd remained at the same orphanage, Saeed had avoided me for years, persuading the Warden to give him a permanent room in the no-access bay upstairs, and insisting on a transfer to another school. I was in the library when he appeared in the doorway. His head was near the top of the frame, and his hair, that had been short, had grown into a collision of waves that were just like my own. That was how I recognised him. He stood transformed, with his paled scar and his jutting shoulders, like the suggestion of wings. He asked me if he could come in and I nodded, dumbly. My heart was punching my chest and I was afraid to look closely at his face. When he sat down next to me and I closed the book on my lap, I continued to stare at the cover.

'Is that good then?' he asked.

'It's all right.' There were other words, such as sorry, that I wanted to say to my brother, but they did not seem big enough or good enough and, on the spot, I couldn't come up with any better ones.

'I made a mistake,' he offered, a few minutes, or possibly seconds later.

'When? *You* did?' I blurted, before both of us realized I had the wrong context.

'It's the anniversary soon,' he added, quickly. 'They're going to ask me if we want to go. They've been asking me every year, and I keep putting them off. I should've told them to stop asking, but I didn't, and now … Look, I know what you think about it.'

'Do you?'

'Well, I expect you don't see the point, given that you can't remember them.'

'Any more than you can.'

'Right.'

'But we should go on pretending that we remember them anyway?'

'I don't see it as pretence, but as a ritual, a mark of respect, perhaps.'

'There's nothing there but bones and plain white headstones.'

'Think of it another way then,' he said. 'You've hardly set foot outside of this place. Not for a long time. You sit here, by yourself, in this dingy room, and it can't be good for you.'

'I'm studying.'

'So have a day off.'

There had been no days off since the accident. My hope of reconciliation had all-but faded. I had not been able to sustain it all these years by myself. I hadn't even dared to dream of this, but I took Saeed's visit as a sign that we might have come full circle. We were back where we started, and whatever he thought of me, whether he'd come to terms with who I was or not, our estrangement, like a sentence, was over. I had done my time.

Saeed's slightly smiling mouth didn't move as I peered into the car. I refused to notice what kind of car it was, but as I was climbing in and closing the door, my right leg jumped and I banged my knee against the handle. Saeed turned away. We travelled in silence, me with my hands on my thighs, pushing firmly down, and he still turned to the window, so that I could see only the cooled imprint of the scar on his cheek. The line of the scar converged with a camera strap that he wore, high on his shoulder. I don't know if it was meant to, but it reminded me of the bag that I'd worn across mine eight years ago, to the day.

We were left alone in the cemetery for an hour. Saeed led me straight to the stones that stood, side by side, still upright among the orderless rows. He stood in front of them, prizing the black leather case like a shell from a chick. With that gaping, discarded from his side, he held the camera carefully his hands, checking its dials before raising the viewfinder to his eye and clicking.

It was a cold, clear day and I shivered, shifting my feet, until he'd finished. I assumed he was using up film or getting used to the light, and he duly turned to me, suggesting we take pictures of each other.

'What, here?'

'Over by that tree. Take the camera. No, wait. I'll set it up then you take it. Take a few shots.'

I took three photographs of my brother in his duffle coat with the collar up, obscuring his face. He told me they'd be in black and white, because he didn't like colour. I remembered the prints that were laid out on the doctor's desk – the odd angles, the awful lurid scar.

'Now you,' he said. 'By the wall.'

I was placed in the low glare of the winter sun.

'Don't squint.'

'I can't help it.'

'Look at me then, not at the light. Stand still, and keep your hands away from your face. Now turn to the left. Just your head! And to the right. Look down.'

'Why?'

'Now look up.'

I realised then that Saeed was giving me instructions that had been given to him when I'd marred his perfect face, and the damage I'd done had been carefully recorded. He was showing me what it felt like to be documented from every

51

angle, an object of scrutiny, a specimen, an example. I didn't like it.

'I'm going.'

'One more Suhail.'

This last was a close-up, so close that I could look directly at him without squinting at all. I still have this picture. I keep it on my desk.

The following evening, Bruno, now large, and with the gait of a Sumo or a bulldog with its testicles manifestly intact, was amusing himself in the recreation room. He had grappled and humped his way through all that was left of the orphanage staff, and was now trying to intimidate the television. This old, fuzzy, teak-effect box was the longest serving, and pretty much the sole surviving item of entertainment in the room, not counting the monopoly set, whose bank notes had been used to make roll-ups. Still the main focus of everyone's attention, the TV was, in its own way, bigger than Bruno, and indifferent to being thumped on the head. Knowing this, Bruno was attempting to blow it up by setting the volume at full-blast. Those present – a trio of twelve year old girls hooked on soap operas, and two older boys pretending to wait for the news – were covering their ears as the door opened, and a runner mouthed my name, repeatedly, until someone noticed and turned the volume down to loud.

'Suhail!' exclaimed the hoarse fourth-former. 'Mr Jackson's office! Now!'

I arrived to find the Head Warden pacing, grim-faced, and accompanied by a uniformed policeman who scanned me, efficiently, from top to bottom, getting snagged, for a moment, on the purple paisley waistcoat I'd found in a second-hand shop.

'Sit down if you please,' said Mr Jackson, who sat down quickly himself, as if at his own invitation. He clasped his hands anxiously and leant towards me. 'I'm er, I'm afraid to say we have some troubling news for you.'

His eyes darted to the only object on his desk other than an empty in-tray, and he caught my alarm.

'Oh, no. No. It's not … your brother has not been involved in another … gosh, in an accident or anything. Dear me, this is difficult.'

'But it appears,' the officer interjected, 'he has absconded from here, and left no indication of his whereabouts.'

'What? He's disappeared?'

'There was a note, you see,' offered the Warden, 'a small note, a very minor one, nothing to tell us where he is. It was attached to one of his personal effects, namely this one here on my desk, the camera. He has taken everything else, all of his possessions. I do hate to say it, but we must assume he has run away, unless I'm quite wrong on the matter, which I most certainly hope I am, and you know otherwise?'

I didn't. I was questioned about what happened the previous day, and asked to sign something. I nodded when the policeman asked permission to take the film and develop it, promising to return any prints that were not useful as evidence. They asked me if I had any questions for them, but I only had the one.

'What did the note say?'

'It said: "give this to Suhail."'

*

Saeed's departure was the first of many at the orphanage. The process of evacuation began slowly, one by one, and gathered momentum. Years of under-funding had led to a neglect of the building which was, in places, structurally unsound. With parts of the exterior threatening to collapse, nobody could afford to worry about the facilities. Inevitably, fewer people, and then no-one new at all came to work or live there. Life was such that anyone who had anything to compare it with left as soon as they could. Those of us who remained had known only this institution, exposed, rendered abject by perceptible degrees of decay. People responded to this in different ways. Mr Jackson, having little in the way of business to detain him in his office, took to wandering about the place, from room to room, as if he were making a final headcount. Two girls who'd managed a C grade in art decorated the second floor, covering the holes in the wall with self-portraits. When he wasn't aiding Bruno in his campaign against innocent objects, Fin was strangely, incompetently driven to try and fix them. He would stand for ages, shoulders hunched, arms slack, trying to shut the door of a wardrobe whose attitude, even more than his, expressed the futility of the task. He fussed over faded curtains, attempting, without the use of a ladder, to lasso some hooks with rings that had fallen off at the ends. As I stood in front of a window so grimy I could not see out, I saw him, as if in a mirror, kneeling in a corner, poking crumbs of underlay back into the carpet.

I had no desire for the company that remained, no longing, even for Bobby Grigson. I would have stayed that way, deadened to the loss of a brother I imagined I had regained, if it hadn't been for one, remarkable arrival. She blasted in to the dim, barren expanse of the orphanage with a force that threatened to raise it, but that brought with it a quality of light and liveliness that our senses were not accustomed to. Bridget was as surprising as the first dip of

54

sherbet before your tongue works out what it is. She was bigger than anyone I'd ever seen, filling my field of vision with the massive sphere of her torso, fringed with the glow of her luminous extremities. She was pristine and vibrant, like a freshly-formed planet, her vitality a result of her closeness to the sun. Her dress was a swirl of colours so bright that she radiated warmth, conserving none of it for herself.

Everyone gravitated towards her, but none more than me. Straight away, we took up our positions, at a distance which depended entirely on our qualities relative to hers. As a new order was established, Bruno found himself displaced, dispatched with some haste to the margins of our renewed society, while I, bypassing even the younger sister she had dragged in her wake, found myself closest. In a very short while, Bridget, who we called B, had become the undisputed Queen of our cosmos – a title I had seemed destined for, but happily conceded.

We fell into friendship as if we were falling in love; involuntarily and with unsustainable intensity. I had gone from empty straight to full, the shadow of my brother blocked out, blindingly eclipsed. We were intoxicated, sharing intimacies without judgement or restraint. We were both inexperienced, equally enthusiastic late-starters in the art of the soul mate. What little remained unsaid was somehow already understood. She was like a sister and I was her just-found brother, or so I believed. Her actual sibling, Suzy, was much younger than us and unlike B in every way. While B's face shone like a perfect pearl, delicately marbled and intriguing as an orb, Suzy was merely pale. She was also so slight and flat that it was easy to imagine that she had been subject to enormous centrifugal pressures as she spun around, orbiting B at impressive, dizzying speed. B in turn seemed to notice Suzy only in passing. They had been transferred from another orphanage that, unlike ours, was too full. It was clearly supposed that B, independent, self-assured and mature for her age, would not only cope but flourish, even here, and indeed she shone in the gloom, ousting it from its furthest refuge.

Our conversations were earnest and properly adolescent. We shared the scope and profundity of our knowledge like first-time explorers in a miniature world. There wasn't much there, but it was all a great discovery. Our thoughts being as elastic and unpredictable as our organs, we sprung with undisguised enthusiasm from the depths of our existential concerns to the weighty matters of fashion, and of course, we were always beyond shock or embarrassment. B responded to the already open secret of my sexuality with a huge sculpture-less shrug, and then asked me if I'd managed to do it yet. While I had not, she stated, matter-of-factly, that she had, when she was fourteen, doggy-style with a teacher. Although she was unimpressed with the experience, she was willing to try again, if only so she could communicate it, in a letter to her mother, a devout catholic. I remarked on the fact that she had a mother, and she said she believed it was customary. She asked me what had happened to mine, and I told her mine was dead. Hers, apparently, had gone to a nunnery.

B's mother had given herself to Christ shortly after her father, an architect, had given himself to his secretary. She and her sister had lived in a strange-looking modern house with a slash roof and odd-shaped windows. She showed me a picture of it, and of her father, who was evidently more perfectly proportioned than any of his creations. A fit man in every way, he had dropped dead from a heart-attack after his usual five mile run. His new wife had wanted neither the house nor the children who came with it, but B didn't bear her a grudge. She wasn't much older than her, she said, and it was all done now. What she wanted to know from me was whether or not there were any fanciable teachers around here. I had to disappoint her, but we made plenty of other plans.

Mere boys were of no interest to B, and that was just as well. Neither of us were exactly leaders or, for that matter, followers of fashion. We had our own style, and didn't benefit by comparison with the girls who boasted feathered hair, starter cleavages, mid-length skirts and ankle socks. I might actually have gone for this look but B judged it to be impractical given the state of the heating system, and wasted no more time on the subject. She was invulnerable, almost immune to teasing, deflecting it with insouciant skill. She was particularly indifferent to Bobby, now largely devoid of his gang, but invariably with at least one admirer under each arm. B would turn away as he passed us by, and look lovingly at me in ways that we thought, at first, were funny.

Within a year, we had mapped out our own and each other's future lives. We had become a couple whose peculiarity was lost on everyone, especially us. I thought nothing of having my hand stroked, or being complimented on my appearance, and I often kissed B on the cheek. It must have seemed logical to her, if not sensible, to take this further, but I had no idea it was coming. One night, in the recreation room, after we'd watched a film and the others had gone to bed, she leant in towards me as if to put her head on my shoulder, but I felt her lips brush my skin at the same time as her hand made straight for my crotch. I threw her off violently, much more violently than I would ever have intended, and she sat forward, nursing her arm in her lap. I apologised, repeatedly, and she said I hadn't hurt her and she didn't know why she'd done that. I tried to cover the awkwardness, fix the connection that had been based, for both of us, on denial, on an innocence we'd outgrown long before our childhood. I tried kneeling next to her and joking about what happened, but though she went along with it, I could see she just wanted to go. I didn't sleep, knowing that I was to blame. I'd misled her, though I had never meant to. I wouldn't have done that deliberately, especially not to B. I went to see her the next day, but she was taken up with Suzy.

We never had time to drift apart. We'd both reached leaving age and, within a few months of each other, we went, not to the same college as we'd planned, but at least to the same city. We promised to stay in touch, but the attraction between us, established in a finite space, an elapsed time, was weaker now, a distant pulse, and I was already accelerating towards other lights.

*

I lived, for nearly ten years in a glittering firmament, as one gay man in a multitude. For most of that time, I believed I had found my home, and for most of that time I experienced the ordinary joys and mundane miseries of a manic social scene, speeding on its hard-fought freedoms and on the pain of what those who are ignorant of it call a lifestyle choice. I taught English at the same college I'd studied it, covering the whole curriculum, doing my research, trying to figure out if I was going to have a career, or write. I worked hard and played hard too, becoming a connoisseur of bodies like, and not like

58

my own. I went to clubs, learnt how to dance; I rarely went home alone. I tried everything, or almost everything, revelling in the permissiveness we granted each other and that cost nothing to anyone but ourselves. I was lucky. Some of my friends were not. I was healthier and in many ways happier than ever before or since, but I discovered, eventually, that my appetites were not commensurable with my desire. They had been satisfied but I was still hollow. I stood naked in front of the mirror as if to check that I was there. I had filled out, just enough. I had grown in to my body, even as far as my ears. I had the physique, I'd acquired the look. As a specimen I would definitely pass, but this was no longer what I wanted. What I wanted was to see my brother again, to ask him why he'd left and what he meant by giving me his camera. As if I didn't know. It was supposed to be a constant reminder, a symbol of my guilt. I didn't look at my face.

At first, I thought of myself as a traveller, as someone who had journeyed to a new and better life. Increasingly, I found myself to be a tourist, footsore, detached and lost. Pleasure I had thought was mine for good began to slip away, its face a mask that no longer fit. Along the star streams, between the bright couples and even brighter trios, I had always been searching for my brother, peering, squinting at the vacuous incandescence. Then I started to imagine that I'd spotted him, and went chasing off in unknown directions only to lose sight of him in a great cloud of indistinguishable faces, like particles of dust. I always knew that what I was seeing was only what I wished for, but I pursued it anyway, into the cloud-like crowds and the lifeless corners of the city. When, finally, this quest came to feel as futile as it was, I took to approaching strangers and asking them if they'd seen anyone who looked just like me. They hadn't, of course, and gradually, reluctantly, I gave up.

Then, one day, when I was reading, I came across a story about *probatimi*, two men who love each other, who are bound to each other and think of themselves as brothers. One of these men, Dmitri, is brave, gentle and widely admired until his home is ransacked, his wife killed and his daughter stolen. Unable to recover his child, Dmitri becomes vengeful and cruel. He is injured in a fight and ends up scarred, wearing *the badge of his daring in a deep gash across his eyebrow and cheek.* I recalled another gash across another cheek, and in that sense at least, I had found my brother.

I read on. In the same volume, I found the story of Guido, compelled, like the Ancient Mariner, to confess his crime. Guido wanders the seashore alone, tormented by guilt and loss. There is a storm, a ship is broken against the rocks and he watches as the sailors drown. He sinks to his knees, covers his face, and when he looks up he sees a chest floating towards him with someone or something on top. This thing is hideous, misshapen, and he's repulsed by its *odious visage.* But then the creature addresses him, offers him a bargain – in exchange for his body.

These stories were like my dreams. They became dreams in which there was always a storm, a fight, an accident and sometimes a bargain or magic spell in which I became the creature and he became me. I watched my limbs distort into unrecognisable shapes, becoming scaly, thick, the colour of no human skin. I tried to walk and realised that I must crawl or slither. Sometimes I caught sight of myself in a lake, or in the rain-slicked tarmac of an isolated country road. I longed to change back, to undo the spell, but first I had to find the monster that now moved freely, living my life while I lived his. It was impossible, he was beyond my reach, but I could no more avoid these dreams than I could avoid sleep. The only way I could think of changing them was to write my own story, and provide them with a different source. I wrote about two men called Marcus and Patrice. Although my story had all the necessary ingredients – a storm, a fight and so on – it still didn't end the way I wanted it to. I asked my friends what they thought of it, but they missed the point, which was that I didn't get the lightning right. I know that now. Lightning always accompanies the magic spell. In some ways it is like a spell, because it changes everything. If a spell can be reversed, then surely lightning can too.

*

I never told my friends what happened with my brother, or even that I had one. When they read my story, they didn't know what they were looking for, and besides, in groups of more than one, they rarely took anything seriously. I wasn't surprised that their feedback consisted mainly of telling me whether they fancied Marcus or Patrice but as a result, I found it harder to conceal the disappointment that had already taken hold of me. It manipulated my mouth and eyes against my will, and when I spoke, or laughed, I sounded like someone else, someone or something that could only mimic conversation. I wasn't seeing anyone, and so it was easier for all of us to attribute my malaise to that. I went on two blind dates that I would not have agreed to under normal circumstances. One was embarrassing, cringe-making, and the other was irritating. Although I could see that both men promised something meaningful to someone, that someone wasn't me.

I was only going out occasionally, when I noticed a man who was new to my circle of friends. He appeared with different groups at different times over a period of some months. What was strange was that he was very striking and yet drew virtually no attention to himself. Far from being surrounded by admirers, he would stand back, close enough to look like he belonged, but not close enough for anyone to talk to him. Similarly, if someone came up to me he might be behind them but not really with them, so that his presence could not be acknowledged. In fact, although I preferred to think I didn't have one, he was so much my type, my ideal, that I half thought he was an illusion. Blonde, muscular and immaculately groomed, his body made subtle impressions in his expensive clothes and though he was inexplicably alone, even ignored, he never appeared self-conscious or less than composed. If anything, there was a slight air of arrogance. He passed me once, in the street, striding towards me with the manner of someone whose place in the world is as certain tomorrow as it is today, and exactly what they intended it to be. He glanced at me, more deliberately than seductively, as if he was issuing a challenge. Come and get me, if you dare.

I did not speak to him until I found myself at a party I'd agreed to go to, partly because I knew he'd be there. We were crammed into the kitchen, as usual, but I saw him, somehow managing to remain aloof from the fragrant, flirtatious scrum. He slipped outside and I followed him, telling myself that I'd have made for the door whether he was there or not. He made no show of interest in the garden, lit-up, though it was only dusk, like a grotto, and any sense of camaraderie was overlaid with expectations that were mutual but already in excess of the norm, and as such, indecipherable. I introduced myself, and said that I'd often seen him, but had no idea who he was.

'I must be the mystery man then,' he said. 'But you can call me Matt.'

'You have an accent. Where are you from?'

'My father was born here, but my mother was European.'

'Was?'

'She passed away, and then I went to live somewhere warm and sunny for a while.'

That explained the tan. I asked him what he did for a living and he told me he ran his father's business after he retired, and then set up his own.

'So why did you leave?'

'I came back because I got tired of the life I was leading. The scene didn't suit me anymore. It never actually did, you know?'

I did know, and by the end of the evening I also understood that each of us had the need for something more that could not be obtained with the help of our friends, or without the help of one, like-minded person.

*

Although he was not much older than me, Matt was a gentleman, and for a while, we dated. It would be more accurate to say that he courted me, as if I was quite the lady. I tried to behave like one, asking about his life story and remarking on his achievements, but my attention often wandered. Matt had come to terms with a father who'd abandoned him as a child, taking his wife's inheritance in order to set up a hotel franchise, and sharing little of the rewards. There had been some help, when Matt's mother

63

became terminally ill, and in recognition, Matt went to work for his father after she died. He became a majority shareholder in the business, and then sold it in order to establish his own finance company. At the time we met, this was obviously successful, and success, I noticed, has maximum impact when it isn't claimed, but left to the body to articulate. I listened, and I wanted to touch him, but he made me wait.

While I waited, Matt devised a schedule of diversionary activities. He took me to galleries, to the theatre and to operas. Though I was never sure if he was enjoying himself as much as I was, his behaviour was always as impeccable as his appearance. My role, I understood, was to match his chivalry with grace, and though I was willing to play it, sometimes I fell out of character, and he would sit stiffly through a performance, pinning my meandering hand to his knee.

As a leading businessman, well-known in his profession even though he hadn't been in the country for long, Matt did not have much free time. We saw each other when we could, and spoke in between. I didn't think I was seeing less of other people than I was before, but I was aware of becoming absorbed, drawn in to a relationship that would redefine me, and I offered no resistance. Matt, in turn, was open about wanting me to himself, a sentiment that disarmed us both, and prepared me to enter an interior life that he assured me he'd never shared with anyone before. He struggled in the company of friends I was already detaching from, remaining watchful and quiet, as if he expected to be blamed. Instead, he was welcomed by groups of never more than four or five, all on their best behaviour, keen to know a familiar stranger. Of course, when he stood up to go to the bar, or phone for a taxi, there was a chorus of nudges, winks and flickering tongues, but it stopped dead on his return.

Only one person was not overtly impressed by Matt. Ben was an old friend, and someone I'd had a relationship with, soon after I left the orphanage. He was training to be a counsellor and keen to practise his listening skills. I'd told him as much as I could bear to about my past, leaving him to surmise the rest. He would sit close, tilt his head and say nothing until I complained about it and threatened to leave. Then he took to holding my legs, pulling them onto his lap and wrapping his arms around them. I left him anyway, but he seemed to take it well. He arranged those dates, picking people he thought would look after me in his place. He remained over-protective and clearly distrusted Matt, though he never actually said so. He just observed him closely, seeing, as I did, the look on his face when he turned and caught us chorusing. Ben's concern was expressed in the form of repeated invitations, attempts to reintegrate me, and earnest statements about how much I was missed. But I didn't take him seriously. I thought his fears were unnecessary, and that he was mistaking Matt's more formal manner for something else. In truth, the only thing *I* missed was the dancing.

We talked a lot about Matt's job and my writing, his aspirations and my dreams. Although we could not have been more different, he seemed to understand, more clearly than I did, exactly what I wanted. He would reflect this back, as a series of insights that were quite breathtaking, and that demonstrated a remarkable power of perception. He pre-empted the confession I would undoubtedly have made about the injury I inflicted on my brother, and his subsequent disappearance. He helped me see that I was not ready to deal with this yet, and that I'd been living a life of avoidance and denial that was only now coming to an end. He said that he recognised my need to stop running towards, or away from something in my past. He perceived a need for stillness, withdrawal and self-reflection that would, he assured me, be a prelude to more meaningful action. He offered to help me in this process that would, he said, be difficult and challenging. He spoke so quietly, and with such meaning and authority that I was defenceless, entranced by his voice, already his.

'You're trembling,' he said, as we sat together in his apartment. 'Let me get you a drink.' He got up, poured us both a brandy and handed me a glass.

'Are you all right?'

'Yes. No.'

'Yes, or no?'

'Both.'

'I see.'

'Not this time.'

'Explain?'

'We've been seeing each other for ages now, and you haven't even kissed me yet. Don't you want to?'

'Of course.'

'But?'

'But nothing Suhail,' he said. 'There's no rush. I want you to be certain.'

'I'm certain.'

'That's good,' he said, sipping the brandy and placing his glass on a side table. 'That's what I wanted to hear. I have to know that this is as special for you as it is for me, and not like before, not a casual affair.'

'I don't think I've ever had one of those! I'm not sure that anybody does anymore, not even straight people. The rest of us have one-night stands or get married and move in within a week. It has been lovely being treated like this, but please, kiss me now before I explode.'

He sat closer and took my face in his hand, stroking my cheek with his thumb. He hesitated then kissed me hard, surprisingly hard, prizing my mouth and snagging it with his teeth. I felt his hairless chest and moved my hand down his body, but the waiting was over now and he quickly removed my clothes before pushing me down on the sofa.

*

It was towards the end of our honeymoon period that we moved here, to this great rambling house. I'd describe my first year as contented rather than happy. The sex may have been a little rough but it was certainly exciting, adding a dangerous dimension to a relationship that might have been too polite, too civilised, and now felt complete. Matt seemed satisfied, but he had his work and his routines. The pattern of his days was already established, and made me more aware of an absence of form, and often substance, in mine. I was always keen to see him at the end of the day but he was often tired, and had work to do in the evening. At dinner, if he didn't want to talk, I'd make something up to amuse him, something I'd pretend had happened during the day. That often worked to loosen him up, as long as it didn't involve anyone else, the postman say, or one of my old friends. When it didn't work, and I couldn't draw him out, I'd settle for gazing at him appreciatively and making silent, obscene suggestions. He didn't like it if I made them out loud.

In many ways, whatever the limitations of our relationship, the imbalance in our financial status for example, and our very different personalities, Matt still seemed right for me. I don't just mean in terms of what he looked like. He was right for me because he was everything I was not – solid, dependable, gainfully employed. In turn, I tried hard to be right for him, to be what he wanted me to be. But I fell short. I couldn't meet his standards, and then, gradually, he started to let me know that he wasn't really satisfied at all.

Where he had always been courteous, he began to get critical. First it was my appearance. He didn't like my clothes, he said, and would I consider dressing more appropriately. When I didn't, because I wasn't sure what he meant, he used it as an excuse to stay at home. We couldn't go to this event, or that, with me looking so scruffy. He didn't want to go on his own either, and I could hardly go without him. I didn't have the money, for one thing, and I wasn't certain who I could call. The idea of going out with someone else, un-chaperoned, would never have taken off.

Then he began to accuse me of neglecting myself. I wasn't taking enough care of my body. I insisted on eating the wrong food and was too reluctant to exercise. I was too inert, sitting all day at my desk when I would have been better off getting up and moving around, doing some press-ups or going for a jog. I'd have been better off still with an occupation, a less sedentary job, a job. That was rich. I'd had one, but he hadn't approved of it. He had encouraged me to develop my writing, and that takes time. It isn't easy, especially when there isn't anyone to teach you how. He wanted me to stop biting my nails as well, and get a proper haircut. Sometimes I think he wanted me to be more like him, but I wasn't, and so he tried to make up for it, to make up the gap by, as he put it, *suggesting* how I could make the most of myself. The trouble is that his suggestions were more like directions about what I should and shouldn't, could and couldn't do. I hate being told what to do. It makes me come over all rebellious. The idea, he said, was to instil a bit of discipline in my life, to get into a habit of self-improvement. This habit would replace my other ones, the bad ones. He claimed that he wasn't actually interested in *telling* me what to do. He wanted to help me know it for myself. But this knowledge, self-knowledge, was not easy to come by and I would have to work at it. I would have to nurture it and I couldn't afford, he said, to waste time hankering for others whose lives were also dissolute.

Matt started acting as if there was no longer any common ground between us because I, not he was changing. I was becoming lazy, slovenly and irresolute. I was letting myself go. My underlying lack of moral character was producing symptoms of stress and anxiety. The worst of these symptoms, for Matt, was the now interminable movement of my legs. The fact that I couldn't control them was symbolic, for him, of a more endemic problem, and I tried to suppress it in his presence.

He continued to assure me, for many years, that his comments, however hurtful, were unintentionally so. They were made for my own good, and would eventually enable me to improve myself in all aspects of my life. To an extent, this was true, and I realised that I could, of course, work harder, exercise more, eat better and so on – and Matt was hardly a hypocrite. I tried to adopt certain regimes that paralleled his own, but they were too rigid and oppressive, and I couldn't stick to them. As a result, Matt's attitude worsened again.

He took it on himself to school me in a way that felt at first bizarre, and then perverse. It was exactly as if I was ten years old, already an inveterate under-achiever; a child who could barely get himself to school, let alone do anything useful while he was there. It was one thing being given tasks and targets and time limits. These could, at a push, be construed as helpful. But having my clothes laid out on the bed for me each morning? That was something else. Matt could no longer criticise what I was wearing because he was deciding it himself. He decided what I ate and when I exercised too. Every day I went to my study as if to a classroom where I was expected to work between set hours. Initially, he made regular checks on me, and I learnt then that it was better to feign compliance than to try and resist his assumed authority. The sibylline scolding of a quietly spoken man can be chilling, like a curse.

As his invective became less plausible and more extreme I wondered if Matt was beginning to come apart. He was doing most of his business from home, working very long hours as well as taking care of all his investments and endowments. He would only use his personal gym in the basement, and rarely went out, relying instead on the postal service, the phone and a regular courier. The lack of fresh air, and perhaps as he said, the strain of living with me, had even affected his looks, reddening his once clear blue eyes and draining colour from his face. His hair seemed somehow coarser, as if it had dried out, or was artificial, a wig. It wasn't. I found that out on the day when the courier failed to come.

It was late in the afternoon, and I was at my desk. Matt barged in without knocking and, glaring at the floor he was pacing, began to complain that his entire day had been wasted,

70

that he had needed some important documents, and that a deal that would have been lucrative and should have been consolidated, was now ruined. He was furious. His speech was like a sequence of strangled hisses and his face, which should have been flushed, was white and blotchy. He was tugging at a loose strand of hair and biting his bottom lip. I stood up, as if to placate him and moved towards the door. He saw what I was doing and stood in my way, asking me, over and over, why this had happened, why people you depended on were feckless, unreliable; useless. As if I knew; as if I could answer. When I didn't, he pulled me to the floor and raped me.

His skin, up close, had a slightly oily texture, an ophidian sheen that enabled him to move against me and manipulate me with ease, while I was rendered motionless, unable to escape. Mentally, I slipped away at the moment I was caught, slowing my breathing as his quickened, and allowing his weight to all but crush me until he was done. I felt nothing while it was happening, but I was in agony when it was over. I hoped the damage to my body would grant me some immunity, at least for a while, but I couldn't be certain of that. The next day, when I was working, I locked myself in.

*

It is winter now, and a long time since I have seen anyone apart from Matt. My days are solitary, and structured by regimes, doctrines that are designed to encompass my work, domestic tasks and even personal habits. I blame myself for my current isolation, for rejecting those who cared for me and for failing to see what drove a man with Matt's incomparable abilities. He has continued to prosper in a new line of work which, as far as I understand it, entails careful negotiations between companies and individual clients and involves him in identifying, nurturing and matching their respective demands and requirements. This work is competitive and confidential, but those who are most successful at it, like Matt, are not only renowned but become legendary, more powerful than those they serve, and more ruthless. If Matt applies standards of extreme order and discipline to me, it is no less than he does to himself. I think he enjoys it. I, on the other hand, have little hope that his mission to improve me, or rather, to instil in me the habit of self-improvement, will have any effect. I may appear to go along with it, but that doesn't mean I don't resent it, that I don't despise him for it. I know where it comes from too – his puritan urge. It comes from his mother.

Matt may have learnt his trade from his father, but he learnt everything else from her. She was he told me, beautiful, devout and dedicated to making more of his life than she'd been able to make of her own. She brought him to this country to educate him, and they had to manage without her inheritance. Since she had sacrificed her own future for his, she left nothing to chance, setting him daily, weekly and monthly goals, and devising a system of rewards and punishments in order to maintain his motivation. By the time he was ten years old, he was already what she wanted him to be, meticulous and committed, both to his tasks and to her. No-one could surpass her in his estimation. No-one deserved his devotion more than the woman who, despite her own unhappiness and physical frailty, was tireless in her efforts towards her son. In her absence, Matt assumed her role and transferred her methods to me. He schools me exactly as she once schooled him. The more he strives to maintain himself to his own exacting standards, the more preoccupied he becomes with what I am and what I'm doing.

However much I have failed to perform, however many admonitions I have earned in place of rewards, Matt will never give up on me. He will never give up on me because his mother never gave up on him. He is as fixated on me as she was on him. Even now that he is revered and increasingly reclusive, even now that he manages me indirectly; he will not leave me alone. He will not let me be. There can be no unresolved cases, no unfinished work on his desk. There is nothing untidy in this house. I rarely see him by day, but I receive written guidance and instructions. They are left for me at the breakfast table, or pushed under my door. Once, in a moment of irony or rebellion, I wrote them all out myself, and stuck them on the wall next to my desk. I made sure they looked like commandments, because that is what they felt like to me:

<u>I shall not</u>
Waste time when I should be working or otherwise improving myself
Lie in bed after 7am
Go to bed after 11pm
Masturbate, ever
Drink alcohol except when given specific permission to do so and then only sparingly
Smoke, especially secretively
Attempt to do anything secretively
Spend my allowance without first presenting a formal itemised account, and never on luxuries
Eat unhealthily
Sit around idly, make the house untidy or go into private rooms under any circumstances

Complain when I am ill since this is caused by lack of exercise
and not adhering to the rule about diet
See anyone on my own
Speak out of turn
Step out of line
Resist his authority
Refuse his requests
Imagine that I am good or attractive or successful
Stop trying to be

<u>I shall</u>
Work to a timetable
Sleep to a timetable
Keep house to a timetable
Be rewarded if I do
Be punished if I don't
Be either in the exercise room or in my own room
Stop locking doors, including in the bathroom
Wash when I'm told
Wear what I'm told
Suck what, when and how I'm told
Be grateful
Be obedient
Be quiet
Come when I'm called
Sit when I'm invited to
Roll over
Play dead
Play nicely, or else

Friends that I couldn't see on my own, but could once,
perhaps, have called on, were never allowed in the house. As
far as I know, Matt has no friends, only associates, and only

one of these, Harry, was ever encouraged to come round. Harry is Matt's solicitor. He is middle-aged, bald and over-weight. I would hear him, panting and wheezing as he followed his employer up the stairs, doing his best to answer questions but struggling to keep up with the pace. I would come down to the first floor, and pretend I was going somewhere. Matt would frown at me over Harry's head but I didn't care. Although we could only exchange banalities, we had a tacit understanding of each other's plight, and I grew to like Harry even before the incidents that could have turned us into more confirmed allies.

One time, when the voices coming from the stairwell were more agitated than usual, I waited until Matt and Harry had gone in to the office, and then crept down to listen. This was risky, since his hearing had always been preternaturally sharp. There was nothing to be gained from muttering or answering back, and there at the door I tried not to breathe too hard.

'How long have I been a client with your firm?' Matt demanded.

Harry paused to think. 'Five years?'

'Six,' said Matt, extending the word to several times its length and sounding like he had dropped it into a pan of hot oil.

'Any firm would have been only too pleased to take me on, but I chose yours. Do you have any idea why?'

'Err …'

'Because I calculated that a small outfit such as yours would value a client such as me and take particular care in handling his affairs. I was clearly mistaken.'

'I really wouldn't say that. The circumstances in this case were out of our control and yet we've tried very hard …'

'Not hard enough!' I could tell that Matt was apoplectic by the further drop in volume. 'I could destroy you just by leaving.' I must have jumped slightly because my elbow brushed against the door. 'Quiet. What was that?' I heard footsteps but was too frightened to move.

'It was me,' said Harry. 'I just knocked into your bureau. Clumsy of me. Sorry.'

'You're an idiot,' Matt concluded. 'You can't you do anything right. I have a good mind to reduce your fee until hunger forces you to stop lumbering around and sharpen what is left of your wits.'

I didn't listen to any more, partly out of concern for Harry. The next time I saw him was in the summer when Matt, somewhat arbitrarily, decided to go boating with some people we had never met. Matt himself had only met one of them. Grant was a financial advisor and a former colleague. He brought along Bernard and Celia, a husband and wife recruitment team, and also his boyfriend, Justin. Justin was everything Matt couldn't abide, an embodiment of camp, an affront to repression and restraint. Justin, hung with delicate layers of haute-couture, smelling of sweet perfume and accessorised down to his fluffy white dog had no place in Matt's world. He was an anomaly, a figure from my past that I thought I'd never see again. If I was delighted by his presence in our otherwise joyless party, Matt, very clearly, was not.

Tensions started to rise during the picnic. Bernard and Celia were dominating the conversation, talking over Matt, about how someone they had recruited, and then released in favour of someone better, had been found out by his employers and fired, as a result of which he'd hung himself from the chandelier in the company foyer. They obviously didn't realise that nobody talks over Matt, especially in ways that are boastful and indiscrete. I could tell he was annoyed because he stood with his arms folded tight across his chest, tall and austere like the spires in the distance behind him, a silent rebuke to everything modern and brash.

Nobody else seemed to notice this. Harry was eating, and Grant seemed to be enjoying the story, but Justin wasn't listening anyway. He was fussing about where to put the various layers he'd removed so that they wouldn't have to touch the grass, and be contaminated by natural fibres. He folded them into a neat pile, and placed them inside a silver messenger bag, opening the flap and reflecting the sunlight straight into Matt's bloodshot eyes. Then he produced a small bottle of lotion, and started applying it to arms that no amount of sun cream could be expected to protect.

At this point, deprived of attention for longer than he could bear, Horace, the Bichon Frise, removed himself from Justin's lap and walked into the middle of the picnic, singling out the pastrami, before parking his behind on Matt's abandoned plate. Harry noted this with a flicker of alarm, but Matt just flared his nostrils and looked away. Grant ordered the dog off and then went round refilling people's glasses. Unfortunately, as he was topping up Justin's rosé, Horace noticed another dog being rowed up the river and ran towards the bank, knocking into Grant's legs in the process. The wine spilt all the way down the front of Justin's apparently priceless white vest, causing him to yap, flap his hands and draw a great deal of amused attention to our gathering.

This was too much for Matt, who flung his arms open, rippled pink, and ordered us all, immediately, into our boats.

By the time I'd helped Harry into ours, the other one had already set off with Justin at the oars. Since Bernard and Celia had agreed to differ about which of them could row with most stealth, everyone thought it would be amusing if Justin, now naked from the waist up and as puny as a pre-adolescent princess had a go. That is, everyone except Matt. We caught them up quickly, but they were tacking from one side of the river to the other, and impossible to pass. Matt issued instructions to Justin (who pronounced his name "Justine") in as close as he can get to a shout:

'Move over to the left, I'm coming past you.'

'You can come all you like lovey,' Justin replied, 'but I can't promise you any control over my movements at this moment.'

'You're pushing me into the bank.'

'What was that about wank?'

'Row forwards with your right oar and backwards with your left to straighten up.'

'But I don't want to straighten up darling, so don't try and make me, there's a good boy.'

'I said row forwards with your right oar and then back down with your left you fool.'

'Tetchy, tetchy. Shall I pat my head and rub my tummy too?'

At this point our boat hit the bank and theirs hit us, knocking one of Matt's oars into the water and the other into his cheek. He broke out in red and purple patches that looked like week-old bruises, and while everyone in the other boat was still laughing and pointing, he grabbed the right oar, and, almost hitting Harry, he stood, reached over him and smashed it repeatedly into Justin's face. Justin screamed and pleaded and kicked and flailed in a futile attempt to defend himself, but Matt was relentless. When Harry and I eventually stopped him, it was as if Justin was wearing a vest again, but it was a different colour this time. The legal services of Cook, Rampton and Jones were better appreciated after that, but no-one invites us out anymore, and nobody ever calls, not even Harry.

*

Matt has taken over from Saeed as the source of my dreams. Not long after the boating incident, I dreamt that I was woken by a storm and went downstairs to find Matt sitting in an oxblood Queen Anne chair, playing chess with someone I hadn't seen before. He wore a cheap suit and his thin waxy hand, like the flaccid claw of a rodent, hung limply over the knight as he regarded his opponent with sly, bright-eyed caution. Matt sat back, a near-empty tumbler of brandy on the table beside him, and ran his finger along the raw rim of his bottom lip.

'Well,' he said, as I appeared in the doorway. 'Look who it is. What do you think, Peter?' he asked, turning to his companion with a wink that brought something resembling a smile to his sharp-toothed mouth. 'Ah,' he went on, 'I see you approve, and why shouldn't you? He is appealing, in his way, and he has a surprisingly juvenile frame. You could do anything you want with it. I do. Wait right there!' He had caught my movement from the corner of his eye. 'I haven't finished. I have a question for my friend here. Peter, what would you say if I gave you the choice between my king and his body? Which would it be? You haven't had the pleasure of either of them before. Will you carry on playing this game with me, or would you prefer to play with him? I am hard to beat, as you know, but he isn't.'

I woke up before Matt got his answer. Another time, I dreamt that he'd locked a young couple who'd been dining with us in his cellar, marching them down with a carving knife because the poor woman had said the wrong thing about his dessert wine. He did it as if it was a joke, but nobody appeared to get it, and besides, they were down there for a fortnight.

Only the other day, soon after Matt had gone out, briefly, on business – which he hardly ever does – I thought I had a visitor. I opened the door, but it was a bright, sunny afternoon and for a moment I was blinded. Then, when the man's features emerged, like the first impressions on a canvas, I froze, allowing him the opportunity to let himself in.

'Good day to you,' he began, sounding, at first, like Mr Jackson from the orphanage. 'Please forgive this intrusion but I had to come. I've not had the pleasure of making your acquaintance, but I've heard a great deal about you and, more to the point, your work. That is what explains my presumption in thus presenting myself to you today. I do hate to be rude, and I hope that you will understand. Let me explain, you see, I am also a writer, like you sir, and I have fancied, for a period of time, that something could happen, something in short involving the two of us, you and I, getting together so to speak in order to discuss and debate, in short to share our thoughts and ideas about this writing business. What would you say to that? I mean, what would you say to the prospect of bringing your thoughts on the subject to bear on my thoughts and vice versa and even, if I may make so bold of bringing our stories together in some way, yet to be determined, since they may have more in common than either of us could have dreamed in our wildest dreams, or at least *intended*.'

He spoke this word darkly, narrowing his eyes, and although I didn't know what he meant by it, I quickly realised that this was not Mr Jackson. He, this figment of my daydreams, or so I thought, was here for a purpose and there was nothing benign about it.

'Oh, now I sense that you are alarmed sir, affrighted, and that I may have gone too far, over-stepped the mark, when what I want to say is really perfectly simple and is this; you are a writer and I am a writer and writing is a difficult and lonely business and here is an opportunity for us to help each other or, at least, for you to help me, to *reciprocate*, once I have offered my services to you.'

'You see, I, standing here as I am and as I hope, in time, you'll take me, have in a nutshell been invited to *intervene* and more than that to stay, to take up residence for as long as is needed, as long as is necessary to afford you some much needed succour in your lonely, but not necessarily singular task. In truth, I am a little early, but I, like you, if I may presume, am somewhat impatient and more than that I wanted to let you know, to make it clear that I understand, I understand completely that when one person is over here and the other person is over there, or when, more to the point, the person who is over here and the person who is over there are actually in the same place, then, under those circumstances things can become awkward and it can be useful, indeed necessary, to find a mediator. I sir, am that man. Think of me as a *double blessing* if you like, because I intend to prove myself exactly that. I will be both a mentor and mediator and, for that matter, *anything else you want me to be*. Now,' he said with a too familiar grin, 'shall we go inside?'

I may have created this person who sounded familiar but who wasn't, who looked like someone he couldn't be, but he was starting to seem distressingly real. I followed him down the corridor into the drawing room, trying to unscramble my thoughts, but before I'd even sat down, he began again.

'Good good. First of all, and now that we're both more comfortable even though, if you don't mind me saying so, you don't look very relaxed, first of all and in order to perhaps relax you a little bit let me outline what I've come to think of as my plan of action. My plan of action is as follows: first of all you are to give me the most detailed possible background of your current project, whatever it may be. Which is to say, how you became interested in it, what, so to speak, were your *motives*, how would you describe it in outline to someone, anyone, a stranger, such as me and finally what is it about the project that makes it at all interesting or important, and *to whom*. These things are important, you see. Then after that it would be useful if you were to enlighten me as to your process of investigation, notably where did you start it all from and why. *Where*, I wonder *did you get it from*, and where on earth do you suppose it is going? As well and in addition you might mention your sources, or should I rather say *your source*, not all of them because we do not have forever, do we, but the principle ones, the ones, excuse me, the *one* that counts, the one that others should know about, should they not? Not a minor question this one, no, not at all. Once you have told me that, we'll really be starting to get somewhere and then the time will be right for me to read, carefully of course, every word you have written, so that I can begin to formulate a response.'

'Ah, I see that I have elicited a reaction there and that you've become alert and wish to speak and you will speak, my dear sir, but bear with me, just a moment or two longer while I explain, as best I can, why I believe myself to be qualified to approach you in this way. For *who am I* to offer you advice;

who indeed? I tell you I am a writer and you take that on trust. I tell you I am a writer of some experience and you may well wonder, you must well wonder what is the precise nature of this experience that is greater, allegedly than my own? I will tell you. I am neither a young man, nor an old man *much like yourself*, but when I was a young man I was successful you see. At a very tender age I was recognised, widely you might say. You might even say that I was celebrated although to say that I was lauded might be going a little too far if only because I liked to use a pseudonym, a *nom de plume*, an alias. Oh, it was a wonderful time, when I was mixing with like minds and taken out and spoiled and made to feel so very special if you know what I mean, and I wish it could have lasted for ever but of course it couldn't because nothing really does and since then I have suffered, suffered torments that shall not be spoken, that shall remain unsaid, that need not be said to one such as you, for we are *kindred spirits*, are we not? As such we are bound to each other, *we are brothers* and fate wills it that our interests henceforth are shared. Yet since I am the elder at least in these matters, in this art, I must first impart the lessons I have learned, inherited if you will from our predecessors regarding discipline, method and rigour.'

'Stop!'

'Stop? But why my dear ...'

'For one thing I've had more than enough of discipline and I do not believe in method. For another thing, why are you talking like that, and what, exactly, are you trying to say?'

'Talking like what? And why would you not care for method when it is an indispensable aspect of your art?'

'Because it makes things predictable and I prefer surprises.'

'But this is precisely where you are displaying your naivety, even ignorance and forgive me but it also accounts for your lack of outward achievement. Do you not wish to succeed?'

He didn't wait for my answer but stood up and marched straight to my room. He could have guessed where the drawing room was, but I have no idea how he knew where my study was located in this maze of sealed boxes. I would have asked him, but I could barely keep up. When he got there he went to my desk and rummaged around until he found the manuscript of Marcus Florian, the story I may not have published, but that was the start of my dream to be a writer, and to transform my nightmares – nightmares just like this. The moment he started to read from it I recognised, not Mr Jackson's voice, but my own, spoken by another. I suppose I had been preoccupied with the surreal nature of our encounter and with trying to decipher what it meant. But now there was no doubt. I was hearing the tone and the texture of my speech. He mimicked it well, and grew in confidence as he read. At times he lowered the manuscript as if he already knew it, and when he reached for a pen in his inside pocket I realised he was wearing my jacket.

'Who are you?' I demanded, 'and why are you imitating me?'

'On the contrary dear sir, it is not *I* who has imitated *you.*'

'What do you mean? What's your name?'

'I do not, for your purposes, have one. But you may call me 'Juvenis'.'

Juvenis. I knew that name from somewhere, from a two hundred year old story in a book I'd read and long since forgotten. Was he saying I had copied it? That I'd copied him? Was he the author or some kind of ghost, here for revenge, and in which case, why was he impersonating me? I tried to wake myself. This wasn't really happening, it couldn't be, but it carried on. From another pocket, he produced a note and handed it to me. It was addressed to Matt and thanked him, at obsequious length, for his hospitality, his generosity, his patience, dedication and so on. At the end of it was my signature.

'So,' said my tormentor, turning back to the manuscript, 'let us see what we have here, shall we? Anything of use, I wonder? Anything that is *not already mine*, that I may have for my own, to square things, to even out our arrangement, to make it fair? First I must mark what belongs to me.' He took his pen and started to highlight sections of the manuscript.

'Leave that! It's my work, not yours,' I protested.

'But my dear,' he said, 'you stole it from me, and now I must take something from you. I have received special dispensation to do so, to do exactly thus, from the master of the house. He told me I might avail myself of anything within it, anything at all. I intend to take this most welcome invitation literally, as I'm certain you will understand. To soften the blow, so to speak, I am prepared to wait and let bygones be bygones. We may forget the past and look to the future! I shall be quiet, and wait until you have finished, quite finished what you are doing now; your current project as it was previously termed, whatever that might be. A mystery! I do love a mystery, don't you? Is it a mystery? No, don't tell me. I don't wish to know, I will have a surprise, yes, why not? I will wait then, as long and on the understanding that the waiting is not interminable, until you have finished writing before I take what I want, *what I'm owed*, and dispense with the rest. Indeed, if you make sufficient haste, in short, if you are quick enough I will make no mention of your less than accommodating attitude and will therefore, as a result, spare you, as it were, the consequences. How about that? Now, I think I shall go to my room, if you will excuse me.'

He took my manuscript and left. I have looked for it since, but I can't find it. What I'd thought was only in my imagination may not have been. It is possible that Matt has played a trick on me, and that someone, some being from the past who can make himself look and sound like me, was actually here. As far as I know, he still is.

*

I must intervene here. I have been quite forbearing, but things are clearly getting out of control. First of all, the tyrant who features in these journal entries, with his so-called regimes and commandments, is an imaginary one. This is not to say that he doesn't have a point sometimes. I personally don't see anything wrong with hard work and self-discipline, or with striving to be a better person, but Suhail obviously does. It was wrong of him to present my efforts to help him in this way, but even though he has made it necessary for me to present a more accurate picture, I cannot take this one too personally.

For the record then, I did, on request, set him targets and deadlines. The list he makes is odd, and looks in places like the kind of thing someone would write in order to motivate themselves. But then it becomes distorted and grossly exaggerated. In fact, Suhail knows, for example, that it isn't good for him to lie in bed in the morning. He needs structure and routine in his day, otherwise he gets lethargic and depressed. That's why

86

he asked me to try and wake him at 7.00 a.m. It's up to him whether he actually gets up or not. He also knows that he gets tired and needs a full 8 hours sleep. Unlike me, I can function on half of that.

Contrary to what he suggests here, I'm not that interested in his personal habits, although I do believe that a healthy mind is the product of a healthy body. Take me for example. As I've stated, I don't drink more than the occasional brandy, I don't smoke or eat badly unless I'm obliged to, and I myself do work out for 45 minutes each day, precisely, and I never get ill. I don't give Suhail an allowance as such, but I do run his account for him because of his poor track record with money. These days, or more precisely for a year or so before he left, I did feed some funds into his account and encouraged him, of course, to use them sensibly.

Neither of us have private rooms as he claims, but as my description of the house will make clear, there are a number of rooms that are and always have been locked up. He could have gone in any of them if he'd really wanted to, although it might not have been safe to do so. I don't know what he means when he says that he couldn't see anyone on his own, but I'll come back to that subject shortly. The rest is absurd, although the last two items under the first heading fit very closely with his psychological profile. You will know better than I do that the psychological profile is a useful means of detection. I will therefore give a full account of Suhail's in due course, but his description of the mystery visitor illustrates some aspects of it quite well.

This brings me to the list of injunctions. I was accused of harassing him if I said anything about cooking and cleaning *etc.* so I decided to draw up a rota which divided all household tasks equally between us on a week by week basis. Suhail ignored it and so he can hardly claim to have kept house for me. I do prefer a tidy house and Suhail, it must be said, is very untidy. Inevitably, in any long-term relationship, there have to be compromises. I have never told him to be grateful or anything else, although I have asked him to be less hostile at times.

He is naturally quiet and was even uncommunicative before he left. If he was out of sight in his own room most of the time it was because he wanted to be and let's face it, it isn't good to sit around in your pyjamas all day long. As for not locking doors, his journal makes his claustrophobia quite apparent so I doubt very much if he would have wanted to in any case. The timetables were provided for his own sake, not mine, and yes, if he made a deadline I'd often give him a reward, although I would not have done if I'd realised that rewards would be taken in this way, and he would subsequently pretend that he was treated like a dog. Suhail was not mistreated, in any way. He had no need of escape, at least not from me.

The figure that really persecutes Suhail is, I suspect, the one that comes calling. The visitor is Suhail's alter ego and everything that he fears and wishes himself to be. On the one hand he is a sinister impersonator and an identity thief. On the other hand he is older, wiser and more successful. Above all, he is a figure from the past.

He embodies the past, like a ghost. The ghost of Suhail's brother, perhaps. This ghost finally takes up residence in an adjacent room, meaning, I suppose, that the past has all but caught up with Suhail.

Apparently, I am the ghost's agent and it, the visitor, is not the mediator he claims to be. Well, I'm certain there are no ghosts in this house, and although we have had one or two short-term lodgers over the years, and the last one was quite recent, we have never had a long-term live-in guest. To the best of my knowledge I have no mysterious associate with whom I have conspired and corresponded either to help Suhail with his writing or to help himself to it although, in the early days when we would leave each other notes and messages, Suhail once thanked me for my support in this area. It saddens me that he has misrepresented this as the visitor's obsequiousness.

A couple of factual corrections: it is not rare for me to be out of the house on business, and we do not have a drawing room. At least, I don't call it that. In general, there is nothing wholly unexpected in this piece of invention. It is all in character, not least the outright rejection of method and instruction which combines, paradoxically, with a longing for direction from somebody close who truly understands him. These internal contradictions are here for all to see, but Suhail's attitude towards friends, especially his intolerance, is unfairly attributed to me.

He once had many friends, as did we, but he steadily pushed them all away. I could see why but I couldn't stop him, try as I might. I would invite people and he would un-invite them. He retreated into himself more and more during the course of our relationship, and as the spectre of Saeed continued to grow, so others became superfluous and often irritating. It wasn't just me who lost out. They cared for him but he gave them less and less to care about, until they struggled to remember why they did and eventually forgot. It wasn't as if I didn't warn him that this was happening, but he wouldn't listen to me. I think he missed them too. He must have been lonely. I'm more gregarious, by nature, but I see people all day long, so I didn't suffer as much. Also, in my relations with him, I could survive on less. I tried to reach him when I could, and to bring new people to him. Hence the boating trip. This is what really happened:

Cook Rampton and Jones, is the name of the firm I work for. Harry is one of our in-house solicitors. I knew Grant from my days as a financial planner and, fair enough, I couldn't really cope with Justin. I wouldn't go as far as to say that I cannot abide campness, though I certainly prefer not to encourage it or engage with it. I don't react well to melodrama or any kind of attention-seeking behaviour. It is alien to my personality. In fact, Justin's dog annoyed me more than he did. It wasn't just that he barked continually and sat his filthy backside in my food. It's that I can't bear pointless breeds like that. Of course, the character and appearance of the breed and the owner are not unrelated. Everyone knows that.

Horace (I need hardly say more) was a stupid creature with no purpose at all, except to look as pampered and prissy as his owner. A miniature poodle with his tail draped over his back. Exactly. What does Bichon Frise mean anyway? Something to do with curls I think. Justin boasted of Horace's long Mediterranean ancestry and went on repeatedly about how much brushing, shampooing and scissoring was required in order to make him look so ridiculous. Allergies were described in graphic detail, not that they needed to be. We all witnessed the scratching, biting, licking and, in addition, snorting, choking and honking for ourselves. Horace, of course, had sensitive skin caused, not least, by too much brushing, shampooing and scissoring. We were informed, whilst eating, that the most revolting symptoms were collectively known as 'reverse sneezing,' the cure for which, as we couldn't help but observe, was massaging the animal's throat while pinching its nostrils. Happily, while perilous for the appetite of the onlooker, the condition is not dangerous to the dog. Give me a German Shepherd any day.

I've looked into the history of this breed and intend to acquire a good example in due course. This won't just be an excellent companion but a very useful guard dog. Developed by a cavalry officer, Captain Max von Stephanitz, at the end of the 19th century, the German Shepherd's talents must be and always have been properly channelled. It's an incredibly versatile animal which served in both world wars as a tracker, sentry, mine detector, message carrier, cable layer, and so on. Since then it has been a police dog, rescue dog, obedience dog, you name it. Cowboy breeders have threatened the bloodline, but there are organisations throughout the world which are dedicated to keeping it clean.

Back to that day out. Justin's outburst at having some drink spilled on him was disproportionate and embarrassing. It wasn't necessary to have known him long to realise it was characteristic of a highly unstable, almost hysterical personality. There were other people picnicking nearby and we disturbed them. They stared at us. I got people into boats as quickly as possible after that. Bernard and Celia did go with Justin. They came with him and Grant. I had not met them before, but Grant thought I might like to. It was a mistake. We didn't get on, and I certainly did not believe their story. Justin's rowing was hopeless, but I didn't think it was particularly funny. He was all over the river and bound to hit somebody eventually. I tried to help but of course help wasn't the point. The point was to create a spectacle. Another one.

Incidentally, in order to move to the left in a rowing boat you would have to do the opposite of what Suhail says or, rather, has me say. That is, you would back down with your left oar but you couldn't, if you were close to a boat on your right, row forwards with your right oar until you'd done that. If you'd already rowed backwards with your left, rowing forwards with your right would just point you in the other direction, so in fact to straighten up you'd need to go forwards with both oars simultaneously. Even then, if the boats are very close, you might need to use your left oar to paddle towards you before doing anything else. All of this was completely lost on Justin who was content just to make a fool of himself.

His idiocy had consequences. We were pushed into the bank and the left oar was knocked out of my hand and into the water. The right blade dug into the bank, causing the handle to fly up and catch me on the side of my face. Nobody wants to be hit in the face, and I admit I was angry at first. Nevertheless what happened next was not deliberate. It was an accident. As I just said, the blade of my right oar was stuck in the mud. I had to tug at it a good few times and with both hands in order to get it out, rising up out of my seat and increasing my effort each time. At the point that it came free there was a lot of energy pulling me over, and as the blade flipped across I slipped on the wet wood at the bottom of the boat. My left leg went under me, and the blade made contact with Justin's nose just as he was leaning in to watch.

I only remember the one blow but it did cause quite an impressive nosebleed. I dropped the blade as soon as I could, but of course Justin wailed and moaned as if he had just been mortally wounded. I scrambled to regain my balance and tried to reach out to quieten him at the same time, but as I did so I slipped again and fell on him. Harry and Suhail helped me off. It was all very unfortunate but really just one of those things. It was bad enough that Justin tried unsuccessfully I might add, to sue me without Suhail making a meal of it too.

I neither wish nor need to comment on Suhail's dreams about Peter and the couple in the cellar. They clearly illustrate that his mind was unhealthy and, try as I might, there was little I could do about that. Suhail has a profoundly weak sense of self, and this is because his identity, unlike mine, is not built on a solid foundation of values and morality. This fact is apparent in the circumstances surrounding his writing and the short story that may or may not have been his. He could only allow himself to reveal these circumstances in the nightmare of the visitor who accuses him of theft, and then steals the manuscript back. Conveniently, Suhail claims that he cannot find his manuscript, but I found it easily enough. I only had to look.

I carried out a systematic search of Suhail's desk drawers and bookshelves. They were a shocking mess. No organisation, nothing in alphabetical order. Books and papers were piled randomly on top of each other. The drawers were stuffed full and the shelves covered in dust. I don't think he ever cleaned in there. With so little floor space, it's hard to see how he could. Nevertheless, there it was, the manuscript, in the second drawer down on the left, buried beneath some notes he'd made toward an article that had, presumably, never been written. Suhail had not managed to publish anything. By his own admission, he couldn't make up his mind as to whether to pursue scholarly research or try to be a writer. I refrained from reading his first attempt at a story. I have no time for fiction, as I've said, and it clearly wasn't any good. Even his friends didn't think much of it.

It was when I was contemplating his erstwhile friends that it dawned on me. Suhail might have been corresponding with them behind my back. I was annoyed that it hadn't occurred to me before. One of them might know of his plans. It was possible that somebody he used to associate with knew where he was. Having discovered nothing useful in my quest for the manuscript, I immediately resolved to check his emails more thoroughly. It had not seemed necessary before. I had only looked at one page, and at nothing more than the subject headings. On this occasion, I noted who the senders were too, and read everything in his inbox, saved messages and sent messages. I realised that I had committed an oversight, and was determined to make up for it. I have to say that this task took me weeks, despite the fact that Suhail did not have a regular job – the truth was that he only ever worked part time and towards the end, not even that – and had become anti-social and relatively inactive. He had not bothered to delete his spam and, sad to say, there was not a great deal else. Had there been a message of any significance either sent or received, he had removed it. I doubt if there had been though. I went through his trash. There was nothing there.

§

Today is an important day, a real day, not a dream one. Not another lost one. How long have I been lost for? I don't know, I don't even care – it doesn't matter now I'm awake.

I went down to breakfast in my usual way; in my pyjamas, unwashed, unshaven, furry of tooth and several hours later than Matt would like me to. He'd done that bloody rota again. Every week he uses more coloured pens and bigger type. I'm expecting bar charts soon. Venn diagrams or whatever they are. I was always bad at maths. He sticks it on the wall above the bin with drawing pins. I'm sure he's not allowed to do that, make holes in the plaster. Like everything else it's listed, and still painted sludge green. They don't sell that shade anymore, but gods forbid we should change it, or add any colour, proper colour, i.e. anything but the colour of swan shit. There is nothing resembling vibrant in this museum piece he calls home. This place is a relic – cold, dead and dull. Just like its owner.

I wanted to deface his handiwork, re-assign all the tasks to him, re-arrange them as I regularly re-arrange the saucepans that hang on a clanky metal frame that has to be winched up and down. They'll never line up in order of size as long as I'm around. I wanted to pull his poster down, rip it to shreds and stuff it in the bin. But that would give him too much to react to, too much to get his teeth into, and as long as it stays there I can pretend I haven't noticed it, that I've been too busy to sit in the kitchen drinking endless cups of tea and staring at the walls. Newspapers aren't permitted. They'd be too much of a distraction.

As I brought my first cup over to the table I saw the letter Matt had left for me, after he'd steamed it open. Inside the envelope were two pages neatly written in a hand I easily recognised to be Ben's. Ben is a full time counsellor now, a behavioural therapist, and he has a new boyfriend, I was pleased to hear. He had been on his own for a while, but he clearly doesn't need to practise on his partners anymore. Other people pay him to look sympathetic and say nothing except 'how does that make you feel?' I don't mind talking about myself, it's not that. It's the inequality, the lack of reciprocity, the artifice. Anyway, Ben always meant well, he was always kind, withholding judgement even of Andrew who'd managed to be vain in a community of narcissists, acerbic when everyone around him was tart. Andrew is married now, apparently – to a woman. Finally, he's met his match.

The others are all doing well, and life is going on much as before with perhaps fewer club nights and more visits to the theatre. There has been a bit more pairing off and settling down. Civil partnerships are the big news, and it looks like Danny and Li are up first. The guest list is already proving controversial because Ed wants to bring Rocco, sixteen years his junior and currently starring in some musical in the West End and his ex, Robin, stage manages the same show, is definitely already coming, but can't stand the sight of the 'little ponce' with whom he is already, so to speak, fully acquainted.

Ben went on to describe the 'his and his' outfits, the bridesmaid's gear etc. But he was too obviously trying to make me laugh. It wasn't him. He was preparing me for something, and then it came, two lines at the bottom of the last page:

Look Suhail, I've been trying not to tell you this, but she wanted you to know. I'm talking about B. She's alright, sort of, but

That was it. The other pages were missing. Matt had taken them. Whatever it was that B wanted me to know, Matt didn't want me to know. She obviously wasn't alright and she needed me in some way, but he didn't want me involved. I couldn't believe it. Even by Matt's standards this was intrusive, outrageous. Who did he think he was, intercepting my mail like that, interfering? The letter was addressed to me. It was private. I had no privacy anymore. None at all. This was the last straw. I was going to confront him the minute he got in. I knew better than to search the house. What I was looking for wouldn't be there. He'd have taken it with him. He'd have secreted it somewhere else, somewhere out of my reach. I'd never find it. I'd have to wait.

I spent the day brooding over Ben's letter, the section that I had, and reading those two lines over and over. B. It had been a long time since I'd seen her, just that once, since leaving the orphanage. She had studied Design and was setting up her own fashion business, specialising in outsize clothes for eccentric, unashamed women. There were more than I'd have thought. She already had a client base that extended abroad and she travelled a lot, buying up fabrics from around the world, the sort Matt would describe as exotic.

He got back at his usual time. I decided to make it look as if I'd never left the kitchen, or had only just arrived. In other words, I was still in my pyjamas and stubble. I was the sort that could grow a full beard in well under forty eight hours.

'Where is it?' I demanded, when he eventually worked out where I was.

'Good evening Suhail,' he said. 'Where is what?'

'My letter.'

'I left it on the table for you this morning.'

'Not all of it, and I want the rest. How dare you …'

'How dare I? How dare I what, Suhail? Pick up your post from the mat because otherwise it might form a mound and block the door? Put it right in front of your nose where, even then, you might fail to see it?'

'I want to know what's happened to my friend.'

'Nothing.'

'That's a lie. Something has happened and I want to help her.'

'Why?'

'What's wrong with you? She's my friend.'

He pointed out that I had not seen her in years, and he knew that because I'd not really seen anyone in years and, what's more, that's how it should be because my friends were all a waste of space, including this one, no doubt. The last thing I needed to do, with so much improvement still to be made, so much work to do on myself and my attitudes, the last thing I needed was to go chasing after people whose lives were of no concern to me, and no real importance. I objected to this, I slammed my hand on the table, and he told me not to make a scene.

Then he sat down and crossed his legs and stared at the ceiling. I knew I was going to get a lecture. The topic, not for the first time or I bet for the last was indebtedness. There were those I owed something to, and those that I didn't. I owed nothing to B as far as Matt was concerned, but then, he doesn't know anything about her or what happened at the orphanage after my brother left. He knew that I had a brother who left, but I hadn't told him anything else. He didn't know the half of it, but he still went on, he still singled out Saeed as one of the people I should, but clearly didn't feel indebted to. He brought me up, didn't he? And I don't even talk about him. I was ungrateful and withdrawn. I had no sense of responsibility or rather, I had a misplaced one. That was it. My sense of responsibility was misplaced. In comparison with him of course, nobody had a claim on me. If my brother had brought me up it was him, Matt, who had put me up, who had put up with me for all these years. And what did he get in return? Nothing. Worse than nothing: sullenness, childishness and a refusal to pull my weight. I expected everything to be done for me, and I wouldn't even contemplate helping him with anything, not even the day to day running of the house in which I lived, rent free.

This went on for what seemed like hours. I hardly got another word in, but when I returned to my room and Matt went to his office, I tried to phone Ben on the landline. Matt was already there. I heard him pick up the receiver and I hung up. I grabbed my mobile but I already knew I was out of credit. I'd run out months ago. Matt had offered to buy me a five pound top-up, but there was a catch. There always is. I had to stick to the rota.

*

I did write back to Ben. I told him what had happened to his letter and that I'd never got the news about B. I didn't know what else to say except that he was right to have been suspicious of Matt. I couldn't tell him the rest. I don't think therapy has a word for what Matt is, for what my life is. He'd started going back to work, to the city, to get away from me I suppose, but after I heard from Ben he stopped again, decided it was more important to keep an eye on me, and that he does. That he does. He keeps an eye on me when I'm eating, to make sure that nothing tasty finds its way onto my plate. He keeps an eye on me when I'm exercising, which I have to do with him, in the basement, to make sure I'm not cheating. He doesn't expect me to do as much as he does because I'm not as strong, but I have to stay down there anyway, until I'm released. He watches me when I'm working, to make sure that I do, and sometimes he watches me when I'm in the bath. I wouldn't be surprised if he inspects my boxer shorts. He's always putting them in the laundry basket for me.

I wasn't going to post this letter that had nothing much to say. I thought I could say it as well in an email, but when I went to log on, I couldn't get a connection. I kept trying, but I always got the same message about the network being down. I hadn't sent any emails for a while, but it had worked fine then, I got online straight away. I've never been able to diagnose problems with my computer. I don't understand the way it thinks. If computers are like brains then I don't know what my brain is like. I felt stupid, hitting random keys, opening windows into what might as well have been the fourth dimension, and being drawn in to a language I had no hope of translating. I shut the thing down and went to put it away. It's a laptop. I like it best when it's in a drawer. That's when I saw, down the side, the card thing was missing, the modem.

I got caught in the hallway, although I'd waited until the afternoon because Matt is always busier then. He must have heard me creeping down the stairs. A double humiliation – having to creep and then getting caught, as if I was doing something I shouldn't be. Matt took the letter, saying he would post it for me later, after I'd helped him with a job he couldn't manage on his own, one that needed two pairs of hands. It was the drains. They were all clogged up. We went round the whole house. He shoved his bare hand down a couple of them, into some rancid gunge, and then he expected me to do the same. He'd taken pleasure in it, slopping the stuff into a bin liner I was holding open, as far from my body as possible. He grabbed the bag and told me it was my turn, and I looked at him in disbelief. So he dropped it, went inside, and brought out a pair of marigolds. I put them on and attempted to clear a drain, holding a piece of slime between my thumb and forefinger and trying not to wretch. He got impatient then, and finished the rest himself. After that it was the guttering. I was

101

allowed to hold the ladder, but detritus kept falling on my head and when I protested he told me to get inside and wait for him. He had something to tell me.

I could not have guessed what that was. Apparently, he'd spoken to Ben, some weeks before, and soon after he'd doctored my letter. There was no preamble with Matt. He just said it: B's nephew Rafe had been killed when he was with her on a working trip abroad. He showed me the picture that he'd taken from the envelope – of a red faced, red haired boy I'd met once before, the time he'd come to visit me with his aunt.

This was in the days before I met Matt, when I still lived among other human beings. B had tracked me down and suggested we meet. I was not expecting her to have an attachment, an accessory, and at first I wasn't too pleased about it. He was rather demanding, and didn't like being cooped up in my admittedly rather pokey flat. So we went for a walk in the park. There is something about walking, moving – it has to be outside – that always unblocks things. B and I had struggled when she first arrived. Not just because of the boy. We hadn't seen each other for ages of course, but we were getting through the obvious topics of conversation too fast. There wasn't any flow. It was as if the link that had broken that night in the recreation room was still waiting to be fixed. That seemed to happen while we were walking. I lost track of time, I became easy and so did she. Without realising it, we were communicating. I don't remember what we talked about, only that we talked. At one point B went to join Rafe, who'd got ahead of us, and I hung back. As she approached him he was pulled in towards her and began to circle her, laughing, running, faster and faster in rings made literal by the after-image of his fiery head.

I understood something then, in that moment, about what it means to be part of the world. It has nothing to do with what we think of as ourselves, questing for something, escaping from something, trying desperately to move on or to belong. Belonging is a given. It is part of being alive, part of being. I don't mean communities or relationships. Not that exactly. It isn't familial or even necessarily social. It's something more physical that happens between planets and particles as well as people. It has to do with gravity, energy and mass. I had become energy when that lightning bolt shot through me, phenomenal energy, and B had phenomenal mass. She was capable of making things happen, of putting them in motion around her. All things are in motion all of the time. They're dynamic or they're dead. They move in relation to other things and they cannot, absolutely cannot, move alone. Alone has no meaning. It's a trick played by consciousness and sight. We interact whether we like it or not.

Well my epiphany, such as it was, kept me up in the air for an hour or so. And then we met my friends for lunch – Ben, Andrew and another guy, I can't remember his name, who was Andrew's latest hanger-on. Andrew was good at being funny at other people's expense, and I must confess that I often enjoyed his performances, but not on this occasion. It was my mistake, arranging to meet in a trendy pub frequented by body conscious, bitchy clientele. Almost every head swivelled when we came in, and stayed locked on as B did her best to negotiate the narrow spaces between trim, prissy little tables. Finding one she could sit down at was an ordeal, and then she had to perch on a ridiculously undersized chair that Ben and I had pushed away into a corner for her. She was game of course. She joked about it, but that made it worse, giving Andrew the excuse for a malicious, mocking apology for a grin. I hated him at that moment. I wanted to throw a tablecloth over her lap so that he couldn't see how much of her over-spilled her seat. Ben tried hard to make things pleasant, too hard, and Rafe ran riot. I would never have planned to bring a child onto those premises, but the arrangement was made before I knew he was coming. I took some satisfaction from the chaos he created, the tête-à-têtes he disrupted, and from the near swoon he inflicted on one old queen who'd clearly never been barged into by a brat before.

B tried to control her nephew from a distance, but that only made her sound bossy. I almost wished she'd never come, but after she'd gone, I felt strangely and totally bereft, as if she had taken everything in the world with her and left a colossal, infinite vacuum in her wake. It had a name of course: Saeed.

Now, after what Matt had just told me, I didn't *think* of how bereft B must be, I could feel it. I tried to find out more, but Matt repeatedly refused to tell me, saying that I already looked upset enough. He was right, but I still wanted to know the circumstances, how it had happened and most of all where she was now and when I could go and see her. Matt was almost sympathetic. He could tell that I was genuine, that I wasn't just trying something on. For once I think he came close to accepting that I might legitimately care about someone else. But it didn't last, he couldn't help himself. He was never going to let me go. He said, and I suppose he was right about this too, that I couldn't be of any practical help. Others could, and there were bound to be others. Ben at least would be taking care of her. He had assured Matt of that. He would put her on to a very good psychotherapist in her area, one who specialised in grief, loss. I was, let's face it, too damaged by my own loss to help somebody else overcome theirs. I couldn't argue with that. He spoke more gently than he had since the old days, the early days. It made me cry.

*

I have a right of intervention here. I wish to state that I sought only to protect Suhail from the information that his friend had unwisely disclosed. He clearly didn't know Suhail as well as he thought he did. Suhail is fragile, easily affected and likely to be overwhelmed by such things. What was I supposed to do? Allow him to read about how the boy, out swimming in the sea on his own, had become caught in the propeller of a speed boat and sliced to pieces? His aunt had been unable to rescue him from the water. It transpired that she couldn't swim. The implication was that she also had her mind on other things, was reading papers beneath an umbrella, and didn't even see what happened until it was too late. If she had wished to prioritise her work, she should have brought another adult with her. Her sister, Suzy I think the name was, had wanted to accompany them but was not permitted to do so. This unfortunate young woman subsequently suffered a bout of 'emotional exhaustion,' which I believe is a euphemism for a breakdown. She was taken to hospital. B, which stands for Bridget, had to visit her there on her return. I dare say it was a grim reunion. Suhail simply could not have coped with all of this. He brooded enough as it was, and that is his word, not mine.

Had the child been my own, I would not have allowed him to go. This Bridget was a single woman on a business trip. His mother was unmarried, worked in a shop and often relied on her sister to take care of the boy. What sort of an arrangement is that? Where was the father figure? It seems to me that he needed one. People should be prepared to give children a proper family upbringing or they should not have children at all. Few women can provide stability and discipline as well as nurture a child by themselves. Fewer still can provide for their offspring financially. I'm not saying that a woman's place is in the home, but unless the circumstances are exceptional, it is either in the home or in the workplace and not both at the same time. It doesn't work. Ad hoc domestic arrangements do not work and are not a substitute for marriage. Neither are civil partnerships in my opinion.

I am not clear why Suhail should place an imaginary obligation to his friend above a real obligation to his family. It is unnatural. Human beings prioritise their own kin, their own kind, they always have. How else would people have survived without social security, charity, benefaction? These things have made us soft and distorted the natural order which is based, as I believe Darwin said, on the survival of the fittest. Suhail was too drawn to the outcasts, the misfits, the no-hopers. I cannot afford to be. Not in my line of work.

As for keeping an eye on him, to an extent I had to. Otherwise he would have eaten nothing but chocolate biscuits all day long. Moreover, he did cheat in the gym, though he thought I didn't know it. I keep a calor gas heater in there for the winter. He must have pressed his face to it in order to make it look like he was hot and sweating. He didn't realise that I'd calibrated the equipment so that it registered whether it had been used or not. I thought it would inspire him to watch me do press-ups, crunches and so on, but it seems that it did not. It should be reasonably apparent by now that he would not work unless I helped him and, frankly, unless I ran it for him, he wouldn't go near the bath. The other statement he made is disgusting. I picked his underwear up because if I didn't it would lie there on the floor exactly where it was dropped for weeks on end. It is as simple as that.

Suhail was not, as he says himself, a competent user of the Internet. He was not a particularly wise one either. He thought he had broken his computer once, and I offered to have a look at it for him. I like computers. They are very logical and to my mind, easy to use. I am not an expert, a hacker or a programmer, but I can find my way around. In order to track his recent moves and see what he might have done, I selected and viewed his list of favourites. There were things there that I'd rather not discuss. Just because pornography sites, chat rooms and so on are readily available, Suhail did not have to let himself be led astray. He could have resisted. He could have abstained. I personally have never seen the like of it, and never wish to again. The Internet can be useful, but it is necessary to sift the good from the bad. A person with a strong moral anchor would have no trouble with that. But for the weak-willed, there is an endless supply of mindless, degrading material. I could no longer expose him to that. He did have an email account, but it was managed by me. I still had to check it after Suhail had gone. He had taken to sneaking around, and I had to allow for the possibility that he might have broken in to my office in order to send or receive a message. You can't be too careful.

I did not post the return letter to Ben. I locked it in my bureau. I make no apology for this. Suhail had totally misunderstood my motives, and I would do nothing that encouraged a resumption in their relations. Ben is harmless enough in himself. I bear him no ill will. But there was no benefit to be gained from their association, only the risk that Suhail would discover what he could not bear and be put back in touch with more of his former contacts. All that drivel about who is sleeping with who and which of them can't stand the sight of the other. Who cares? Have they nothing better to do?

I told Suhail that I'd spoken to Ben because I thought he had a right to know. I decided that the news would be better coming from me, not least because I knew more than anyone how much he could and could not take. I knew how little he could take and also how little he could give. Suhail could not have helped his friend. He wasn't capable, and it would seem he understood that in the end, although he never quite stopped probing.

§

I dream about the accident almost every night. My brother is sitting there, utterly still, blood oozing from the hole in his face, the ghastly flap hanging, dripping great fat reproachful tears, but worst of all, the look in his eyes. It wasn't only his beloved car that had betrayed him. I wake up and I'm tangled in sheets, everything is stuck to me, and as I loosen it I feel the chill of the air on my damp body and I reach back further into my memory for another dream, a better one in which I am innocent and no damage has been done. I lie, thinking about the moment in which I am embraced by my brother again. I see it, in an instant, in a flash, and I feel – if I really concentrate, if I channel every molecule of myself towards it – ecstatic, redeemed.

It was lightning that blew us apart that day in the car. It separated one twin from the other and changed a boy into a man burdened and haunted and filled with nightmares about his past. Then let lightning bring us back together again, just exactly as it had before in that one precious moment of brilliant light and outstretched arms. I knew it could because of its infinite, magical power to create as well as destroy living things, to turn men into monsters and back again. I knew it could, but I didn't know how.

I had some books, but I needed more. I had no choice but to ask Matt to help me. I think he was as surprised as I was, but it had to be done. I told him I had an idea for a story, and that I needed to do some research. I knew he wouldn't want me to go to the library, because that would involve being out for hours at a time, and who knows what I might get up to, who I might meet in the cafeteria or brush past in those narrow, secluded shelf stacks. He wouldn't want me to go to a bookshop for the same reason and besides, I had no money. I couldn't bring myself to ask for that, but he enjoyed it anyway, I could tell. He strung it out for as long as he could. What was the story going to be about? Lightning. What was so interesting about that? Everything. What did I mean? I meant the origin of life, the universe – everything. Oh, he said, it's going to be a long story then. Sarcastic bastard. How long did I

109

think it would take me to write it? Did I have a plan, a structure, a timetable? What did he think. Had I a publisher in mind? No. Look, I said, it's still an idea, and I don't know how long it will take to develop it, but it won't develop at all unless I can do some more reading.

Matt is not a fan of reading, but he had to accept that it was necessary, given the topic, given my ignorance of the natural world around me, of the world outside my room, outside my head. I think it even occurred to him that I might learn something useful, but he still pretended to disapprove so that I had to work harder, so that he could add restrictions, conditions. Oh yes, there were conditions. I was going to have to pay in kind, I knew that. I saw that one coming. The restrictions were ostensibly to do with cost. My favours, unspoken, weren't going to buy me much. I would need to provide him with a list of titles, and these titles would have to be approved if they were not readily available in the local library. I was to be allocated a budget, and it was up to me whether I spent it wisely, carefully, or blew it all in one go. He would expect a regular progress report once the research was underway, and he reserved the right to judge for himself if the outcome of all this bookwork was a success, as he very much hoped it would be.

I made the list. He said it seemed rather eclectic and it was. I was searching for the link between lightning and transformation, and this search had to be wide. There was science as well as fiction, media as well as mythology. That's where he really put his foot down. What did the media have to do with anything? I was supposed to be writing a story, not wasting time watching films. I told him I needed a contemporary perspective as well as a historical one, and it was going to be more like documentary anyway. He still grumbled about it. He doesn't like me watching television. He thinks it's bad for me. I persisted, and in the end he grudgingly agreed to get hold of one documentary about how people survive lightning strikes, and one film, *Act of God*, which was, it turned out, more interesting to him, though he complained that it was unnecessarily quirky and could have been done in a more straightforward way. I said why didn't he contact the director and tell him that because I'm sure he would find the feedback fascinating and Matt told me to shut up and show a little gratitude.

I stuck to reading afterwards. I was allowed to do that on my own. I went for classic fiction because I already knew some of this. *Frankenstein* was one of the books I'd brought with me from the orphanage. It was inspired by galvanism. Victor Frankenstein learns first how to use electricity to make the legs of a dead frog, the fingers of a dead hand twitch, and then he uses lightning to bring his human composite to life. His 'creature' is never given a name of his own. He is never given a chance. He is completely innocent, knowing nothing of good and evil until he learns it from human beings. It is *them* that corrupt *him*, not the other way round. He only becomes monstrous when his creator rejects him. Poor Gregor Samsa is rejected too. Even his sister, who once loved him, leaves him in his filthy room to starve. Kafka doesn't say how Gregor changes, what causes his transformation – whether or not there had been a storm in the night.

Ovid is more of an optimist. He says that 'all things are always changing, but nothing dies.'
The spirit comes and goes,
Is housed wherever it wills, shifts residence

111

From beasts to men, from men to beasts, but always
It keeps on living.

In his poem, metamorphosis is not about horror or shame, becoming some kind of zombie or insect. Dante might have interpreted it that way, but really it is about vitality, life itself. All things are always changing, but what *makes* them change? Again, we come back to lightning. Science has merely proved what the Navajo already knew. Life comes from lightning. Life – not death. A lightning bolt struck the primordial soup, and the process of evolution began. Stanley Miller proved this in an experiment. He put together the same chemicals that were in the primordial soup, and used an electric charge to simulate lightning. In doing so, he generated amino acids, the building blocks of life. That was a long time ago, but there are still experiments, even more of them that imitate lightning in order to create or alter life. There would be no genetic engineering without lightning, no clones for example, and no way of combining the cells of different species. From beasts to men, from men to beasts: it keeps on going. It will never end, and the key to it all is lightning, the magic ingredient, the science and the spell.

Once I'd started I couldn't stop. The more I read, the more I knew it would happen. It wasn't just possible, it was inevitable. Change is what happens, and lightning is everywhere. One hundred bolts per second, as it said in my primer. Eight million chances of being hit every day and, as long as it's raining, you're almost bound to survive. But Matt, predictably, put a downer on it. He didn't like my progress reports. He found them inadequate, insufficiently detailed and poorly organised. He asked to see my notes instead. I thought he was frowning because of my handwriting, but no. He was quiet for a second, looked up at the ceiling, and then proceeded to rant at me about the immorality of my ideas. They weren't even my ideas! What, did he think I was making them up? Could I somehow be held to account for centuries of thinking, investigation and imagination? I wish I could. I wish I could take some credit, but I'm only the messenger, the conduit. Matt's eyes were burning and he kept scratching at his face, hands and forearms as if the irritation I was causing him was real. He even talked about religion, and how we had to save our souls from meddling scientists like the ones that had cloned that sheep and would do the same to us if someone didn't stop them. I really do think he's losing it.

*

Believe me, I am not losing anything. Neither am I about to. I am not the one who harbours a deluded hope, and is so desperate for redemption that he cannot see he risks the very opposite. Although I now wish I hadn't, I agreed to buy him books purely in order to keep him occupied. It was obvious that he needed to focus his mind. He needed a purpose and though I could think of much better ones than writing, I hoped it might at least do. I ought to have detected a certain feverishness about him. He had been more than usually withdrawn – I would say depressed, although I never had him diagnosed. Sometimes depression is accompanied by anxiety, but it is possible for the sufferer to alternate, so that they are depressed one minute and manic the next. I am not a physician, but if Suhail was not suffering from a clinical disorder, he was clearly not right. I do not think he even understood what he was reading.

The alteration of human life is wrong. It transgresses the laws of nature and yes, of God. I do not hold extreme views in this regard, and neither do I make a show of them. I would not describe myself as a pious man but as an ordinary citizen who, like countless others, believes that we were created in God's image and if He wanted it to be otherwise He would have designed it that way. But we are the superior species, each of us in possession of a soul and a consciousness. We are all unique. This knowledge is fundamental to human civilisation. It should not need to be restated. It should be beyond challenge or contradiction. It seems to me that Suhail misinterpreted his books, for what was the fate of the man made from other men's limbs, or the one who turned into a dung beetle? His fate was torment.

A similar fate would befall a clone, or any product of an experiment in genetics. That is why such experiments are, and should be confined to animals. Animals are not conscious of who or what they are, but a human being would be tortured by their loss of identity. Had Suhail's sense of identity been stronger in the first place, he would not have been so drawn to the material that I unwittingly supplied.

I had understood that he was investigating lightning as the basis for a story, and at the time, I could not see the harm in that. It was more beneficial than what he had been doing, which was nothing. He had been lying in bed feeling sorry for himself. In the few short hours between getting up and going back to bed again he had not spoken, except to plague me with questions that, for his own sake, I had no intention of answering. I

114

sought only to distract him with some activity, albeit of little to no actual use. Ironically, I was trying to keep him out of trouble. I thought at least if he was reading he could not be trying to make contact with Ben. I had relocated the phone from his room just in case, and was regularly checking the bill. I had suggested relocating his study too, so that it would be closer to mine and more companionable. But he refused and then, to spite me, he virtually shut himself in.

§

There is a side entrance and a front entrance to this house. The back entrance is reserved for Matt's own special use. From the side it is approached via a winding single track road. This dips down into a deep valley and then rises steeply up to the original chapel and extensions to the main building. From close by, these appear to be either submerging into, or emerging from the dark vegetation at the far end of two fallow fields. At the bottom lies the recently reinforced perimeter wall.

But this was not my first view, which was of the central clock tower and its two impressive spires. Either side of these there were four-storey gabled buildings, two more towers and sloping wings, each with its own arched doorway. Hundreds if not thousands of small regular windows overlooked a well-tended lawn and beyond that the sea. A completely cloudless blue sky contrasted with the red roof tiles and seemed to draw a flush of pleasure from the century old concrete walls. I felt like I was in the presence of royalty or even better, that I was about to meet a still glamorous if haughty film star from an earlier era. If I played my cards right I would become her favoured young companion, indulged, and idolised solely for my beauty.

I tidied my hair behind my ears as we passed through the elaborate iron gates and mentally rehearsed my introduction. I was wasting my time. Appearances had deceived me and I singularly failed to impress. I was never exactly embraced and now, nearly a decade later, I am barely tolerated, even here in my room with its shrinking walls that are steadily leaching the life out of me. Back then, as I stood at the far end of the circular driveway and looked up past the great oak door, the arch, the flying buttress, the five front and two side windows like a thin-lipped smile and above that the two milky eyes and the clock hands at twelve; back then, I almost believed I was home.

It has been a while, I don't know how long, since I had the freedom of the house. I've been moved further and further in, through unlit corridors I could never find my way out of. I'm not even sure which part of the house this is. My energy seems to fluctuate, and I've developed problems with my breathing. My legs jump less, but tremble continuously. I haven't seen Matt for months on end, though I know he is still here. I hear him talking and laughing with the visitor, although I can't hear what it's about. The floor boards in here are sticky with grime and edged in something like bitumen. There is a cast-iron radiator painted a thin watery brown that hisses and gurgles and long ago dribbled its contents, so that it no longer emits any heat. The walls have a revolting texture. They are grey and thick like the membranes of a giant cadaver, streaked with straw-like veins blown out, here and there, like a bladder filled with congealed blood. They leak too – something like acid that bleaches white tracks like ulcers and forms toxic pools along the skirting.

I once believed that the movement of this hideous sac was just a pulse, or at worse a contraction, but now I realise it's a thickening, a growth within the walls themselves, which are closing in, compressing the foul humid air, increasing the pressure, reducing the oxygen, and slowly suffocating me. My existence inside this room, inside this relic, this corpse of a house is insufferable. It is no symbiosis, but a living death.

I am not completely alone. There's a picture of a woman on the wall right in front of me. It's mine actually, one of the few things I was allowed to bring with me. It's a print of a painting, oil on canvass, though it looks like a charcoal drawing with strong black lines, sometimes broken, sometimes smudged, and around the face incredibly fine and intense. The woman is sitting properly on a stool or chair which you can't see, and her hands are folded neatly in her lap. There's no angle of vision, no pose, no expression as such. She seems to just give herself up for inspection, looking straight ahead without ever quite meeting your eye. She's inside a rectangle, a tight-fitting box, which touches her arms and cuts her off at the knees, but leaves a lot of space above her head, as if it was a badly framed photograph. The space recedes into the corner of what looks like an attic room.

There's a shadow behind her, and a sloping roof, and what looks like a window to one side. I never noticed that before. Her figure isn't coloured in, but somehow she has substance. She's wearing a scooped round-neck dress which finishes just above the knee. It fits her closely, and you can see she has a bust, and a belly. Your eye is drawn upwards from

117

her hands which, unlike the rest of her, don't appear to be still, towards a down-turned rosebud mouth, straight nose and large staring eyes. Her forehead and chin gleam in the light, suggesting an oily complexion or, perhaps, alarm. Her non-expression changes as you get closer. From a distance her chest and throat, and especially her face, appear to be charred and immobile, like a death mask in ebony. But as you get closer you make out the whites of her eyes, the creases in her forehead, and the lines like cracks running down her face. I used to think this was a portrait of melancholy, but now I see, coming through the cracks, that she is frightened, and something else too – she is changing.

I often fall asleep at my desk, and just now I dreamt that I was running. I wasn't alone, there were lots of people, all strangers, and I seemed to be leading them. We were being chased, and we were in trouble. I was terrified, but I had to find a path, a route through all these buildings and open areas littered with rubble and debris, as if there had been a bomb. Then we had to get through tunnels, and trap doors, and windows so small, that you could barely fit through them. I've dreamt this before, some kind of storage room which is a dead end, except for the narrowest possible opening to who knows where. Everyone else is going through, one by one, until it's only me left behind, and I'm panicking, and really don't want to go, but I have to, so I do, and the dream goes on and on, even though I know I'm dreaming. Then I'm in charge again, and everyone is following me. I usually wake up before we get there, wherever there is, but today I ended up in a loft space with a white painted floor, white walls, and a large and inviting open window. There were no strangers any more. I woke up panting, sweating, exhausted, and there she was, the woman in the picture, much closer now, and almost life-sized.

She sat opposite me, as if she had come for an interview and was waiting for me to ask my first question. Since she wouldn't or couldn't look at me, I looked at her. I examined her face which now appeared neither sad or scared but expectant, and a lot younger than it did before. Her skin was smoother, and her lips were full and very slightly open, as if she wanted to speak. She is there right now, and her knees are almost touching mine under the desk. My breathing has slowed down, but hers is speeding up. Her chest expands and contracts like a bellows, and I'm afraid she might use up too much air, and leave me with none. She isn't frightening in herself, not at all. She's keeping me company, though she doesn't seem to notice me, and she hasn't said anything yet. I don't want her to go away. She looks lovely, very beautiful. Maybe she'll stay and help me. I need to get out of here.

I want to run along a pure white sandy beach with no-one chasing me, but the house wants me to stay, inside this putrid room, which is shrinking to fit, and in which I'm bound to end up unconscious, or worse, unless I do something, unless I can act.

*

I'm afraid it is going to be necessary for me to contradict and correct another glaring factual inaccuracy in Suhail's journal. He has already misrepresented my character and intentions towards him, and distorted a number of events, happy and otherwise. Now it appears that he has fabricated a description of this house, and his own existence within it. I find such deceit unacceptable. It is one thing to make things up, but quite another to pass them off as reality. Our values, as I've said, are not the same. I believe in the truth, and the more he corrupts it, the more important it is for me to restore it. I have not indulged in a tit-for-tat. I have not answered every single falsehood. In fact, I'm sure you'll agree that I've been very restrained, under the circumstances. However, as the underlying abnormality of Suhail's character becomes increasingly apparent, I will require more extensive opportunities for intervention. Suhail has had his say. Now I intend to have mine.

Is this house in which we have lived together for many years a mansion? No it is not. It is merely quite big in comparison with the average house. Is Suhail's room small? Relatively, yes, but he chose it. Is it dirty? Yes, because he wouldn't clean it, or open a window so that it smelled better and wasn't full of condensation. Were the walls bare? Only because he had peeled off all the wallpaper. Was he confined? By his own volition, and clearly not anymore. Is this house haunted? Ghosts live in the imagination. There is only flesh and blood here. In short, I do not recognise the building Suhail describes any more than I recognise the characters which allegedly inhabit it.

Suhail had far too much time to theorise and fantasise, and if I'd known he was writing such nonsense in his journal I would have given him something better to do. I wish he had been good with his hands, and prepared at least to try and pick up some practical skills. The house always needs work doing to it, and builders and so on can so rarely be trusted. I do what I can, and

I've never had much help. I am fond of this house. I thought that Suhail was too. We chose it together after all. It is a good example of a Victorian brick gothic, and he was attracted to it immediately. I myself have always been interested in architecture more generally. I once thought of training as an architect, and I know a little of the subject. Rather more than Suhail by the look of it. We have no towers here, and not only does the real house have no flying buttresses but neither, I would suggest, has the imaginary one. The feature he describes sounds more like an oriel window to me. We do have one of those.

If I can just make my point a little more fully, as I think I am entitled to do. Suhail is clearly describing a massive Victorian structure with one or two gothic features, but it is not this one. Fully-fledged gothic architecture is of course associated with the cathedrals and churches of the medieval period but, following the Renaissance, there was a marked revival in the 19th century and it has not entirely run its course. Although it is not the derogative it used to be, the term gothic is not well understood. The style of architecture it refers to becomes contaminated by the style of fiction it gave rise to and is thus associated with darkness, claustrophobia and danger in the form of either the living or the dead. In fact, the first gothic church was designed to be a representation of heaven on earth, and thus to be suffused with light. The characteristic height of this and subsequent buildings in this style brought us closer to God, and those tall arched and stained glass windows were intended to admit His presence. The remaining features were a consequence of this desire for the vertical and the ethereal.

Basically, if a load-bearing wall is effectively weakened, by having significant sections removed in order to accommodate glass, other forms of support are required in order to prevent the building from collapsing. The strongest support is the buttress, which is like a pillar or a column built against the outside of the wall or placed at a distance from it. It acts against the lateral forces produced by the roof.

The flying buttress is one of three elements that work in conjunction with each other to allow the construction of higher and wider roofs. Another is the pointed arch. The third is the ribbed vault, which is also a form of arch extending across a floor space and rising to a central point. This has a downwards and sideways force, and where it pushes the walls out, the flying buttress – a semi-arch extending from the buttress to the wall – exerts an equal and opposite force. However, its effectiveness depends entirely on the strength of the pier (the buttress and the flying buttress may be regarded as one unit which has both a vertical and horizontal element), which must act as a vertical deadweight, transmitting the weight of the roof down the semi-arch and into the ground. The pier, or the buttress itself, does this by being taller than the end of the flying buttress furthest from the wall. Here is a useful illustration:

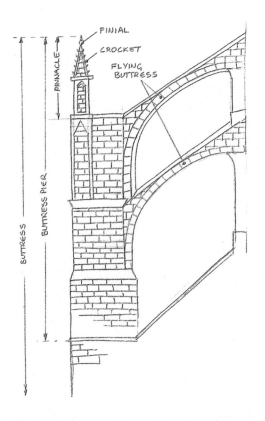

Without this extra height provided by the pinnacle, the line of force would not be carried as far as the ground but would exit some way above it, causing the entire unit to crumble. It is then the roof and the pier which balance each other out, and the flying part of the buttress, although it creates nice aesthetic cloisters and so on, is useless without its deadweight.

My house, as I've said, is an example of brick or Backsteingotik, a less ornate style developed in, for example, the northern mainland, where I was born. I have no recollection of my birthplace, but there is something comforting and familiar to me about its historical architecture. This is another reason why I resent its misrepresentation. Originally, Backsteingotik was associated with a league of medieval merchant towns which extended eastwards towards the Baltic. It began in the 12th century as an alliance between two towns. One was in a position to trade herring, but it had no means to preserve it. The other had salt acquired from nearby mines, and salting the fish made its transportation and distribution possible. Trade duly opened along the salt road between the towns and was of benefit to them both.

In fact, even after a total of more than 60 other towns had joined the league one retained the upper hand – in part because it was an imperial not a feudal town. This advantage over the others caused resentment, and the politics within the league were always divisive. The alliance was loose but did serve to govern trade relations and establish a predominantly protectionist common policy which assured the country's market monopoly. So the origins of at least the brick gothic style of architecture are associated with the mainland and with economic superiority in the north.

However, other countries contend for this honour during the gothic revival period, which is characterised by both romanticism and nationalism. The rise of romanticism in the mid-18th and 19th centuries led to a reappraisal of gothic architecture and other arts of the middle ages, and included a new-found appreciation of tomb monuments, ruins and other picturesque elements of the landscape that emphasised the effects of time.

It would seem that Suhail avails himself of this romantic iconography in parts of his journal. Horace Walpole, author of the first gothic novel I believe, was a slightly more ironic admirer whose taste for the gothic and the picturesque resulted in the playful adaptation of his Strawberry Hill villa. This was given gothic details as effective add-ons without ever having followed the structural logic of true gothic architecture. This predominantly ornamental style was termed 'gothick' and needless to say it has never been taken that seriously. Even though my house may lack the structural elements of the true gothic, I prefer to see it as part of the Backsteingotik rather than the gothick tradition, native to the country of my birth.

The true gothic is not all about style and ornamentation any more than it is about dark deeds carried out in dungeons and attics. It is about innovative engineering, and has been referred to as the honest expression of the technology of the time. Suhail's description destroys the honesty of that expression. His imaginary house is purely anthropomorphic and it represents a suffocating, demonic, mother-type figure. Apart from raising one or two questions about his psychological make-up, to which I will return, it has no counterpart in the outside world.

To continue my own narrative, which pertains exclusively to the realm of reality – far from rejecting or supplanting the neo-gothic architecture of the 18th and 19th century, the modernists, with their steel frames, electric light and lifts, were its heirs, and so the notion of gothic revival is more properly understood as that of gothic survival. The line of inheritance stretches from the 12th to the 20th century and beyond.

Suhail did not see fit to detail the dimensions and features of rooms other than his own. I, on the other hand, will supply more comprehensive information about the rooms in this house. In this way, it will be possible for you to gain an accurate impression of where Suhail lived, and where I continue to live, alone. But first, and in order to prove beyond doubt that his house and mine are not one and the same, I include here the original architect's plan of the front elevation:

FRONT ELEVATION

It is now plain to see what type of house this is. Note the location of Suhail's room, which is adjacent to one of the gargoyles. I'm surprised he didn't mention them. He thought of them as companions. He gave them names which are not, however, relevant here. This is certainly not what the architect had in mind for them, as their ancestors were rather more functional and served as a mode of drainage, conveying water away from the gutters. This same architect, Mr Caste, was required to indicate the drainage and waste system in a block plan and in February 1888 submitted a Notice of Intended Building.

I am unable to supply the notice at this time. However, although it indicates that detailed plans were never deposited, I doubt if they differed much from my estate agent's description. This stated that the property was unique in its class in that it had not been converted into flats. Moreover, the vendor stipulated that the house should never be altered in any way. I have adhered to this condition of purchase, and the estate agent's details that follow describe the house exactly as it is now. Should you require further confirmation, I would be willing in principle to let you inspect it.

CELLAR:
Dry vaulted cellar extending beneath basement rooms and retaining extensive brick wine racks. Used for storage.

BASEMENT:
Staircase descending to:
- **Utility – 26' x 24'**
  Original black and red quarry tiled floor with a range of free-standing units. Butler sink. Mangle (functioning). Wood frame windows. Door leading to passageway and cast iron manhole to coal store with wall-mounted coal-crusher. Door with narrow stone staircase to cellar.

- **Storeroom – 20'5 x 19'**
  Currently used as an exercise room.

GROUND FLOOR:
- **Lobby and reception hall – length 27'**
  Steps up to original outside entrance door recessed in covered brick porch. Two interior pillars either side of hall. Tiled floor. Original staircase with oak banister and painted balustrades. Carved newel post.
- **Kitchen – 25' x 23'**
  Range cooker, large period dresser, fitted cupboards and table plus hanging saucepan rack. Windows to rear. Feature archway leading to range of free-standing cupboards and service hatch. Dumb waiter. Door to scullery.
- **Scullery – 13' x 12'**
  Two butler sinks plus slate work-tops. Larder off with marble slab. Door with narrow stone staircase to utility.
- **Cloak room and W.C.**
  Small window to side. White W.C. with overhead cistern and pedestal sink.
- **Sitting Room – 26' x 23'**
  Wood frame bay windows to rear. Open coal fire, marble hearth. Ornate ceiling rose. Bell pull to kitchen and bedroom 6.
- **Dining Room – 23' x 21'**
  Bay window to front. Coal fire. Original marble Victorian fire surround. Ornate ceiling rose.

FIRST FLOOR:

- **Landing – 19' x 10'**
  With stained glass arched feature windows to sides. Carved newel post.

- **Bathroom – 17' x 15'**
  Wood frame window. Original bathroom furniture with deep free-standing cast-iron bath. White toilet and pedestal sink. Glazed ceramic tiles.

- **Master Bedroom – 22'11 x 19'9**
  Wood frame bay windows. Fireplace with oak fire surround and cast-iron insert. Original stripped wooden floors. Door to dressing room.

- **Dressing Room – 13'4 x 9'**
  Large fitted original wardrobe. Wood frame window.

- **Bedroom 2 – 22' x 18'10**
  Bay window. Cast iron fireplace and original stripped wooden floors. This room is currently not in use.

- **Bedroom 3 – 20'5 x 19'5**
  Bay window to rear. Cast iron fireplace. Stripped wooden floors. This room is currently not in use.

- **Bedroom 4 – 20'6 x 20'**
  Bay window to rear. Cast iron fireplace. Stripped wooden floors. This room is currently not in use.

- **W.C.**

SECOND FLOOR:

- **Landing – 18'5 x 14'**
  Carved newel post.

- **Bedroom 5 – 26' x 19'10**
  Currently locked up.

- **Bedroom 6 – 25'4 x 17'**
  Currently locked up.
- **Bathroom – 10'6 x 9'**
  Not in use.
- **Attic Room – 12' x 11'2**
  In need of decoration.

Other Period Features:
The house boasts a remarkable breadth of original features with high ceilings, deep cornices, picture rails, dado rails and deep skirting boards throughout. It is an unparalleled example of an immaculately preserved period property.

Outside:
Large mature garden to rear, enclosed by 8'7 wall and very private. Narrow stone driveway to front entrance shielded from street by 6' hedge.

The house had only ever been owned and occupied by the architect and his immediate family. It had, as the property details indicate, been preserved but never modernised. I have never thought of it as a museum piece, but as a home that I'm proud to own, and even if some of the rooms remain shut up and perhaps a little damp, the house as a whole is welcoming, not cold and certainly not malevolent.

The remainder of Suhail's description is laughable, or would be if it weren't disturbing. I have read it a number of times and contemplated, at length, what it is really about. I can only conclude that it is an expression of fear, stemming from his own, internal environment, and that the fear is a reaction to precisely that which he claims elsewhere to desire, namely change and a new beginning, a new life. Suhail is in terror of metamorphosis as, in effect, re-birth. Gestation resembles suffocation. Parturition resembles excretion. As the inanimate object in his room comes to life she also begins to extinguish it – to extinguish his.

I am not a fan of Giacommetti's portrait of Caroline. It is not to my taste. I find it strangely vulgar, but Suhail insisted on bringing it in to the house. He clearly spent too much time staring aimlessly at it, when he should have been working. The image took root in his wandering mind which was increasingly preoccupied with both life and death. Caroline is his maternal angel of death, just as the house he invents is his smothering symbiotic life-source. Whoever he is with, whoever triumphs of the two – he is faced with the promise of extinction.

§

Yesterday, I may have been asleep at my desk again, but there was a dog lying in the corner of the room. It was white and definitely dead. Its tongue lolled from the side of its mouth, and there was a great big gash on its side, stretching from the front legs to the back. The poor thing had been ripped open. I knew it was dead, because it didn't whimper or bleed. I carried on. I was looking for something on my desk, but I couldn't find it, so I checked in a drawer. The drawer was empty. I checked in another drawer – also empty. Where were my things? I glanced at the floor. Perhaps I'd put them there. I saw a patch of red, a blood trail leading back towards the corner where the dog was, only now there was only a head. It was disgusting. I could see the stump of its neck bone, and straggly tubes like worms. Why would someone cut the head off a dead dog?

I looked at its face once more and noticed it was baring its teeth. I couldn't see a tongue anymore. Maybe it wasn't dead when they cut it. Suddenly there was blood everywhere. I went to grab something, anything, to defend myself. The paperweight – but it was a paw. My pencil – but it was a leg bone, skinned and slimy. Where my books had been, there was now a heap of what looked like untreated swatches of leather, but the hide was human, not animal, and very, very pale.

I shoved my chair back, but it caught the side of the open drawer and spun me, so that I was looking right down into it. It wasn't empty. There was another head: Justin's. He'd been choked with Horace's tongue. I looked up, screaming, and there right in front of the desk where Caroline should have been, looming at me, screaming silently back at me with his white face all cracked, was Matt. I was reading his red-raw lips. He was blaming me. He was saying I killed them, and I was saying I didn't, I didn't. Two red tears ran down from his blood-shot eyes as if to drain them, but then they ran upwards and sideways too, making clown eyes to go with his clown hair.

The usual whispering, conspiring and laughing is much louder, but I still can't make out what it's about. I hear distant sounds too, like the fading cries of a child or an animal. Underneath me the floor taps and chugs to the rhythm of a wilful old engine. All around me the walls groan with the effort of consuming me, and then there are the footsteps. They come from the opposite direction to the voices, and from deeper inside the house. They form a pattern, as if they were on a loop. The same boards creak in the same way and in the same order every time, only the speed picks up as the steps near my room, and they seem to be getting closer. If I'm imagining them, why can't I stop? Someone is banging their fist on the door. It sounds like its splintering. That sounds like my name. Is it you? You can't come yet, I'm not ready. I need to write my story. It may save me.

*

The story is finished, but I'm still here, unchanged, all but consumed inside this carnivorous cavity. Perhaps I have to wait until I'm starved, like Gregor Samsa, or suspended between life and death. It's hard to believe, but this room was a refuge for me once, and I still prefer my chances in here, rather than out there, where I am out-numbered by Matt, his associate, and the vengeful ghost of my brother.

I went on many expeditions in the early days, each time venturing further and further into the depths and corners of this endlessly empty, hollowed out house. I went down unlit stone staircases into the cellar, the mangle room and even the coal store with its nasty metal crusher. I dared myself. The last time was supposed to be the best; a night-long tour taking in every room, locked or otherwise, mapping every shape, shadow, smell and echo. I was prepared for my task; nervous, but excited. I set off well, but then, as I was making my way along a narrow corridor that zigzagged the whole length of one floor, I felt a sensation behind me, an unfamiliar one, like a presence, or a light pressure. It increased every time I branched off to the left or right. The effect was to lighten and quicken my step, and at first it wasn't unpleasant. It was as if some benevolent hand was guiding me, assisting my adventure. As soon as I went into a room though, this assistance became much less welcome.

I broke into a square room, containing nothing but dust, spiders' webs and a broken bed, up-ended in the middle. I walked from corner to corner, and as I did so, the pressure built behind me until I was being propelled. I turned and scanned all the space around me, in a vain attempt to catch whatever, or whoever, was pushing me. I couldn't see anything. Quickly, I walked out of the door, crossed the corridor and went in to what looked like an old dressing room with a scattered pile of wood from a dismantled wardrobe, and a rusty shirt rail on the floor. Something tripped me, then something else buffeted me, and I lost my balance. It was as if the planks, immobile in themselves, had mischievous kinetic abilities. Either that or someone was hiding under them. I hurried on, but the rooms were getting bigger and so was the invisible force that gathered, always right behind me.

I can't count how many times I staggered forwards with my arms in the air. Eventually I was even lifted from the floor, and thrown down like a discarded doll. Every time I got up and turned to face my tormentor, he stopped. I tried to run, but there was nowhere to run to, and my speed only increased his power. I was hurled across dressers, and into walls. I was battered, and bleeding. One time, I was lifted, turned and dumped into a desk chair which skidded backwards, but didn't tip over. It was as if someone was determined to teach me a lesson. Would that have been you, Saeed? Do you hear me? I hear you! I see you, I hear you, and I know you are there. There is no need to knock my door down, and there was no need to knock me down. I know what you want and I'm coming. I'm going to make everything all right with you – so back off.

You won't kill me – you just want me to think you will. You almost had me convinced when you flung me along the corridor, and I found myself grasping the banister and trying not to fall down the stairs. I could see the tiled entrance hall and front door below me, and then Matt appeared, carrying a pile of papers. He looked up, dropped his things, and ran up the stairs as if to stop me from jumping. He thought I was suicidal, and I must have looked a mess. He had to take some credit for that. He had criticised and controlled me. He had locked me away from my friends. He hated me, though he'd never let me go. My arms were rigid, and my knuckles were white, but he prized me from the railing and made me sit down. I started to shake, and I couldn't control my body. The thing that had persecuted me was possessing me now, and it wanted to speak. It had something to say and as Matt sat down beside me, it started to say it. It told him what I'd never told anyone before. The words came out, one by one, and dispersed. I didn't want to listen, but there was nothing I could do to stop them:
     accident
     car
     door
     bang
     brother
     children
     fight
     fault
     blame
     road

bumper
blood
hospital
photograph
face
scar
gone
left
loved
sorry
sorry
sorry

The thing that was in me was done. The last word hung in the air, then evaporated. I stared at the space where it had been, and then I turned to Matt. His head and eyes were lowered as if there was something there he didn't want me to see. Without raising them, he whispered:

'I know. I know everything about you Suhail. I know how you think, and what you feel. I know you're afraid, and also that you should be. You did a terrible thing to your brother, but you must remember that you belong to me now. You are mine. You try to hide from me, but I am always with you. You don't need to tell me anything. I know what you did and what you will do. I know you as surely as I know myself.'

*

I trust that little more evidence is required in order for me to fulfil my goal of demonstrating that Suhail is an obsessive and dangerous liar. In my opening statement I indicated that he is consumed by guilt and the fear of punishment and revenge. This could be no clearer that it

137

is in his account of being pushed from room to room by something behind him which he cannot see and which therefore doesn't exist but that he attributes to the vengeful ghost of his brother. I enter this account at the moment the supposed ghost is about to propel Suhail down the stairs. Apparently I interpret what I see as an attempted act of suicide stemming from my own unkind actions.

This is all, needless to say, pure fantasy. The facts are as follows. I came home carrying a bound bunch of *curricula vitae* which related to the job descriptions and institutional prospectuses filling my briefcase. I'd set the briefcase down to open the front door and as I stepped inside I saw Suhail clinging to the banister and in some distress. I dropped the package and ran up the stairs. He was not bleeding or bruised although he was marginally more dishevelled than usual. I did not, in fact, think he was suicidal although he had become increasingly overwrought of late. I was concerned for him. He was barely coherent, but I understood well enough that he was talking about his brother's accident and his own involvement in it. I already knew about this because he'd already told me. He must have forgotten. My words were intended to comfort him, but he was obviously losing his mind.

My opening statement also reported that Suhail's fear drove him further into his imagination where he envisioned a dramatic act of transformation that would physically reunite him with his brother and enable him to start his life again as a biologically changed man. There can be no doubt now about the nature of that act.

Suhail refers to it continually. In his mind, the transformative act is electrical. He has merged what is real with what exists only in his mind. At least, he refuses to perceive the difference between fantasy and reality, even if he is still capable of doing so.

We must not excuse him of his responsibility, especially since the evidence leads us to suppose that he left in order to act out his delusion. What could be more dangerous, more violent than a man intent on subjecting himself and another to certain electrocution? Unlike Suhail, I fail to see how being struck by lightning could have a positive outcome. If it does not result in death, it must surely result in terrible injury and so far from repairing the damage he has done he wilfully risks repeating it. The stark reality is that Suhail may have murdered or further mutilated his brother. If he himself has survived, which I have reason to believe he has, I alone am now responsible for the monster he has become. I blame myself for knowing that this could happen and failing to prevent it.

I have had time to ponder my failure in this regard. Perhaps I was too complacent regarding the extent of my knowledge. I could have been more thorough if I had applied the same method of analysis to Suhail as I regularly do to my clients and colleagues. It did not occur to me to do this at the time but I have done it retrospectively in order to see what it reveals. The findings suggest that Suhail's psychological condition was at least as bad as I had thought and that it might therefore have been impossible to stop a calamity from occurring. Nevertheless, for all the things I did – whether or not they were appreciated – it is clear now that I could have done more to help him. He would have refused point blank to see a counsellor or therapist, but I have expertise of my own. I applied it too lightly and I regret that now. I should have tested him. I should have insisted. My method is sound.

The method I use at work is called psychometric testing. It may not be familiar to you, but would undoubtedly be useful for the purposes of recruitment at least. It has been scientifically validated as a reliable means of measuring personality. Application forms, *curricula vitae*, interviews and references can only tell you so much and are by no means immune to invention, distortion and dishonesty. Psychometric tests have a built-in distortion filter and are a standardised mode of assessment, making it far easier to compare like with like than an interview, which could never be run or responded to exactly the same way twice. The test reduces this variability, making it a very useful tool for determining aptitude, attitude, values and ability, and therefore how an individual is likely to behave in a given setting.

Psychometrics refers to the measurement of psychological characteristics. This can be traced back to World War Two and the need to select men who were suitable for flight training. Pilots etc were mainly given IQ tests, but the larger scale personality tests coincided with the development of computers and the ease with which they could compile statistical analyses. What these tests do is ask questions which are designed to gauge an individual's typical ways of thinking, feeling and acting in a range of circumstances.

The questions are not necessarily direct or transparent, since if you ask somebody how they perform under pressure, they are likely to say they perform well. Questions, which are referred to as items test the different aspects of a personality type. Then you or the computer combine and cross-reference them. We want a broad picture and we want to know how someone will behave at work, with their peers, their superiors, their subordinates and so on. If we can measure their personality or their typical ways of thinking, feeling and acting, then we can predict their behaviour. I have never produced an inaccurate profile and believe me; it would be costly if I did. It really would.

The items on a test are always structured as a pair of binary opposites, so, for example, introverted and extraverted. Generally speaking, in the process of assessment and selection we are interested in someone who is average for a given personality trait, because if they were either extremely introverted or extremely extraverted they would be difficult to work with. I have administered and scored many psychometric tests using various software programmes that can provide you with a detailed narrative report of a particular personality, highlighting strengths and weaknesses and recommending relevant self-development measures.

After Suhail left, I self-administered a test which I completed as if I was him. I drew on all my years of knowledge and needless to say I answered questions truthfully and scored them objectively. The results, as I've indicated, are extraordinary. I have certainly never seen a psychological profile so extreme that the programme I used struggled to interpret it using the terms available from its database. This has, for example, 'aggressive' but not 'violent,' and 'destructive' but not 'murderous.' Even then, it has a tendency to accentuate the positive and so prefers to use 'depressive' (low score) for 'aggressive' (high score), 'creative' (low score) for 'destructive' (high score) and so on. Look out for 'radical' and 'innovative' which are as close as the computer can get to 'dangerous' and 'liar.'

Before looking in detail at what I'll present here as Suhail's psychometric psychological profile, I need to say a little more about the main psychological functions and types that have been identified. As I said, these were always presented as opposing pairs. We will need some flavour of them in order to see exactly how severe Suhail's case is. Carl Jung in the 1920s and Hans Eysenck in the 1960s were both leading figures in the examination of human typology. Eysenck identified three main sets of types: extraverts and introverts, the emotionally stable and the emotionally unstable and the tough-minded and tender-minded (a set which addresses psychosis). These will certainly be useful in understanding the core elements of Suhail's personality.

Jung was interested mainly in the way people characteristically receive and process information. For 'receive' Jung said 'perceive' and for 'processing' he said 'judging.' He saw two ways of perceiving information and two ways of judging it; sensing and

142

intuiting and thinking and feeling. The four functions of sensing, intuiting, thinking and feeling can be directed either towards the external world of people and things (extraversion) or towards the internal world of thoughts and imagination (introversion), creating eight possible types.

The thinking and feeling functions are fairly self-explanatory and refer to either a rational or irrational, logical or emotional way of dealing with information. A sensing form of perception indicates a preference for detached observation, facts and hard data, whereas an intuitive form of perception goes beyond or ignores facts and data, preferring to seek out patterns, ideas and theories which are not particularly grounded. Suhail largely corresponds to the introverted-feeling type, but it is important to remember that there is always variety within each category and that each dominant function, used in the preferred external or internal world, always brings it's opposite or subordinate with it.

Moreover, the subordinate function must come from the opposing pair, so while Suhail feels in his preferred internal world, he intuits in the external world, so explaining his impracticality. In addition, where he is conscious of being emotional he is not very aware of, or concerned with the effects of his intuition on others. That much is obvious. Thus he is already not as considerate as his type would suggest, and other more detailed characteristics will push this aspect of his personality still further.

Personality is understood partly through beliefs, which make up attitudes and attitudes which amount to values. Values maintain the concept of the self and may be interpersonal (relating to others), extrinsic (relating to work) and intrinsic (relating to the individual). These value categories will be useful in organizing Suhail's profile. This shows, for example, that his work is, or rather would be, if he did any, driven more by a desire for achievement and aesthetics than by a desire for economic status and security, and that he himself is a highly independent outsider, rejecting both moral and traditional values outright. Had Suhail adhered to these values at all, neither he nor I would be in the position we are now.

Some of the newer tests have brought back the category of intelligence, but have renamed and reconstructed it as *intellectance* which is more about how clever people think they are, rather than how clever they actually are. These newer tests have also developed even better distortion or faking filters plus ways to avoid culture, sex and age biases. Previously, in seven out of ten pairs of traits, men would occupy one pole and women the other. The same applies to the old and young, although there were never really any meaningful statistics on ethnicity. Luckily, Suhail is predominantly the kind of person that psychometric tests are aimed at anyway, and so we can expect any imbalance to stem from the answers, not the questions. Some of the key questions relate to what are called 'global factors.' These include: low anxiety/high anxiety, pragmatism/openness, agreeableness/independence, high self-control/low self-control. It is relevant to note that the high anxiety factor may produce manic-depressive tendencies, a sense of extreme vulnerability and occasional ill-tempered and impulsive outbursts.

Independence is connected to an underlying wilfulness. Those who lack self-control are also immune to social and parental expectations. Each global factor is composed of a number of primary factors and these include: low intellectance/high intellectance, emotionally stable/affected by feelings (such as depression and anxiety, which can produce psychosomatic symptoms such as breathlessness), conscientious/expedient (where someone prefers to be creative and spontaneous rather than persevering and dutiful), tough-minded/tender-minded (the axis of psychosis that also accounts for obsessions and paranoid delusions), trusting/suspicious, concrete/abstract (where someone can dwell on ideas that have no grounding in reality), confident/self-doubting (where the person is prone to feelings of guilt and often dwells extensively on past mistakes), conventional/radical, self-disciplined/ informal (where someone is inclined to ignore rules and follow their own urges, regardless of the consequences), composed/tense-driven, empathetic/lacking empathy. Emotional people are, paradoxically, more likely to be aggressive or violent and to lack empathy for others.

Lack of empathy is what lies behind all crimes against the individual. On the other hand, self-controlled people who appear to be emotionally rigid are not only sensitive but far more concerned with what motivates and, indeed, affects others.

§

Suhail's Psychometric Psychological Profile

The subtlety of a psychometric test stems from the inter-relation between all of the factors and chiefly from inconsistencies in a given personality profile. However, what stands out in Suhail's profile is the absence of any inconsistency whatsoever. This is emphatically not normal. Every trait indicates every other trait, and none complicates the others. At no point does he produce an average score, which would indicate that he exhibits behaviour associated with both traits in a given pair. It is remarkable, and I've never seen it before. The following report was written by a computer program and must be considered in light of the aforementioned limitations in its database of terms. I have highlighted the computer's text in bold.

Intrinsic values

Suhail's strong tendency towards independence suggests that he vigorously defends and maintains idiosyncratic ways of thinking, feeling and acting. He is unlikely to have any regard for authority and will not like being told what to do. If he finds himself in a submissive position he will be resentful and will look for ways to get out of it and regain what he will see as his freedom. He will do this at any cost.

Suhail does not live by a strict moral code and regards social conventions as a challenge. He believes that it is desirable to change existing laws and rules and will break them himself if it is expedient for him to do so. He may do this in pursuit of some personal goal or esoteric truth, which will engage him more than religious, materialistic or logical truths, which he is likely to question.

On the whole, Suhail is amoral and highly driven. He is single-minded rather than self-controlled. Rather than being influenced by parents, teachers and those in a position of power in society, he will be influenced by new ideas and other intangibles. He is very open to possibilities and to subjective experiences, which he will respond to on an intuitive and emotional level. Lacking any concrete or practical tendencies and without logic, materialism or religion to guide him, he is vulnerable to the excesses of his own imagination.

Extrinsic values
Suhail would have to work on his own, and although lacking in self-discipline and the ability to persevere with routine, un-stimulating tasks, he will be driven to achieve his own goals. He will not adhere to established methods and will work sporadically rather than systematically, preferring to initiate than to complete a project and choosing ad hoc rather than tried and tested means. Nevertheless, his sense of his own commitment and even sacrifice will be absolute and he is more likely than not to produce results.

Suhail is highly competitive although he might struggle to identify who his main competitor is. Without necessarily having what others might recognise as a high standard of work and behaviour, he will set his own bar very high. Desperate for success and recognition, he will never feel that he has it and never stop trying to get it. He will not consider himself to be ambitious or career-orientated because he will not necessarily distinguish between his work-goals and his life-goals.

Suhail's work will not be orientated towards the real world of people and things, but will be introspective and abstract, having no bearing on everyday life. He will not want to get his hands dirty. Conveying a high intellectance, which does orientate him to the external world, he cannot help but process information internally where he is subject to his own emotions. He is likely to become anxious and depressed or over-stimulated and will be easily drained of energy as he struggles to cope with his own feelings. Temperamentally highly unstable, Suhail is tense-driven and prone to emotional outbursts. His intensity promises radical innovation and Suhail is a natural experimenter but his creativity is constrained by feelings of self-reproach. The fear of what is behind him will determine his path ahead. He will be unable to share this with anyone else.

Interpersonal relationships
Suhail is exceptionally wary of interpersonal relationships and spends many hours alone. Cut off from real relationships, he is preoccupied with imaginary ones and it is only within the realm of his imagination that he is able to display any insight into the thoughts, feelings and actions of others. This may be because his imaginary characters are merely vehicles for his own thoughts, feelings and actions. This lack of empathy is a consequence of his emotional volatility and alienation from his own core values and sense of self. Self-doubting, he is driven by guilt not sympathy and having become isolated from friends and family, he is also motivated by

a keen sense of rejection. On the whole, he will be unable to shift his attention from the object of his guilt, so producing an unhealthy personality.

Conclusions

Suhail has an unhealthy personality. Although a combination of intellectance and intuition could make him an effective problem-solver, and his love of literature could make him a good communicator, he is too anti-social and inclined to let his feelings and imagination run away with him. Lacking discipline, interpersonal skills and respect for authority, he must be considered to be unemployable except as an academic or independent artist.

Capable of radical innovation but plagued by guilt and rejection, even Suhail would not know if his efforts would be beneficial or detrimental and to whom. He would be unlikely to concern himself sufficiently with this question, since he seeks creativity for its own sake and as a means of escape from his past. Where a course of therapy might assist with his depression, Suhail should not be considered suitable for any routine self-development measures. On the whole, it is unlikely that he would benefit from any form of intervention at all.

§

Suhail's profile condemns him as it exonerates me. There was probably nothing I could have done to stop him. While he was here, under my roof, my qualities counteracted his, but he slipped away from me, as he was bound to do. It would have made no difference whether I'd locked him in or not. He was going to find a way out in the end, because he was compelled to find his brother before his brother found him. This almost completes my evidence pertaining to Suhail's character and the reason for his disappearance.

It remains for me to establish, in as far as possible, where he is and what has happened to him. I have endured many sleights and distortions of my character but I remain wholly faithful to the truth about his, however unsavoury that might be. He is right about one thing though. Whoever he is and whatever he has done, I will never give up on him. I will never let him go. He is all I think about. Looking back, he is all I have ever thought about.

§

The stories work while I'm reading or writing, but then they finish, as if they were only dreams in which the dead come back to life, and no longer wish to harm me. I wake up, and it's dark and I realise where I am. I'm still here, still me. I don't want to be here anymore. I don't want to be me. Now I know, really know that I will not have to be, not for much longer. Lightning will strike us, the spell will be cast, and we'll be re-born as the one cell, one embryo, one person we were always meant to be.

I found a newspaper pushed under my door. It was out of date, several months old, maybe more, and well-thumbed, but that doesn't matter. It was folded open to a story about a wealthy middle-aged businesswoman who had lost a cherished nephew, in tragic circumstances, on a business trip abroad.

150

That was B, of course, but there was more. It said that she was unable to have children, but had approached a fertility specialist who was known for his interest in cloning – human cloning. She wasn't just *a* candidate, she was *the* candidate. Good for her! B had suffered enough. I didn't even know she was infertile – a result of fibroids, it said in the article. Nothing should have been able to hurt B, but it seems that everything did; first her parents, then me, then Rafe and even her own body. Losing Rafe would have been like being hit by a meteorite. She would be carrying an invisible crater. She'd have been damaged, seriously off-kilter, reeling on her axis. This would steady her, mend her; make her whole again.

Of course there was the usual hand-wringing about ethics, and should-we, shouldn't-we, and what would the status of a clone be, and wouldn't it suffer an identity crisis and so on and so on. All rubbish, as if we didn't all have identity crises, as if we didn't already live in a world where some people, some groups of people, weren't already regarded as inferior and weren't already used as spare parts for the rest. As if it wasn't already possible for one person to be identical, at least in appearance, to another. Then there was the legal stuff, but human cloning isn't illegal everywhere and they didn't say which country the procedure would take place in. I hope its here, right under our noses. I hope they find a loop-hole, a way for B to have her baby at home. They could do it secretly, privately, and no-one need know. Suzy was going to be the surrogate, and they would bring the child up together, share her as they'd shared him, their red-haired boy. That's forgiveness.

I kept reading and they talked about how it would be done and guess what – they are going to use lightning! There was a drawing. It showed a cell being taken from the donor and fused with an empty egg cell to make an embryo. They illustrated the fusion part with a lightning bolt. It is the lightning bolt, the electric spark that kick-starts life, merging the two cells into one and, get this, *reprogramming* the nucleus from the donor cell so that it forgets it ever had an adult life and starts all over again, from scratch. It may have been a skin cell or a heart cell or whatever, but it gets rewound, like a clock, back to the start of the day, back to when it was a stem cell and could still be anything – anything at all.

So that was it. At that point I understood exactly how it was going to work. Saeed and I would be together, side-by-side, touching, like two cells on a slide and BANG – we'd be fused, then reprogrammed and effectively, re-born. They don't know how that works, the reprogramming, and I'd like to find out more about it, though I don't see how I can. Matt wouldn't buy me any more books, or go to the library for me, even if I could find him, even if I asked nicely. He said I'd wasted my opportunity and would not be given another. I would have to make do with what I had. Well fine then, I will. I know what I'm going to write about now. I will do it quickly and quietly. My efforts will be invisible. I will appear to be compliant. I'll let the visitor take whatever he wants. I'll let the house take whatever it wants, but I will retreat, and they won't even know where to look for me. I will become what I was already being forced to be. They starve the donor cell before they transfer it. They suspend it so that it is quiescent, and no longer developing and dividing. They interrupt the cell cycle, and I will interrupt all of mine. I will co-ordinate them so that my whole body is in a state of arrest. I will become one cell. Down and down I'll go, until I'm microscopically small. Then further, until I'm an infinitely small black dot, a singularity, a nucleus. I will be still, suspended, quiescent, and very soon, puff – I'll be gone.

*

What is it about Suhail's sorry state of mind that clings so desperately to the illusion of escape? It is guilt, in a word. Unable to face up to the reality of who he is, and what he has done, he has indulged in a sequence of fantasies in which he transcends his present circumstances and even his own body. If the house was not consuming him, then he claims that, at some unspecified point in the future, he will starve. He encounters the subject of cloning and wishes to disappear into his past, so that hi s life may begin again. When he is talking about reading, or writing, he imagines that he may be transported directly into a world that he, or another, has created, as a person or an entity that he or another has created.

For Suhail, everything is a potential time machine in which he can travel forwards, back or just elsewhere in a whole other zone. But who is it that haunts him in the present? Who must he escape from? It is not some ghost at his door, but only himself and his barely acknowledged crimes. His writing will not save him from anything. A story is just a story, even if it is about change. See for yourself. I read it, and it has done nothing for me. I have not changed, and neither, I trust, will you.

§

The Mysterious Case of Mr Charles D. Levy

My name is Charles D. Levy and I am a heart surgeon at the Great Ormond Street Hospital, which cares for sick children. I am at the farther end of middle-aged and would say that my figure is comfortable but fit enough. Beyond these most rudimentary details I would struggle to describe myself – either my appearance or my personality – in the present tense, so let me tell you briefly what I was like before the events which I am about to relate occurred.

I was a principled, respected and though I say it myself, successful man. I was brought up in an ordinary lower-middle class household by parents who encouraged me but could afford me no special privileges. I worked hard at school to get in to medical college and hard at medical college to become a doctor. I made sacrifices and I earned my position as one of the hospital's senior practitioners; trusted and rewarded as more than a safe pair of hands. In these days of targets and audits my published mortality rate is comparable with that of anyone in the country. We all undertake private practice, but I retained and honoured my commitment to the National Health Service, and believed wholeheartedly that medicine should always be free at the point of delivery. I don't honestly know what I believe now; about anything.

Medicine is a competitive, class-ridden, hierarchical institution and my steady advancement within it, inevitably at times at somebody else's expense, did not please everyone. Indeed I left many people behind, people who considered themselves more entitled to status than me, as well as people who considered themselves my peers. Needless to say, most of them were men, or as one of my female colleagues would have

154

it, pompous public school boys. I cannot name one in particular, but there are a few who tried and failed in small and petty ways to impede me. One individual may have said too little in response to a favourable comment about my work made by a retired consultant and member of the board of trustees, on which I serve, at a drinks party. Another may have omitted to circulate new and significant research to me, so that by the time I read it in *The Lancet*, the findings had already been utilised elsewhere. Once I had a paper of my own turned down by the *BMJ* and I found out later, because you always do, that this was due to a particularly negative review by a person who was named and was known to me. But these were just minor irritations and I ignored them. Even if I hadn't done so, I cannot see what difference it would have made.

On the whole I enjoyed excellent relations with my colleagues who generally, as I've said, held me in very high esteem. I did not seek the good opinion of those who envied me or those whose professional standards and ethics were questionable. I refer to the gold-diggers and glory-seekers whose activities besmirch the good name of medicine and science in general: those who would do and say anything to obtain funding or publicity and who raise people's hopes for cures and remedies which may one day be possible, but which are far from tried and tested and might indeed be dangerous. Stem cell research is a case in point. Used precipitously as a treatment for Parkinson's Disease, this appeared at first to reverse the condition, but then it came back ten times worse, depriving the patient of what remained of their mental and motor functions. I believe, or believed, in proper clinical trials following extensive animal testing. I had no time for the anti-vivisection or animal rights case and had only contempt for those who risk human life through, for example, the use of

155

explosives in cars or buildings, for the sake of rats or rabbits or even dogs, cats and monkeys whose welfare is, in any case, strictly attended to by ethics committees. I am, or was, a traditionalist in both my methods and my values. I adhered to what I had been taught, to the precepts of the Hippocratic Oath obviously, but also to those of professional and personal progress wrought by patience, and a degree of perseverance.

There is no room for magic in medicine; any risk of harm should be carefully assessed and minimised, and nothing at all should ever be done which might threaten human dignity and integrity. Worthy sentiments, you might agree. Would that they had not been compromised by those who sought to undermine me and my beloved science, and would that I had not allowed myself to become corrupted by their act. You see I have lost everything I had, as well as everything I knew. There may be something in its place now, but I still do not understand it. I don't know what it means or what I have become. I have not fully arrived at this new place yet and neither have I totally left the old. I pine for what I remember, even as my own mind, if it is that, tries to distort the memories, to turn good things to evil and vice versa, so that I don't know where I am.

So whether it was a good thing, as I believed, or not, I was, as they say, part of the system and I was recognised as such. I even made it in to the Royal College of Surgeons and I was proud, not of myself exactly but of what I had achieved. My work was my life and my legacy and I had given up everything for it; everything. I said I had made sacrifices, but there was only really one. My devotion to my career was such that there was only one other thing I wanted that I didn't have. I may have liked to have children, but I see children every day.

156

I did not see her every day, Lucy, and I could have done. We were eight years old when she asked me to marry her and I promised that I would as soon as we were eighteen. Our eighteenth birthdays passed but we did not get married, because I went to college and left her behind. I broke my promise and by the time I came home at the end of the first year she had married someone else. I thought before all this happened that it was a noble and necessary sacrifice. I nurtured the pain like a virtue. And now, now I suspect it was the cornerstone of my folly: my self-love.

The story of my current misfortune begins with an ordinary day, an unremarkable case of a little boy with a hole in his heart. This is a common condition, and indeed one which I suffered myself at the same age. The hole is easily repaired and the procedure may be described as routine from a surgical point of view. The hole was small and did little to compromise the child's general health. He was a bit pale and could become short of breath if he exerted himself or became over-excited. Otherwise he was fine and any slight physical fragility was more than compensated for by a personality that can only be described as robust. He would not be confined to his bed on the ward, and when he wasn't playing with literally anything he could get his hands on except the other children, he was playing hide and seek with me. I assumed that he was an only child, but was never able to confirm this.

He was checked-in to hospital by a man, assumed to be his father, but who subsequently could not be traced. The boy's registered name was false and when I asked him about it he said that he had never heard it before and it didn't belong to him.

'So what is your name?' I asked him, 'and who brought you here?'

He replied that he didn't know the man who brought him and, looking directly at me said:

'My name is Charles David Levy.'

Well, it was easy enough to assume that he was merely reading what he saw on my name badge, which was clearly within his line of sight and had been on previous occasions. This reads 'Mr. Charles D. Levy,' and it is not such a hard middle name to guess. Naturally I phoned the police to check any reports of runaways and so on, but there were none matching his description. I ruled out amnesia, mental illness and, as far as possible, abuse. I could not perform the operation because there was no one to sign the consent form, and I became concerned for this boy who had adopted my name and who did resemble me if only in appearance.

My concern was obviously a professional one and I paid no attention to the attendant unease while he and I addressed each other like two unpractised quiz masters in want of contestants. He:

'Why is a heart in four sections, or is it two sections of two? Why isn't it one? What does ventricle mean? Is the hole the size of the inside or outside of a polo? What are you going to fix it with? Why isn't the hair on the back of your hands the same colour as the hair on your head? Why don't children have grey hair? What is your favourite colour? Did you know you've got a mole in the same place on your neck as me? Can I play with that (of the monitor beside the adjacent bed)? Why not?'

Me:

'Who looks after you? Where do you go to school? Who gives you lessons? Where do you live? Are your parents alive? Why won't you give me your real name?'

His answer to the last question was that he had, and the only other one he offered was: 'some friends.'

I learned only that he was eight years old and that when he grew up he wanted to be 'a famous heart surgeon.' Children mimic adults. That is what they do: how they learn. But still, why me? And where were the other adults in his life? His evident desire to impersonate me was troubling, but not yet as alarming as his parents' absence from his bedside and also, seemingly, from his mind. Perhaps my initial assessment was wrong and he had suffered in their hands, perhaps his reluctance to disclose information about himself was the result of some kind of trauma. However, there was simply no sign of physical trauma and none that I could diagnose of any other kind either apart from the apparent withholding of details that could identify him. Without them I was faced with the bizarre situation of a patient on my ward that I couldn't treat, and would have to discharge if he carried on insisting that he and I shared the same name.

He, the other Charles, was in no way unsettled by this situation, even when I tried to explain, as carefully as I could, that if I was unable to find his parent or guardian he would not have his operation and would have to be taken in to care and looked after by strangers. That was all right, he said, because the hole never really bothered him and he liked being with strangers. But it was clearly not all right, and while he slept one night I searched through his clothes in the hope of finding a clue as to who he really was. It transpired that my quest had been anticipated, by who I cannot be certain, and what I found was not a clue but confirmation in the form of a birth certificate.

I had this document authenticated. If it hadn't been, I would have taken it, and the appearance of this boy on my ward, as a highly dubious and exploitative prank designed to provoke me with false evidence of what science could do if people like me did not stand in its way. But the effect and the intention was a lot worse than this, and even when, at first glance, I did not know that the certificate was authentic, I experienced what I can only describe as a sense of utter crisis in my entire being. I do not know how many times I re-read this, or for how long I simply stared at it, my breath and seemingly my whole life in suspension.

Charles David Levy
Born: April 12 1998
Father: Edward Charles Levy, Civil Servant
Mother: Margaret Levy, née Stanworth

Same name, same birthday – only fifty years later – and same parents. My parents, had they both been alive at the time would, I hardly need to point out, not have been of reproductive age, and in fact my father died three years before that and my mother then went in to a residential home. She was eighty, and becoming senile. She is dead now, mercifully. When I did eventually recover something of myself, I gazed at Charles David Levy and for the first time recognised him as being more than similar to me in appearance. I do not have many family photographs, and it is surprisingly easy to forget exactly what you looked like half a century ago. I remembered then, and the effect was that of a virus, a completely alien strain, overwhelming my body in an instant. My penultimate and hopeless act of self-preservation was to take a sample of his blood in order to obtain a DNA test. Like an innocent man who had just received a non-commutable death sentence, I walked it at a funereal pace to the lab along with a sample of my own blood. Somehow I made up a story of a possibly inherited condition using false names, and then I found a place where my dulled terror could not be observed, and waited. The result this time was much more dreadful than the confirmation of a blood-match – diseased or otherwise. That of a father and son would match. My samples were, they said, contaminated. They were not a match. They were identical: clones. Clones are twins, separated in time.

I am not a paranoid man and I have not set out to prove who did this to me and why. It is obvious why. Cloning is everything that science should not be, and my convictions are well known to my enemies. Even if I could not prove who did it, I could prove that it had been done. But this would give them exactly what they wanted – a scandal, publicity – and it would result in public knowledge of what the public most feared to know about unregulated, unethical scientific practice carried out by mavericks. There is a human clone living among us and although I did not willingly create him, he is mine and I have taken responsibility for him. At least, I have now. My initial response was to flee the hospital for the sanctuary of my own home. Who discharged him and in to whose care I do not know, since at that point I broke all further contact with the hospital and lost, as I've indicated, so much more than my job. My friends were there too, good people who could advise me, but who could not be told for fear that they would force the matter in to the light and inadvertently satisfy the perpetrators' intent. Human cloning is a crime in this country and I was prepared to protect the criminals in order to spare the victim:

not me, not my reputation, which was already condemned, but that of my profession.

I had my reservations about therapeutic cloning above and beyond that of stem cells, but reproductive cloning, cloning a human being is an abomination simply because it destroys that which defines us; our uniqueness. It is also very bad science because the process, though seemingly quite simple, is not at all well understood and the risks are manifestly too high. The process involves the fusion of a donor cell with an enucleated egg by means of a tiny electrical charge which kick-starts the formation of an embryo and a new life. How it does this is not certain, but what is certain is that it does so unreliably. A more than 50% failure rate may be acceptable in sheep, goats or cattle, but it is not in humans. As much as the image of my surviving clone haunted me, I did not like to think about the fate of those who did not survive. His existence undermined everything I believed in, and threatened to undo everything I had done, but it was not, strictly speaking, his fault. I had underestimated the strength of feeling against me and against what I represented. If I could not defend one, I was determined to defend the other, and this I had to do alone.

It did not take him long to find me. For a while, maybe a month, I watched him through the window, lurking in the street and around neighbouring houses. I observed him as he became increasingly wild and bold, breaking in at night and soon in the day to steal food and clothes. He slept in garages or cars and he played with dogs and dustbins, machines and tools and whatever else he could find. I am surprised nobody heard him or saw him because he made no attempt to hide himself and would sometimes just run around aimlessly yelling at the top of his voice. He did not seem to fear any adult intervention or authority and carried on by himself, inventing his own rules to his own games. By this time it was autumn and the weather was getting cold. I could see the condensation on his breath and an unhealthy tinge to his skin. He panted and he coughed and for a few days did not emerge from the shed next door. When he did, I let him in. I fed him, bathed him, and let him sleep until he was stronger. I had a little time to get to know him for who, not what, he was, and although I cannot say that I disliked him, I became convinced that he was dangerous.

He was inquisitive, intelligent – and reckless. He read my books and showed a great aptitude for science. I had no reason to doubt that he would fulfil his stated ambition to become a great, a 'famous' heart surgeon. He was going to be a pioneer, he said, like Christiaan Barnard who performed the world's first heart transplant. Of course, heart transplants are common now, so he would come up with something else. Though he did not know the word, he spoke of xenotransplantation; the use of organs and tissues from animals to benefit humans. He might use pig hearts he said, because he had heard that humans and pigs were quite similar species. But it shouldn't be all one way, he went on. It wasn't fair if pigs were used to heal people without ever getting anything back in return. If a person got mangled in a car accident but their heart was ok, why shouldn't it be used to help another animal if we're all related after all? He didn't believe in eating pigs and sheep and cows and so on, so that didn't present him with any problems of reciprocity.

So that's what he would do; he would lead the world in performing heart transplants between species and he would put an end to human favouritism, or what the animal advocates term speciesism. Even allowing for the excesses of a young

163

mind, this worried me deeply, for not only would he do what he would do for glory, he would do it in my name. Imagine it: a brand new version of yourself whose life would run contrary to everything you have done and hold dear. Your achievements would be erased one by one, your decisions would be reversed and the coherent account you have given of yourself to date would be scrambled. Unbearable! How can I have been expected to let this happen? Was I not entitled to act? I had heard that a cloned child, if it survived, would be no more than a vehicle for the parents', or more precisely, the donor's (since the clone's parents are the donor's parents) dreams of immortality. Not so! It is not me who would live through him but vice versa, not so much a twin but a parasite separated in time, a self-virus who would destroy what constitutes me, who would take over, grow fat at my expense, occupy me like a shell, use me and deny me my humanity, my right to individuality. He would live my life again but he would not replicate it. He would cancel it and leave me with nothing.

Charles and I were still discussing his future late in to the evening when our conversation was interrupted by a brilliant white light followed immediately by a huge bang of thunder, which shook us physically in our chairs. He rushed to turn out the light, and ran to the window shrieking with excitement and seeming not to notice his own efforts to breathe:
'I love storms. I love them. Do you?'
'No.'
'Can we go out in it? Please? Can we?'
'No. Stay away from the window. It's dangerous.'

I hadn't noticed the storm approaching and he waited for it to pass over our heads before coming away from the window and switching the light back on. He went up to the mantelpiece and looked at the two photographs I have there; one of my mother and father on holiday, and another of Lucy and I aged 16, holding hands. After all that had already occurred, what he said then still shocked me:

'Where did you get that photograph?' he asked, pointing to the one of my parents. 'Did you take it out of my bag? I brought it in to hospital with me but then I lost everything. It used to be by my bed. I want it back. They're my Mum and Dad. I don't remember them and they're dead now, so I didn't tell you about them before.' He went on to the next picture before I had a chance to respond. 'Is that you? She's pretty. Did you marry her?'

I told him the story of Lucy and me. I took my time. My eyes glazed. I nearly forgot that he was there. She was the last part, the only part of my life now that was truly mine and I wanted to be with her, with both of us right up until the end, however painful, however unnecessary that now was. 'Oh,' he said, 'I have a girlfriend and she's very pretty too. She's going to be a surgeon as well as me and we're going to live together and when we're famous we'll go on TV and travel to other countries and it'll be more fun that way.' Enough: at this point I had had enough. He wasn't going to take everything. I slumped down in my chair, my head in my hand and closed my eyes. This time I heard the storm as it returned, and I watched the red of my eyelids turn to black and then white again as Charles took up his station.

What happened next was neither reasoned nor insane enough to reduce any plea to manslaughter. Jumping up with an excitement that paralleled his, I said:

'Let's go. Let's go and play in the storm.'

165

He didn't hesitate and we both ran from the house. We were some distance away when he tired and I lifted him on to my shoulders, holding his arms above my head and running in the downpour. I think, no, I know that I wanted to be struck and that I had made him the taller and so the most vulnerable of us two. I cannot tell you whether he was killed or not because I never saw him again. There must have been a strike because I woke up on the ground with a severe pain in my chest and gasping for breath. I lay there for a while, watching the storm play it self out, and then got up with some difficulty. In my confusion I never searched for him or for his body, but made my way slowly home where I sit now, many years later, waiting.

I do not know if Charles David Levy is living my life as the wrong kind of surgeon, but it doesn't matter any more if he is. I have changed, and probably, if he is alive, so has he. We may not be so different now and we were never really the same. Little boys change what they want to be all of the time, and big boys can do it too if they have to. Lightning taught me that.

§

I cannot proceed with this case file without passing one or two further comments on Suhail's final journal entry. It is strange, even by his standards, to claim that he is becoming quiescent, like a cell or nucleus that is about to be transferred, fused and reprogrammed. I suppose that this undoubted delusion was necessary to his fantasy of metamorphosis. It was also preliminary to its attempted actualization. In other words, starving and becoming motionless was what he thought he had to do before he left to be reunited with his brother. It was the precondition for change as he saw it.

It is sad. At this point he seems to have lost the ability to rationalize altogether. Not only is he not thinking straight but he is not thinking at all. His emotions may be in control of him, but this does not give him the right to abdicate responsibility for the state he is in, or for the things he is about to do. I have said, and I emphatically repeat that he was not mistreated. Neither, I can assure you, was he starved, although he had not eaten as much as usual in the previous week or so. This was only because he had let things get on top of him. If he was stressed, then this was his doing, not mine.

Contrary to what he said, I did go to the library on his behalf. This is where I acquired the newspaper. They were only going to throw it away, as I pointed out to the assistant at the reference counter. I passed it on to Suhail when I judged the moment to be right. True, he had stopped asking me for more information about his friend, but he'd already made it abundantly clear that he wanted to know. If I'm honest, I was also being realistic. The damage was, to an extent, already done. Suhail had already found what he thought was confirmation of his fantasy in the appalling experiments conducted in the name of modern science.

Human cloning is perhaps the worst among these, as I'm sure you would agree. The very idea is an abomination, and I struggled to believe that a reputable, if left-wing broadsheet would deign to print a piece that appeared to take it seriously. In my opinion, speaking as an ordinary citizen, this was a classic example of irresponsible journalism. The journalist in question was exploiting this woman's grief as much as the charlatan so-called specialist who had promised her a healthy baby. Everybody knows that there are terrible risks involved when human beings misuse technology to intervene in nature. It is going too far. The potential benefits are outweighed by the real prospect of death and deformity. This is why human cloning is illegal in this country and quite rightly restricted to animals and to therapeutic outcomes alone. I am sure there are reputable individuals engaged in cloning animals for commercial and medical purposes, and mindful of the strength of public opinion. However, there are also a number of mavericks that seek the headlines and are, unfortunately, granted them.

Am I not correct in thinking that one or two of these more disreputable types have already featured in the press? Have they not already claimed that they've cloned the first human? Did they provide any evidence? Was there proof? I don't think so. As I understand it, the claims made so far have been hoaxes, and I see no reason why this one should be any different. It is tempting to feel sorry for Suhail's friend, but she should have known better. Suhail should know better too, but he doesn't. Indeed, despite my efforts to help him raise the standard of his behaviour and establish his own moral compass, he remained stubbornly susceptible to deception. He lied about everything, including my background and character. It was all made up.

Fact – I have never been either rich or poor. Fact – I earn a very good income from my job but I do not have inherited wealth. Fact – I have lived overseas but he doesn't really know where or why. I do, as a result, have a slight accent and yes, I choose to speak quietly. So what? Nobody has ever accused me of hissing, not to my face and believe me, I could shout if I wanted to. Fact – as I said in my opening statement, I generally work in an office. That is, an office away from home. If I decided to work at home at all, it was only to keep Suhail company. Even then, I didn't bother much in the end because he would neither come out of his room nor let me in.

As for my appearance, it is hardly a revelation that I am neither the blonde-haired god nor the white-faced devil he conjures in his dreams. He used to find me attractive. He clearly doesn't any more, but he couldn't just say that, could he? Of course not. We did meet roughly as he describes. That is, we met in a garden at a party, but not until I'd watched him for a while and done my research. I found out who he was and talked to some of his friends. They never let on about this. They pretended not to know me, on my request. I gave my reason. It's the same reason I didn't approach him directly. It was important that he chose me. Suhail would never have responded to a cold-call. I'd have been turned down flat. I could put myself in his way, as indeed I did, but he had to come to me, not the other way round. That tells you something about who was really in charge, despite everything he says.

§

I stand accused of being controlling and cruel. If this wasn't bad enough, which it is, I am accused of acting in such a way in all aspects of our relations, including the most private. I need hardly say that I regret this airing of our private life more than I regret anything else Suhail has said and done. The sense of embarrassment and humiliation is almost unsupportable. It is not at all mitigated by the fact that what he describes is untrue. How could it be true? What he describes is, in his own words, perverse. It is sadistic. He does not speak of two men making love, but of a reptile embracing a child. What is perverse then, is Suhail's imagination.

It is clearer here, more than anywhere else, what a dark place his imagination is. The image of our union that he creates is primitive, and possibly has a mythical origin. As I've said, it is likely to be derived from literature, since this constitutes his preferred realm of non-reality. It is possible, on the other hand, that he made it up himself. Either way, it says more about him than it does about me. Much more. For that matter, everything he depicts about our relationship says a great deal more about him than it does about me.

I will admit to being organized and making plans and lists and timetables and so on. I do these mostly for myself. They help me to work more efficiently. If I also did them for Suhail, it is only because he would not do them for himself. Similarly, if I appeared to cosset him it was only because he could not or would not look after himself. I did not want to do it. I had to do it. He made

170

me. What was I supposed to do, let him sit there and rot in his own filth? Let him carry on believing in his own wild inventions? It was my duty, my right, but that is all. I took no pleasure from it – I can assure you of that. If someone close to you will not take responsibility for themselves then they force you to do it for them.

That is why I had to help him organize his life. If he became dependent on me, as he claims he did, then this was through his choice, his doing. He had a job once. He was an academic in an English department, but he cut back his teaching hours to virtually nothing in order to concentrate on his writing and eventually he didn't bother to show up at all. He was due to teach a course, I forget what it was called. It is not of any consequence, although the students were reportedly disappointed when he did not turn up. I provided for Suhail financially because I had to, because otherwise he really would have starved, wouldn't he?

I also admit as if it were an offence, that I did lay out his clothes for him. I did it to make sure he got dressed in the morning. After he left, I carried out an inventory of his wardrobe. From this, I was able to deduce exactly what he was wearing, and what he took with him on the day he disappeared. He was wearing jeans and a white t-shirt with a stone-coloured cotton jacket and dark brown trainers. I asked him not to wear trainers when he was in public. He took with him a black canvas bag containing two spare t-shirts – one yellow and green, one faded red – an old black v-neck sweater with a hole at the elbow, a pair of sport socks, three pairs of boxer shorts and some basic toiletries. Suhail was unshaven at the time. I trust this will be helpful to you in your search.

After putting clothes on the bed for him, I used to put his breakfast out, to try and ensure that he ate properly, at least at the start of the day. I alternated between cereal and muesli in order that he had some variety. Since my rota wasn't effective, I either had to do all of the shopping, cooking and cleaning or pay someone else to do it for me. For a while, I had to regulate his viewing habits by circling one programme a day in the guide. But he gave up on television anyway. I said that I had to do his accounts. I established a weekly budget, and tried to get him to balance his own cheque book. Of course, nobody uses those anymore.

We used to have a social events diary, but he kept crossing things out, and eventually I threw it away. I helped him do a 6 month, 1 month, 1 week, and 1 day timetable. The aim was to produce a certain number of words a day, though he never did. He was supposed to check targets with me on a Friday evening. He generally wrote, or sat in his room, from 9.00 a.m. to 5.00 p.m. I was just trying to help him structure his day. He never showed me what he produced, and I never asked him to, except on that one occasion when his progress report was unreadable. I see now that he produced painfully little, for all his supposed ambition. He has left behind him no more than a few pages of pointless meanderings. He is a dreamer. He has neither the stability, nor the talent to see things through.

Despite my efforts, Suhail's routines broke down, with inevitable consequences. I should never have let them. They helped him, whatever he says. I supervised Suhail emotionally as much as I did practically. I held him, even though he resisted me. I did it because I had to, and because it needed to be done. I provided him with the security he lacked. This meant that I had to tolerate his outbursts, verbal and otherwise. I was not hurt by them, because they were not about me. None of them were, not really.

I put my own needs to one side as I'm accustomed to doing. I did not count in our relationship. I did not matter. It was I, not he, who slowly became invisible and ceased to exist as a person. At best I was his shadow. A pale shadow, as he says. I admit that my skin is not right. I have a pigmentation problem which has worsened over the years. White patches appear and then spread unevenly. It may also have affected my hair and eyes. I may not be quite so appealing to look at anymore, but I cannot help that. It was cruel of Suhail to draw attention to my affliction in the way that he did.

§

I am starting to get weary of this. I do not have much more to say for now. When Suhail left, as bad as that was, my sense of who I am, if not my colour, gradually started to return. I won't say that this was easy for me. I began to realize what I had lost. I also began to realize how much I'd been taken for granted, or worse. Suhail claims to have been assaulted by me, but he provides no evidence. On the other hand, I have evidence that he has assaulted me, verbally, at least. He has written scandalous things about me when all I ever tried to do was help him. As for the rest, well, if and when he is found, if and when I get him home, things will not carry on as before, I can assure you. I no longer wish to be anyone's shadow.

As I look at myself now, at the back of my hands while I type this page, I see the skin of someone I do not know. It is unnaturally pale, yes, but it is dull not shiny. It is dry, not slimy. It is paper thin, scaly, lifeless and starved. It looks like it's coming away. I raise both hands to my cheeks. They feel hollow and they are not smooth. The loosening skin sags and then stretches. There is a crack which stings and feels hot to the touch while the flesh around it is cold. These are not my hands. This is not my face. I need to stop this now. I have only one more thing to say. I will say what happened the night before Suhail left, and then I will proceed with the remainder of my case file.

§

The last time I saw Suhail was at dinnertime. Well, actually, no. I did see him that morning but he didn't stir. I had got up at the usual time. Did I mention post before? I think I did. I always collected this myself and placed anything for Suhail on the table or under his door so that he could read it before he started work. We are one of those few lucky households who still have post delivered first thing, when you actually need it. There was something for him that day, although of course I thought

174

nothing of it at the time. Now I suspect it might well be relevant.

There was a letter – I suppose it was a letter – in a white envelope. It was not handwritten and I don't recall a postmark. He had not received any correspondence for some time. I put it under the door, as I had with the newspaper, and made sure it was face up so that he couldn't miss it. Then I went to work. Needless to say, there was no sign of the envelope or its contents after he'd gone.

On my way home, I thought I'd make him something nice for dinner as a treat, but when I got there and called up the stairs, he said he didn't want anything. Neither would he come down. He was withdrawn to say the least, and completely monosyllabic. I'm afraid he'd been like that for a while. He said it was because of his work. He said that he was just stressed and that he'd be fine when he finished his current project. He made me feel like I was fussing or nagging if I said anything about how he was behaving, so I stopped doing it in the end. I accepted what he said, let him get on with things, and occasionally tried to distract him, draw him out of himself for a while. It wasn't easy. As I said, if you care for a depressed and unstable person, you have to be prepared for quite a lot of abuse.

Suhail's behaviour was not unusual that evening, although in retrospect he might have been somewhat more anxious. It's hard to tell – I went upstairs and knocked, but he wouldn't open the door. I think perhaps his voice was more strained, but I might be reading too much into it, knowing what I do now. It is hard to engage someone in conversation through a closed door, especially if they don't talk to you much anyway, but after I'd had my meal, I sat on the floor outside and I did my best. More for something to say, than from any real need for his advice, I told him about a client I'd had some trouble with recently.

This client was quite the high-flyer already and he was ambitious for more. He was on the verge of making a big move to a very lucrative job with one of the top recruitment agencies in the capital. They were my clients too (I'd been out-sourced), and for obvious reasons, it was an important deal for me to broker. I genuinely thought it was the right thing, that he was the man for the job. He had all of the desired characteristics after all. I'd tested him myself, and he was exactly what he needed to be: extraverted-thinking but with good signs of balance around factors such as dominant/accommodating, sober/enthusiastic and restrained/direct. I couldn't reveal his name, because confidentiality is a habit I do have to bring home with me, but I described him as being quite tall, athletic and blonde with light blue eyes. Not my type, but in earlier days I might have expected a raised eyebrow from Suhail. I doubt if there was one, even though I couldn't see. I continued regardless.

This young man, who in fact wasn't that young but still looked it, wanted the job very badly indeed. He, I shall refer to him as x, was going to stop at nothing, and I respected that. He did all the preparation he could possibly do. He researched the company, networked with key individuals within it, and began to mould himself into their shape. Not that he had to do too much in order to fit in. I was helping him, grooming him, as well as making the practical arrangements such as lunches and so on. It was all looking very good indeed until it started to mean too much to him, and he began to act as if getting the job was a matter of life or death.

There is a line between saying that you really want something and saying that you have to have it. I don't know when he crossed it, or why, but he did. He started to look drawn, and told me that he wasn't sleeping. He became overly concerned with his performance during what were, after all, informal as well as strictly off the record meetings. He was ringing me up more often than he needed to, and taking the risk of being found out at work. He worried that he had said the wrong thing, or made an unfavourable impression on one of his potential employers, and constantly sought my reassurance. I told him he was trying too hard and rather bluntly advised him to leave it for a few days, since there was still nearly a fortnight before the interview and his efforts were becoming counter-productive.

He did seem to take this on board, but precisely three days later he phoned me in a state of despondency, saying that he knew he'd blown it already, that he couldn't believe he'd ruined the opportunity of a lifetime, and that he was a complete failure *etc*. He was being melodramatic, and I was tempted to hang up, but I'd invested a lot in this person already and I owed myself a result. So I talked him through it.

Since his job would essentially be the same as mine, I told him more than I've ever told anybody about what it's like to do it, and more importantly, what you have to be like in order to do it. This was what he hadn't been able to research, and what was causing him such difficulty. This is a job, I said, which is not about you. You are a mediator, a go-between, a match-maker between client and client and your only goal, your only ambition is to bring them together successfully. Anything else is superfluous and worse; it will get in the way. So this is what you need to be, what you need to become, and you must forget everything else. You are a conduit. That is all.

It doesn't matter what you want, or what you are afraid of. You must not look at yourself that way, or ask yourself those kinds of questions. Rather, you ask what he (or she) wants, what they want, and you must sense what both parties fear about each other in order to circumvent that fear. You are only there to make things happen, and you do whatever you have to do in order to guarantee that they will. It is important that you are always there when you need to be, but that you are not really visible. If you appear at all, your appearance should be tailored, so that you do not stand out and draw attention to yourself.

Your clients are not interested in you, but in your other clients. You should be transparent, ideally. Your movements should not draw attention to themselves either. Indiscretion would be costly to all concerned. If you move in on someone, do not leave a trace. Finally, I said, if you cannot keep yourself in check then you should give up right now.

This was calculated to push him the other way. I knew that he didn't want to give up. I knew that he had it in him. Sure enough, my pep talk worked and he got the job on the salary we were both hoping for. This was both a result, and the end of it, as far as I was concerned. I generally didn't have to reveal anything about myself in order to complete a transaction, and so in my mind I'd done more than enough for him. But he thought otherwise. He continued to call me even after he was in post. He was not experiencing any particular problem as such. It's just that he'd formed a habit – I suppose that's the word, and couldn't stop doing it.

He'd ask for advice about this and that, even though he clearly didn't need it any more. He wanted to arrange lunches as often as twice a month, and seemed to think that we should initiate some kind of support group for others in our profession. I was taken aback at first, and wasn't sure how to react. He made it difficult for me to detach myself from him, so in the end I agreed to meet, in the hope that this might go some way to getting it out of his system. I thought that if I, in person, embodied the balance between group-orientation and self-sufficiency, he might learn from my example.

I couldn't believe it when he started to question me about my affairs. That is something you just don't do, and I regretted then ever having given him such an insight into how I operate. I should have just let him fail after all. He was a parasite, a leech, and he wasn't getting any more. I would not tell anyone, even in general terms, who I was working with or how it was going! He had crossed the line again, but it was much more serious this time. This time he was prying and I had to put a stop to it. So I told him. I said, and this was true in a way, that I was disappointed in him, that I thought he had understood me, and the rules of the game, but that he obviously hadn't and I couldn't help him anymore. I said that the idea of a regular group outing was preposterous, and that he should stop phoning me. I said that I had never expected to be probed in such a way by someone I had considered to be a colleague, and that it would be a good idea if we gave each other as much space as possible from now on. Then I left. I didn't hear from him, and work life returned to normal for the next couple of months.

Subsequently I found out, from a contact, that he had approached one of my clients. Of course! I could have predicted, if not prevented this. I had created him and now he had turned on me. He had made us competitors, rivals, and he left me with little choice. It is about survival, after all. I simply could not afford to let him steal my clients, who are my livelihood. There is generally honour among thieves, but this is only good for as long as they do not steal from each other. And then, well, as I said, what choice did I have?

I exposed him. I alerted everyone who counts in this industry to the presence of a poacher on their land. I pointed to someone in their midst who was working against them, and in doing so made it impossible for him to work for them. You could say that I destroyed him.

Mediating includes walking the line between sometimes complementary, but often competing interests, and this time I made sure he went over it and was widely seen to do so. The revelation of your true identity will betray you in the search and selection business. He should have kept his head down as I told him to, and he should never have crossed me. He really shouldn't.

By this time I had tried the handle on Suhail's door and, finding it unlocked, I'd gone in. Standing over him as he sat at his desk, I asked him what he would have done in my place, but he wasn't listening. He was just staring blankly up at me, and when I passed my hand in front of his eyes and said his name, he started, stood up, and left the room.

§

The next day he had gone and I didn't hear from him again until the email on June 15th. I will send you an item of Suhail's clothing for the sniffer dogs, and a sample of his DNA. You will decide, in due course, which of these is most useful, but I suspect it will be the former.

Email messages June 15th – June 24th

From: "Suhail B" suhailb100@yahoo.com
To: Matt_1@fsmail.net
Date: Jun 15, 8:10AM
Subject: (no subject)

Matt

I'm in another country and I'm a long way out of your reach, so don't even think about trying to find me. I don't owe you an explanation, but if you were thinking I'd gone to find Saeed, you'd be right. I haven't found him yet, but I will.

I wasn't going to contact you at all, but I need to know something. What were you trying to tell me that night? What was the point of your story? You never told me anything about your work, so you must have had a reason. If you were just trying to frighten me, and keep me captive, for once, for the first time you failed.
Suhail

From: "Matt" matt_1@fsmail.net
To: suhailb100@yahoo.com
Subject: RE:
Date: 15 Jun 13:33:51 +0200 (CEST)

I don't know what you're talking about. I was just making conversation. But never mind that now. Where are you? It is a relief to hear from you. It really is. But I beg to differ. I think you do owe me an explanation.
Matt

From: "Suhail B" suhailb100@yahoo.com
To: Matt_1@fsmail.net
Date: Jun 15, 8:36AM
Subject: RE:

I don't owe you a thing Matt, and I'm never going to tell you where I am. Don't you get it? I'm free of you now, I escaped. Just the way I thought I would. You tried to rattle me at the end, but it was already too late. I was already slipping between the bars and guess who loosened them for me? He did. Ironically, he helped me get away from you, your hateful house, your friend and even his own ghost.

That letter you put under my door was from Saeed. It had a ticket folded inside it. I didn't believe what I was looking at, at first. I must have stared at it for hours. It had never occurred to me that it was all very well being ready for my transfer, but there still needed to be a means of transfer, a mode of transport. What am I like? There's not a practical bone in my body, just as you always said.

Well, there you are, you were right about one thing, at least. And here I am. I expect to hear from Saeed again very soon – any day now. The letter said that I should come here and that someone would meet me at the airport and take me to a hotel. He would contact me later. The letter also said that it is hot and humid here, but that there are lots of places of interest, and not so many people at this time of year. Saeed said that you can wander for hours completely undisturbed, and in the afternoon there are spectacular storms. I wouldn't say the storms have been spectacular yet, but they're brewing day by day and I know I'm not going to be disappointed.

I haven't found the places of interest so far, or the quiet, but I'll tell you this much, it's as hot as hell, and a thousand times as sticky. You can take this as a clue if you want Matt, but I'm just making conversation.

Saeed said I had to come straight away, so I did. Who knows, perhaps we'll both come back one day – together. This may be an expedition that my body can't survive, but only in its current state. Imagine – you might never even recognize me.
Suhail

From: "Matt" matt_1@fsmail.net
To: suhailb100@yahoo.com
Subject: RE:
Date: Thurs, 15 Jun 13:41:34 +0200 (CEST)

What exactly do you mean by that, Suhail? Believe you me, I would recognize you anywhere. It is quite an understatement to say that you do not have a realistic idea of what it's going to be like when you see your brother again after all this time. He may have invited you out there, but you should not expect a fairytale reunion. You don't even know what he looks like now, let alone what kind of person he is. You have taken all that for granted. You have a habit of taking people for granted.

When you left and you told me nothing of your plans, I had to decide on a course of action. I decided to wait for a few days and then call the police if you didn't come back and I didn't hear from you. I was unable to tell the policeman why you had gone and so, apart from making me feel foolish, he was also unable to help. It then became necessary for me to try and find out more for myself.

I searched your study, and read your journal. I had to. You gave me no choice. I trust that you can see that. I was right to think that your motive was to find Saeed more than it was to leave me, but you are wrong to think that in finding him you will somehow be reborn or, as you put it, reprogrammed. This is not thinking at all Suhail. This is madness. I know what you are planning to do, but you must stop, immediately.
Matt

From: "Suhail B" suhailb100@yahoo.com
To: Matt_1@fsmail.net
Date: Jun 15, 9:07AM
Subject: RE:

I'm not planning to do anything anymore. He's doing all the planning now. Thinking about it, he must have been doing the planning all along. Why else would he mention the storms? This place attracts more lightning than almost anywhere else in the world. He must have known that. He must have known what I was writing about, what was in my mind. I don't know how. Do you? Did you tell him, Matt? Have you spoken to him like you spoke to Ben, in my place?

It doesn't matter now anyway because I'm here, and so is he, and it looks like we both want the same thing. You may not like it, but there's nothing you can do to stop it. I am going to go back, and I am going to start again. I have to. Since you claim to have read my journal, you really ought to know why. I hurt him very badly and I have had to live with the consequences for too long. Only it's worse than that. What I did is worse than I said. I said it was an accident. But it wasn't.

For a start, when it happened we were already teenagers, not children. It happened just a couple of years before he left. He'd been taunting me since he realised who I was – not just his copy, but a bad one, a deviant one. The teasing had become a way of life, a habit. It almost felt normal, but I suppose the effects were cumulative.

We had fought before but never like we did that day. That day something got in to all of us, the supervisors, Saeed and especially me. I know what it was. It was my destiny. The time was right. The conditions were ideal. The tensions inside that car could have generated lightning all by themselves, but instead they conducted it through me to him. You could say I was possessed. Maybe that explains why I had enough strength to kick him out of the door. Perhaps I was filled with the energy of a demon. I don't know. But I meant to do it. In that fraction of a second I wanted him dead, or at least gone, so that I could be free to be myself.

In a way I got what I wanted, even if I had to wait a year or so. In a much bigger way I didn't get what I wanted at all. I got just the opposite. I'm not free. Ever since the day he left I've been tied to his reproachful ghost, and he was going to get me back. He had every right to, as you already pointed out. He had every right to and he was clearly going to. That's why I'm here. Lightning changed everything for the worse when it separated us. It will change everything for the better when it joins us again. When it joins us again I'll be reprogrammed and what I did will be undone. I'll be free, finally. Do you see?

From: "Suhail B" suhailb100@yahoo.com
To: Matt_1@fsmail.net
Date: Jun 16, 8:33AM
Subject: (no subject)

Hello. Are you still there?

From: "Matt" matt_1@fsmail.net
To: suhailb100@yahoo.com
Subject: RE:
Date: Fri, 16 Jun 13:46:32 +0200 (CEST)

Oh I'm still here all right. I've been thinking about your confession and your remarkably unorthodox choice of reparation. I wonder, will your brother's situation improve as a result of your actions, or just your own? Do you somehow imagine that he too will be freed from the past?

From: "Suhail B" suhailb100@yahoo.com
To: Matt_1@fsmail.net
Date: Jun 16, 8:58AM
Subject: RE:

He must somehow imagine that himself Matt. I told you, he got me here and when I arrived there was a message at the hotel reception telling me to look around for a while. I wasn't sure what he meant at first and I've been reluctant to go out. I'm still weak from not eating and as you know, I've grown somewhat accustomed to darkness and confinement. I can't think why, but I feel out of place here. The light outside is blinding, and besides, I didn't know where to go. I decided to research the area first by reading all the various books and brochures provided by the hotel. It took a while. My first outing was to a nearby theatre last night. Well, it's called a theatre but it's actually an old cinema. I liked it, once I'd found it. I really don't do maps, or directions. It's quite possible that I've become slightly agoraphobic. Thanks for that.

Anyway, this place was fabulous. You'd have hated it. It was completely over the top inside; columns, arches, statues and carvings all in red and gilt. There was a massive Wurlitzer on the stage. A tiny old man in a tuxedo shuffled on to play it before the film started and then they both descended through the floor. The film itself was dull in comparison. I don't even remember what it was. I was staring at the ceiling which was covered in tiny stars. It was beautiful. I could quite happily sit there every night.

Nothing else appeals to me in the least, but now I understand that's not the point. This area is devoted to commerce, families and tourism. It's all glass and steel monstrosities, residential housing and theme parks: hideous. Talking of hideous, you should see the clientele around here. I don't know why he put me up at this hotel. It must be costing him a fortune. I feel significantly under-dressed.

I'm going. There could be another message for me today and if there isn't I understand what I'm supposed to do now. I'm not supposed to be sight-seeing – I'm supposed to be finding us a venue, or should I say a stage for the event to take place.

From: "Matt" matt_1@fsmail.net
To: suhailb100@yahoo.com
Subject: RE:
Date: Fri, 16 Jun 14:02:51 +0200 (CEST)

I don't think you are Suhail, but if it stops you from wallowing in your room, then so be it. I don't doubt that you've been provided with a very comfortable room. Perhaps you should be more grateful. Your brother has clearly taken some trouble over your accommodation. What exactly are your objections to the clientele: is it simply that they are well-dressed or has somebody offended you in some other way? You could always make more effort yourself of course. Tell me is your hotel large, or small?

From: "Suhail B" suhailb100@yahoo.com
To: Matt_1@fsmail.net
Date: Jun 16, 01:22PM
Subject: RE:

It's huge Matt, massive. There are more than 30 floors and hundreds, possibly thousands of rooms. It is as you say, very comfortable, even luxurious, but in terms of style it's not my kind of thing at all. It's austere, restrained; conventional. I dare say you'd like it, but I feel like people are whispering and laughing and it's all too obvious that they don't approve of my sort around here.

The lobby is a vast colonial landscape with palm trees and columns growing in an orderly fashion out of square tiles which appear to have been polished to infinity. It's all very regimented. The ceiling is so high that the click of expensive shoes echoes on forever, bouncing and distorting like the light from the high bay windows that face the waterfront with its row of neatly parked yachts. It's like an enormous hall of mirrors.

I sat for a while at one of many clusters of armchairs and sofas precisely arranged on a plush red rug. I tried to read by a table lamp, but I couldn't concentrate and my heart started racing. My eyes shot from the page to the floor, to the glass table, to someone's patent leather bag, to the white light from the open doors, to the windows, the walls and then back to the page which I could no longer see. They started to sting and water and I had to shut them.

The sounds were worse. There was a cacophony of small splintered voices, which might actually only have been one or two voices, discussing something of great importance they didn't want me to hear.

Then, I know you'll think I'm paranoid, but there was someone, a man, I know there was. He kept looking at me. He looked behind him at the reception desk and I thought for a second that I was being given the eye after all, but it was too quick and his expression didn't seem that friendly. Then he walked around the lobby as if he was searching for someone, but he kept glancing at me from behind people and columns and trees. He even sat near me and pretended to read a paper but every now and then I caught him peering at me over the top of it.

He had a good look at me, but I never got a proper look at him – not at his face. He was very careful about that. I got out of the lobby but then I think I spotted him again at the end of the corridor when I went back to my room. I stayed in here for a little while. There is a computer and a television and I can pull the blinds and lock the door. I'm not paranoid. He was real. Who was he? What did he want?
Suhail

From: "Matt" matt_1@fsmail.net
To: suhailb100@yahoo.com
Subject: RE:
Date: Fri, 16 Jun 18:30:49 +0200 (CEST)

How would I know? Why are you asking me? First you imagine that there was a hidden message in my account of what passed between my self and my client. Now you imagine that there is a hidden connection between me and this mystery man, but how could there be? You read far too much into things Suhail. Far too much.

Whatever happened to reason and common sense? Reason and common sense would tell you that there is no mystery man. He doesn't exist. You are imagining him. Reason and common sense would also tell you that if he doesn't exist, I can't be connected to him.

Never mind the simple fact that I still do not know where you are. If I knew where you were I would go there myself because somebody needs to intervene. You are going to have to tell me, Suhail. I will not play your game of clues and guesses. What do you think this is – a child's game of hide and seek? Grow up. You do not seem to have grasped the consequences of the action you intend to take. As usual, you have attempted to shift the responsibility, but I cannot accept this.

I repeat the question I asked you earlier and that you failed to answer. Who will benefit: him, or just you? Why can't you see that you are indulging in a selfish fantasy and that this is dangerous? Wake up Suhail! Snap out of

it before it is too late and one or both of you gets hurt, as you surely will. Do you really want to hurt him again?
Matt

From: "Suhail B" suhailb100@yahoo.com
To: Matt_1@fsmail.net
Date: Jun 16, 02:03PM
Subject: RE:

No! Of course I don't want to hurt him again. What kind of a question is that? I didn't want to hurt him in the first place. I didn't want the blood, the scar, the screaming. What do you think I am? I just wanted to be left alone. I told you that. But we were never meant to be alone, Saeed and I, Saeed'n'Suhail. We are twins. If I'd been an ordinary twin, a perfect twin, he would never have resented me, and none of this would be necessary. But it is. It's the only way.

He couldn't forgive me for kicking him out of the car, and he couldn't forgive me for being born the same, but different. So I have to rub out the kick, rub out the copy and give at least one of us the chance to start again. Otherwise we are both lost, we are both dead. Why can't you see that? I already destroyed him, and if I don't do this, he will destroy me.

There is no way forwards, only back. I can't run away from him. I've tried that. I can only run back to him, and perhaps that movement, that gesture, will save him too in some way. Perhaps then he'll finally be able to forgive me. When lightning strikes us we'll be together again, at last.

Now, with or without your blessing, I have to go on looking for a location. By the way, you were wrong about that man. I saw him again this morning.
Suhail

From: "Suhail B" suhailb100@yahoo.com
To: Matt_1@fsmail.net
Date: Jun 16, 06:26PM
Subject: (no subject)

I found myself at the aquarium a mile or so away from here along the waterfront. I thought I might as well go in, but if the waterfront was too crowded, this was nothing in comparison. Once I was in the foyer, I couldn't have turned round if I'd wanted to. If we didn't move as a shoal, we didn't move at all. At least it was relatively dark, although the humidity was unbearable. The air conditioning must have broken. I could hardly breathe. Through a myriad of human forms, large and small, I caught the merest glimpse of sea dragons, cypress swamps, mangroves and manatees.

Am I teasing you? Trust me, I'm not. I know you've probably already worked out roughly where I am, but I won't be specific. I hate to frustrate you Matt – it brings out the worst in your personality, and does little for your complexion either. But the last thing I want is for you to come after me as well. I'm nervous enough as it is.

We were at the coral reef gallery and I sensed him closing in on us, like a predator. I turned and I saw him between two heads, fixed on me – unshakeable. I tried to communicate my alarm to the others but caused only local agitation and we, as a whole, continued at the same pace from one window to the next, passively ingesting the contents as we went. By the time we got out I was fairly frantic, pouring with sweat and unpopular with the people whose backs I'd jabbed but who still wouldn't let me through. After that I came back here and spoke to you.

This afternoon I was walking through town, not really knowing what I was looking for when I arrived at the art museum. There was a man, sitting on a step outside, reading a guidebook. It was the same one. There was no doubt about it. I turned straight away but he'd already seen me. I tried to shake him off. I jumped on a bus. I had no idea whatsoever where it was going. The bus crossed a river. He was not on it. I'm sure of that. I checked.

I got off again at another museum that was once a hotel and was probably worth visiting back then. I sat outside with my back to what was, admittedly, a glorious construction with silver minarets and domes and other things of a purely decorative nature. I did my best to calm down. I watched the crowds for a while to make sure he wasn't among them, and then I went inside where it was cooler.

I took in very little information, but then, why should I care about the history of this area or the lives of wealthy foreigners? It's not as if I fancied any of them or anything and even then, I've had my fill of wealthy foreigners, haven't I Matt? I've learned not to go there again.

There was only one interesting piece of information as far as I could see. Back when it was a hotel, the building was the very first one in the entire region to be electrified. Having learnt this, I found myself walking rather absent-mindedly down something called the Grand Hall.

Someone brushed past me. He brushed my shoulder with his as he walked in the opposite direction. I hadn't seen him approaching, but I turned as he passed me, and so did he, just a fraction. It was definitely the same man, wearing exactly the same clothes as before; a dark suit. I don't think there are many people wearing dark suits out here at this time of year. Most of them wear garish shorts and short-sleeve shirts. Even the businessmen are without jackets. It would horrify you. This man is smart though, with short black hair and about my height and build. I still haven't had a proper look at his face, but there is something about him. He seems familiar. He is quite dark skinned. He makes me feel queasy. I think it could be Saeed.

I don't know though. Who else could it be? Why would anyone else follow me? If it is Saeed, I don't know what he's doing. Perhaps he's checking me out first, having a look at me before I have a proper look at him. If he's trying to frighten me, he's succeeding. I don't know what to make of this at all. Why doesn't he just come up to me, or at least leave me another message if he is not ready to meet? Before I left the museum, I scanned every single room, and I thought I saw him again, disappearing around a corner somewhere. This time I pursued him, but I didn't catch him up. Then I left.

My head was throbbing, as it is now. I don't know what's going on. I took the bus back across the river, and then I got confused. I got lost. I hate getting lost. I hate this place. I stood in a square, and it was as if the sun, reflecting from so many tall shiny buildings, was throwing hundreds of spotlights on me. I felt as if everyone could see me, but I could see no-one and nothing. I couldn't tell whether he was there or not. It probably wasn't him anyway. It was probably just a stalker, some creep.

I was standing there, sweltering and starting to hyperventilate. An old man came up to me and gave me some water. He took me to a bench and sat next to me for a while. He gave me directions back to the hotel, and I found it in the end. I threw up when I got to my room, and lay down on the bed for an hour or so. The usual late afternoon rumblings give me a headache at the best of times, and they're getting much louder now. Suhail

From: "Matt" matt_1@fsmail.net
To: suhailb100@yahoo.com
Subject: RE:
Date: Fri, 16 Jun 23:49:09 +0200 (CEST)

It is indeed unfortunate that your explorations have proved to be so traumatic for you and that you've felt the need to retreat to your room. If you are so perturbed by the appearance of this stranger, why don't you confront him and ask him who he is and what he wants instead of asking me?

Matt

From: "Suhail B" suhailb100@yahoo.com
To: Matt_1@fsmail.net
Date: Jun 16, 06:55PM
Subject: RE:

I told you, I tried that. I went after him in the museum but he got away and I haven't seen him since. He wasn't in the square, as far as I know. He wasn't in the hotel lobby or in the corridor outside my room – as far as I know.

From: "Matt" matt_1@fsmail.net
To: suhailb100@yahoo.com
Subject: RE:
Date: Sat, 17 Jun 00:04:37+0200 (CEST)

It would seem that it was nothing after all then, and you should forget about him. Your sightings of this person are most likely to be a pure coincidence. At most he could be an admirer, or a stalker as you put it. But I doubt that. It takes time to build up that much of an interest in someone.

There is of course an outside chance that it's your brother, and that for some reason he is unable to make contact directly. He may be too apprehensive himself, although I would not expect you to consider that.

From: "Suhail B" suhailb100@yahoo.com
To: Matt_1@fsmail.net
Date: Jun 16, 07:12PM
Subject: RE:

You do seem to have a theme going there Matt. Shall I tell you what I think? I think you've appointed yourself my brother's spokesman so that you can carry on persecuting me, even from a distance. I think you can't stand it that I got away from you, and that you're trying to control me by playing with my mind. I think you started doing this the night before I left. Perhaps you sensed that I was going. Wasn't the story of you and your client some kind of allegory of my brother and I, and wasn't it you who once described yourself as the mystery man? I think it was.

You might as well come clean now Matt. I've seen through you. I may not understand what really is going on out here, but I guarantee that it's no coincidence, and I'll tell you another thing – I've changed my mind. I do think it's him.

I've just had another idea. There's no stopping me this evening. There's a bridge near here. I read about it. It has a very wide span and the best views of the bay, but that's not what's interesting. Apparently it was hit once, by a tanker during a storm. A section of the bridge fell one hundred and fifty feet into the water, along with the passengers of a greyhound bus, and now they say it's haunted by ghostly hitchhikers. I don't know why I haven't been already. The bridge was rebuilt with brightly coloured steel cables that fan out from a central support, like two-dimensional pyramids. It's much stronger now but it still has an ethereal look, especially when it's lit from the roadway at night. The books say it's an ideal suicide spot but I'd say it's an ideal location for a spectacular reunion, wouldn't you? I'm going to go and see.

From: "Suhail B" suhailb100@yahoo.com
To: Matt_1@fsmail.net
Date: Jun 16, 11:14PM
Subject: (no subject)

I sat on the wall in the middle of the bridge and I swear it was swaying in the wind. Nobody came, but there was a fantastic storm. What a waste. I was soaking wet and disappointed, but when I got back to the hotel there was a message.

I'm going to see him tomorrow night – at last. I've waited so long for this that I don't even know what to feel. There is excitement, mixed with a million other things, but more than anything, there is a sense that this is right. This is what has to happen. By tomorrow night I will finally have got back to him, and the scene will be set for a transformation that will make everything better again. I know it will. We're going to meet on a quiet stretch of beach an hour or so away from here by road but not far from where the bridge ends. A beach – I should have thought of that. There are enough of those around here.

I'm going to start looking in to transport first thing in the morning. I'm not going to wait for him to sort that out for

me this time. I'll make sure I get there somehow, even if I have to hitch a lift in a car. I wouldn't expect to hear from me again, but you never know. Since you evidently don't approve, I won't expect you to wish me luck.
Suhail

From: "Matt" matt_1@fsmail.net
To: suhailb100@yahoo.com
Subject: RE:
Date: Sat, 17 Jun 04:44:11+0200 (CEST)

Good luck. You don't always get what you expect Suhail.

From: "Matt" matt_1@fsmail.net
To: suhailb100@yahoo.com
Subject: RE:
Date: Sun, 18 Jun 04:12:31 +0200 (CEST)

Well?

From: "Matt" matt_1@fsmail.net
To: suhailb100@yahoo.com
Subject: RE:
Date: Sun, 18 Jun 18:58:52 +0200 (CEST)

Look, I know you are still out there, all right? I know you are. I insist you tell me what happened. I demand it. It is my right to know. You have no business cutting yourself off from me, and do not pretend that you no longer know me because you have changed. That would be ridiculous. I've told you that all along.

I want to know what happened on the beach. I am presuming that you managed not to get lost. I want to hear about it from you. I have no doubt that your fantasy has not been fulfilled because there is no way it could have been. Logic defies it. But I want you to tell me what you have done. What have you done? Where is your brother? Tell me. I don't want to wait any longer.
Matt

From: "Matt" matt_1@fsmail.net
To: suhailb100@yahoo.com
Subject: RE:
Date: Mon, 19 Jun 10:08:45 +0200 (CEST)

Suhail!

From: "Matt" matt_1@fsmail.net
To: suhailb100@yahoo.com
Subject: RE:
Date: Tues, 20 Jun 13:20:58 +0200 (CEST)

I see. I am prepared to wait only a few more days and then I intend to come after you. I think I know where you are. You have dropped enough clues and besides, I could always get your emails traced. I will come if I don't hear from you. I will search the area myself if I have to.
Matt

From: "Matt" matt_1@fsmail.net
To: suhailb100@yahoo.com
Subject: RE:
Date: Wed, 21 Jun 11:11:07 +0200 (CEST)

I am going to book a flight for the end of this week.
Where the devil are you?

From: "Suhail B" suhailb100@yahoo.com
To: Matt_1@fsmail.net
Date: Jun 24, 02:12PM
Subject: RE:

here, don't. d on 't c o me, having, sh i t, some troub le
typin g. Ha nds won' t w ork pr op er ly. D if f icult finding
som e where . G ot lo s t. not quite sure now, a m havi
ng some trouble. pain. Constant ly in my back. hands
shake , tremble , very tired , been asleep slep t on
beach   H e w a s t here, right there , in front o f m e
on the   beach. I w as n early there, nearly it was h
im. It was .   Must go to s leep now, sleep a lot . not
here. can ' t.   found thi s plac e can't reme mber ,
can't do all   . been trying d am n I t. Can't. B ack,
hurts. Woke up and it hurts . Back. Bad ears and still
white .   Everything .   H e was g on e a g ain. H e wa
sn't there an y more . w hy did n' t h e w a it? Sle e p
now. T hen

From: "Matt" matt_1@fsmail.net
To: suhailb100@yahoo.com
Subject: RE:
Date: Sat, 24 Jun 19:21:25 +0200 (CEST)

Wake up! You are not making yourself clear. Did you see
him? Was it definitely Saeed? Are you quite sure about
that? Stop complaining about your hands and your
back and your ears and just tell me what happened will
you? Did you get drunk? You sound drunk.
Matt

From: "Suhail B" suhailb100@yahoo.com
To: Matt_1@fsmail.net
Date: Jun 24, 02:35PM
Subject: RE:

Not d runk y ou mi ser a ble b as tard . Hit. ha! Must
have b ee n but st il l no no no. Too soo n
okuo[uir45tdsrt45l;,'l,;lk[,

From: "Matt" matt_1@fsmail.net
To: suhailb100@yahoo.com
Subject: RE:
Date: Sat, 24 2006 19:41:47 +0200 (CEST)

Now what? What are you doing? Have you lost control
of your faculties altogether?

From: "Suhail B" suhailb100@yahoo.com
To: Matt_1@fsmail.net
Date: Jun 24, 02:55PM
Subject: RE:

n ot qu ite . y ou k n ow I ha t e to d is appo in t y o u .
got s h ou t ed d a t fo r hi tting keys and I o ok in g a t
otal m es   s th ou gh, must b ehave be tter or e lse.
Takes su ch long t ime to   do things so slo w. like ol d
man wa lking   rollin g Funny. Fu nny r ou n d here . q
u ite hokey! can sleep o k be fore g e t ting moved on
.   Don 't car e . I t w ill b e o k w hen I g e t ba ck t o
th e be a ch.

From: "Matt" matt_1@fsmail.net
To: suhailb100@yahoo.com
Subject: RE:
Date: Sat, 24 Jun 20:02:37 +0200 (CEST)

It doesn't sound like you'll be going anywhere in a hurry.
You didn't answer my question. Was Saeed definitely
there?

From: "Suhail B" suhailb100@yahoo.com
To: Matt_1@fsmail.net
Date: Jun 24, 03:11PM
Subject: RE: Re:

y e s Ma tt. H e wa s def in i te ly t he r e. in fro n t o f
m e in t he rain. I r an toward s h im . h ea vy r ain. Bi
g s ea: ploplop loplop lopploploplop lopl opp
loploploplopCTUSHHsss s sssssssssploploplop lopl

oplopCTTUSHsssssssss   BANG !   white o ut. gone. I w
an t t o k now   wh e re w e   wer e. I w an t t o go b
ack. N ow. A s so on a s I'v e h ad s om e sl eep.

From: "Matt" matt_1@fsmail.net
To: suhailb100@yahoo.com
Subject: RE:
Date: Sat, 24 Jun 20:20:54 +0200 (CEST)

You are not going to sleep. You are going to tell me
what I want to know. Now let me try and get this straight:
you are saying that you were running on the beach and
that Saeed was in front of you. It was raining and you ran
towards him. Then you were hit. By lightning?

From: "Suhail B" suhailb100@yahoo.com
To: Matt_1@fsmail.net
Date: Jun 24, 03:32PM
Subject: RE:

yes , id iot . b y l ig ht ning wh at el se? ploploplop
lopllopploploploploplop opCTTUSSHHss sssssssss
BANG!!! in fr ont in t he r ai n wavi ng a light h e w as.
Ligh t out. White o ut, w ok e   up , g o n e. I t ha p pen
ed t oo so on. W e wer en't re ady. HOkey o ve r h er
e though. W alk ed o ver t h e br i d g e   to ok da
y s c alled G u lf s om e th in g. Do n' t c ome I' ll
b eg on e a gain soon. Puf f. Y ou wo n't ev en re cog
n is e me.

From: "Matt" matt_1@fsmail.net
To: suhailb100@yahoo.com
Subject: RE:
Date: Sat, 24 Jun 20:45:50 +0200 (CEST)

Don't bet on it. Surely you don't still believe in all that nonsense you wrote about? You cannot still believe that you will change: not now?

From: "Suhail B" suhailb100@yahoo.com
To: Matt_1@fsmail.net
Date: Jun 24, 03:55PM
Subject: RE:

I d o . I s a w him

From: "Matt" matt_1@fsmail.net
To: suhailb100@yahoo.com
Subject: RE:
Date: Sat, 24 Jun 21:00:45 +0200 (CEST)

I don't think you did Suhail, but either way, it is finished now. You're done. All right?

From: "Suhail B" suhailb100@yahoo.com
To: Matt_1@fsmail.net
Date: Jun 24, 04:11PM
Subject: RE:

N O . IT' S . NOT ! D a m n y o u m att .   Th is is n
ot f in i shed . i' m n ot d on e y et. I h av e to go
ba c k t o th e be ach .

From: "Matt" matt_1@fsmail.net
To: suhailb100@yahoo.com
Subject: RE:
Date: Sat, 24 Jun 21:15:36 +0200 (CEST)

Why are you so determined to go back to the beach?

From: "Suhail B" suhailb100@yahoo.com
To: Matt_1@fsmail.net
Date: Jun 24, 04:31PM
Subject: RE:

b eca us e he'll m eet m e t he re

From: "Matt" matt_1@fsmail.net
To: suhailb100@yahoo.com
Subject: RE:
Date: Sat, 24 Jun 21:34:11 +0200 (CEST)

He won't.

From: "Suhail B" suhailb100@yahoo.com
To: Matt_1@fsmail.net
Date: Jun 24, 04:44PM
Subject: RE:

Ho w the fu c k wou ld y ou   kno w? ho
w do yo u kn ow th at   ma t t? D a mn y o
u ol.i9iu,oi4ees45td5e.kk.l,jnjki

From: "Matt" matt_1@fsmail.net
To: suhailb100@yahoo.com
Subject: RE:
Date: Sat, 24 Jun 21:50:36 +0200 (CEST)

Calm down for heaven's sake. You are making a show of yourself again.

From: "Suhail B" suhailb100@yahoo.com
To: Matt_1@fsmail.net
Date: Jun 24, 04:59PM
Subject: RE:

Y up . jump ed up two t s aid d on't do th a t D ON'T DO THA T   te ll me whe re th e be ac h   is

From: "Matt" matt_1@fsmail.net
To: suhailb100@yahoo.com
Subject: RE:
Date: Sat, 24 Jun 22:03:50 +0200 (CEST)

I don't know where the beach is.

From: "Suhail B" suhailb100@yahoo.com
To: Matt_1@fsmail.net
Date: Jun 24, 05:11PM
Subject: RE:

Y es y ou do . I de ma nd to k no w . I h av e t he rig ht. T e ll   me

210

From: "Matt" matt_1@fsmail.net
To: suhailb100@yahoo.com
Subject: RE:
Date: Sat, 24 Jun 22:20:53 +0200 (CEST)

I told you, I don't know. You're imagining things again.

From: "Suhail B" suhailb100@yahoo.com
To: Matt_1@fsmail.net
Date: Jun 24, 05:27PM
Subject: RE:

Th en h o w do y o u k now h e wo n' t b
e th er e ? T e l l m e wh er e t he be
ach is I can 't r e me mb er my way b ac k

From: "Matt" matt_1@fsmail.net
To: suhailb100@yahoo.com
Subject: RE:
Date: Sat, 24 Jun 22:34:46 +0200 (CEST)

There is no point in going back. It is finished now. You are
done.

From: "Suhail B" suhailb100@yahoo.com
To: Matt_1@fsmail.net
Date: Jun 24, 05:43PM
Subject: RE:

T E LL M E W HER E T H E BE AC H
I S

From: "Matt" matt_1@fsmail.net
To: suhailb100@yahoo.com
Subject: RE:
Date: Sat, 24 Jun 22:50:37 +0200 (CEST)

Be quiet. I'm getting weary of this. I don't have anything else to say for now.

From: "Suhail B" suhailb100@yahoo.com
To: Matt_1@fsmail.net
Date: Jun 24, 05:58PM
Subject: RE:

W ai t wh er e a re   yo u   g oing ?

From: "Matt" matt_1@fsmail.net
To: suhailb100@yahoo.com
Subject: RE:
Date: Sat, 24 Jun 23:04:08 +0200 (CEST)

Nowhere. I'm still here.

From: "Suhail B" suhailb100@yahoo.com
To: Matt_1@fsmail.net
Date: Jun 24, 06:13PM
Subject: RE:

y ou 're sti ll   th er e an d I' m st ill h ere

From: "Matt" matt_1@fsmail.net
To: suhailb100@yahoo.com
Subject: RE:
Date: Sat, 24 Jun 23:18:26 +0200 (CEST)

So it would seem.

From: "Suhail B" suhailb100@yahoo.com
To: Matt_1@fsmail.net
Date: Jun 24, 06:25PM
Subject: RE:

S a ee d . W h e r e is   he ? Is he de e d?

From: "Matt" matt_1@fsmail.net
To: suhailb100@yahoo.com
Subject: RE:
Date: Sat, 24 Jun 23:31:53 +0200 (CEST)

If he isn't dead, its no thanks to you. So why don't you just stop it now?

From: "Suhail B" suhailb100@yahoo.com
To: Matt_1@fsmail.net
Date: Jun 24, 06:38PM
Subject: RE:

B ec au se I can 't

From: "Matt" matt_1@fsmail.net
To: suhailb100@yahoo.com
Subject: RE:
Date: Sat, 24 Jun 23:44:48 +0200 (CEST)

Then tell me where you are and I will.

From: "Suhail B" suhailb100@yahoo.com
To: Matt_1@fsmail.net
Date: Jun 24 2006, 06:54PM
Subject: RE: Re:

I 'l l te ll y o u if y o u t ell   me   ma t t

From: "Matt" matt_1@fsmail.net
To: suhailb100@yahoo.com
Subject: RE:
Date: Sat, 24 Jun 23:59:08 +0200 (CEST)

What? Tell you what? Look, forget about the beach and forget about meeting your brother. He was probably never there in the first place. Did that ever occur to you? Did it ever occur to you that it was all just a trick: a hoax?

From: "Suhail B" suhailb100@yahoo.com
To: Matt_1@fsmail.net
Date: Jun 24, 07:11PM
Subject: RE:

tri c k ?   I d on 't un d er stand w hat   you 're sa yi ng . wh y no. no. Te ll   m e w he r   e   t h   e b ea c h   is   ! h av e to go no w , ba c k to th e be a ch

From: "Matt" matt_1@fsmail.net
To: suhailb100@yahoo.com
Subject: RE:
Date: Sun, 25 Jun 00:18:08 +0200 (CEST)

Wait. I didn't mean to say that. There is no need to go back. Perhaps he will meet you again after all, on a different beach, somewhere else, some other time. You should stay where you are and rest for a while longer.

From: "Suhail B" suhailb100@yahoo.com
To: Matt_1@fsmail.net
Date: Jun 24, 07:20PM
Subject: RE:

N o

From: "Matt" matt_1@fsmail.net
To: suhailb100@yahoo.com
Subject: RE:
Date: Sun, 25 Jun 00:22:23 +0200 (CEST)

No?

From: "Suhail B" suhailb100@yahoo.com
To: Matt_1@fsmail.net
Date: Jun 24, 07:28PM
Subject: RE:

no . ah u h . Sh s s s Sh s s s . h ave to go m u ch to do m any m a n y be a ch es

215

no tso mu ch pain now . I wo n' t g o
ba ck. M an y m an y b ea che s

From: "Matt" matt_1@fsmail.net
To: suhailb_100@yahoo.com
Subject: RE:
Date: Sun, 25 Jun 00:34:14 +0200 (CEST)

Too many. You'll never find him. Wait. I think you should
wait with me.

From: "Suhail B" suhailb100@yahoo.com
To: Matt_1@fsmail.net
Date: Jun 24, 07:50PM
Subject: RE:

Lis ten: S h s s s sh s s s sh s s s sh s s s S h sss S   h
s   s   s S h sss   s h   ss   s S h   s s s Sh s   s
s S hs s s Shs s s Shs s s S h ss   s   Sh s s   s
S   h   s s s Sh s s s Sh s   s   s sh s   s s s
S   h ss   s   S   h sss s h   sss S h   s s
s S h sss Sh s s S h s s s S   h   s   s s S h
sss S   h   s s   s   S h s s s S   h s s s Sh s s s S
h s s s S h   s   s   s Sh s s s   S   h s s s
S   h s s s Shs ss   S h s s   s S h   s s Shs s
s   S   h   s   s s
BANG
****   ****   ****   ****   ****   ****   ****
****   ****   ****   **** ****   ****   ****   ****
****   ****   ****   ****   ****   ****   **** ****
****   **** ****   ****   ****   ****   ****   ****   ****
**** **** ****   ****   ****   ****   ****
****

216

From: "Matt" matt_1@fsmail.net
To: suhailb100@yahoo.com
Subject: RE:
Date: Sun, 25 Jun 01:07:42 +0200 (CEST)

Suhail ?

From: "Matt" matt_1@fsmail.net
To: suhailb100@yahoo.com
Subject: RE:
Date: Sun, 25 Jun 19:08:41 +0200 (CEST)

Suhail?

From: "Matt" matt_1@fsmail.net
To: suhailb100@yahoo.com
Subject: RE:
Date: Mon, 26 Jun 15:09:30 +0200 (CEST)

Suhail?

The Newspaper Report

This completes the transcript of our email exchanges which ceased approximately one year ago. Two weeks ago, I came across this local news report. It is the one I mentioned in my opening statement.

Photo Reveals Lightning Strike But No Body

Errol Jonathan's photo, shot through the car window, reveals lightning strike but no body

BY PAT MOORE
Friday June 30th

Somewhere between ████ and ████ a figure, thought to be male, was struck directly by lightning two weeks ago Saturday. Police Department searched the area since then but no body was found.

Area hospitals reported no casualties from the storms a fortnight ago, but due to the delayed effects of some lightning injuries there is now concern for the safety of the survivor.

Sole witness, photographer Errol Jonston took the shot through his car window but failed to notice the contact until the image was scanned and enlarged for printing. At this point it appears that the lightning victim was running - the figure in the photograph is slightly blurred - and that his arms were raised, torso forwards and head thrown back as if he had received a blow from behind.

Where it is not unusual for victims to survive a lightning strike, it is highly unusual if not impossible to escape injury even if the injuries are not immediately apparent such as burns, concussion or paralysis. Medical experts say that physical effects of lightning are not predictable, ranging from minor through moderate and severe.

LIGHTNING INJURIES - Minor injuries may include confusion, amnesia, temporary deafness or blindness, or temporary unconsciousness at the scene. Burns and paralysis are rare and recovery is generally gradual and may not be complete.

Moderate injury includes coma, disorientation, motor paralysis, mottled skin and diminished or absent pulse (the heart may recover automatically from

arrest). First and second degree burns may be apparent or develop within hours and post-traumatic stress is indicated.

Severe injuries include cardiac arrest and blunt trauma and prognosis here is poor.

Though death is usually a result only of a heart attack, clearly even minor injuries can produce long term detrimental effects such as pain, decreased mental function and psychological damage including changes in personality which may lead to suicide.

National Weather Service advises that mental changes in a lightning survivor are functional (to do with how the brain works) not anatomic: "To use an analogy: if an electric shock were sent through a computer, the outside case would probably look ok (similar to a photo or x-rays of the person), the computer boards on the inside would probably look ok and not be fused nor melted (CT, MRI for the person), but when you boot up the computer it would have difficulty accessing files, making calculations, printing, etc. This situation is similar in a person with brain injury who has short-term memory problems, difficulty accessing and coding information, difficulty organising output, etc."

LIGHTNING STATISTICS - Across the nation lightning is a significant problem, being the second largest storm killer for the last 40 years, exceeded only by floods. Still only approximately 10% of people struck by lightning are killed leaving 90% with different and in many cases ongoing degrees of disability.

Dr Mary Ann Cooper reports that lightning can injure a person in 5 ways: direct strike, side splash from another object, contact with a struck object, ground current or by being part of an upward streamer where lightning from cloud to

earth is met or attached to that from earth to cloud. Neurological damage may affect the brain and other parts of the nervous system.

Even though, year on year, lightning kills around a hundred people, injures many hundreds more and causes millions of ████ of damage to property and alone, lightning prediction is still more art than science and the pathology of lightning ('Keraunopathy') is little known. Incidence of lightning strikes are often delayed and limited to the isolated individual. Statistically, most individuals struck by lightning are male.

STRIKING IMAGE - Photographer and storm-chaser Errol Jonston was out driving the ████ area in search of a lightning shot at dusk and heading towards ████ for a clear view of the Gulf. He cannot recall the precise location but claims he was driving perpendicular to the beach when he stopped and turned the vehicle.

Jonston, who uses a window clamp tripod for safety said: "Being on a beach and close to water is pretty risky activity during a storm and most people know that. For a start you are the tallest thing in the area which is not a good idea. I cannot believe someone would just go out for a run like that. Especially in this area", ████ of course, attracts more strikes per year than any other ████ and has twice as many casualties. It is one of the world's lightning spots.

Jonston strongly rejects any suggestion that his remarkable image was in any way altered: "I never manipulate my photographs digitally either by putting elements in or taking them out. I am personally opposed to digital composites and manipulation even where they are admitted to openly".

He went on: "What you see here is what there was. It just happened to be more than what could be seen with the naked eye".

SUPPORT - Any victim of a lightning strike or severe electric shock is urged to seek medical advice. Other support can be found through groups such as:

████
████
████
████
████

PREVENTION - Prevention measures include attention to weather forecasts and conditions before embarking on outdoor activities and may be guided by the 30-30 rule. This states that if the time between seeing lightning and hearing thunder is less than 30 seconds, danger is indicated and shelter should be sought.

Open air activities should not be resumed within 30 minutes of the last lightning flash or burst of thunder.

Safe shelter is provided by buildings and cars (not convertibles) but not shelters (bus, golf or rain) due to the risk of side flashes. Trees pose a similar risk and the poles in tents can act as lightning rods.

If no shelter is available the Lightning Safety Group recommends the following lightning position: crouch down in the lowest possible spot keeping your feet together and placing your hands over your ears to avoid damaging the ear drums.

TREATMENT - If helping a lightning victim or victims, always treat the apparently dead first. Perform mouth-to-mouth and cardiopulmonary resuscitation.

Sadly, the only witness to this incident was not on hand to help and his stunning photograph tells its own story of the worrying scale of under-reported lightning strikes, the effects and occurrence of which we still know very little about.

I have incorporated this whole page report into my case file, and you will see that it has been censored. I will explain why in due course, but it was not me that did it.

The censored photograph shows lightning striking somebody on a beach. It happened on the night of June 17th when Suhail went to meet Saeed. The report says that the victim was running, and that therefore the figure in the photograph was blurred. It says that his arms were raised up, his torso was bent forwards and his head was thrown back 'as if he had received a blow from behind.'

According to the person who censored it, the photograph shows a lot more than this, but before I say more on that subject, I should first explain how I found the news report. I found it when I was searching for further information about where Suhail was and what happened to him. I had to search for further information because the evidence in the emails was inconclusive.

It will be apparent from the email transcripts that I attempted to ascertain the exact nature of Suhail's whereabouts, and that he prevented me from doing so. I obtained a number of clues as to the climate, vegetation, wildlife, local architecture and so on, and was even able to extract information about the hotel Suhail was staying in. However, following the events of June 17th he did not return to that hotel but made his way, by degrees to a place he referred to as 'Gulf something,' where he was able to obtain access to the Internet. It took him a week to get there, but he only stayed for one day.

This was as close as I came to being able to pinpoint his location. As I said, it was not for want of trying. I realised that there was no point in tracing the emails because Suhail had already moved on. There were, however, numerous indications of his general whereabouts, and I used them in order to carry out a Google search into:

- areas that are hot, humid and prone to storms
- areas with theme parks and other tourist attractions
- large, high quality hotels – minimum four stars – with waterfront locations and within proximity of an aquarium
- wildlife and vegetation including swamps, manatees etc
- beaches near a bridge (wide-span) that has collapsed in the past

Each search was a refinement of the previous one. Once I had refined my search as far as possible, I employed Google Earth. This activity was certainly time-consuming, but not uninteresting. It enabled me, in principle, to observe anything, anywhere. Yet unfortunately it yielded no results. All of the beaches appeared to be deserted. I could not see Suhail. I blame myself for failing to keep him in one place, and letting him get away.

I tried to put a stop to his fruitless desire to return to the beach where he claimed to have seen his brother, and been struck by lightning before he reached him. As a consequence, I inadvertently encouraged him to continue his quest elsewhere. If my deductions and his assertions are correct, then Suhail is in a region so replete with beaches that he could not possibly be found by means of a routine police search. I am certain you will agree with this and with my conclusion that, in the emails, I had at best circumstantial but insufficient proof as to where he was, and no real evidence at all regarding what had happened to him.

I reasoned that if Suhail's claim to have been struck by lightning was true, then there had to be a record of the event. He was clearly suffering from some form of injury, and so I used the Internet to compile a list of hospitals he might subsequently have visited. Since I was unable to specify the area, my list was very long. I telephoned every hospital on it. The process was very slow. The receptionists were either unwilling, or unable to tell me anything. The most I could hope for was to be put through to the relevant ward. This did not always happen. When it did, I had to establish my identity and my relationship to the person about whom I was inquiring before any of my own questions were answered. These were regarded as being unusual, and were treated with suspicion. I was unable to discover if anybody had reported any lightning related injuries, because I was told that nobody matching Suhail's description and condition had presented themselves for treatment.

Many months passed before I had worked my way through the list. I then resorted to gathering general information about lightning incidents in the hope that something would come up. Eventually it did. I entered the words 'lightning' and 'strike' into the search engine, and made my way through the entries methodically. There were one million two hundred and sixty thousand entries, and on page eighty nine I found one that highlighted a newspaper headline reading 'Photo Reveals Lightning Strike But No Body.'

There is both circumstantial and more concrete evidence that the 'no body' in the picture is Suhail. He was able, just about, to leave the scene after he was struck. He had been running on a beach after dark in an area known for the frequent occurrence of lighting strikes. More substantially, the incident happened 'two weeks ago Saturday' from the date the report was published, Friday June 30th. Working back from June 30th, the incident happened on Saturday June 17th. This date corresponds to Suhail's last coherent email message. I have submitted the local news report as evidence because it describes what happened to Suhail. However, when I found this report it was part of a longer feature article entitled 'Of Murder and Metamorphosis' by S. J. Kay.

I should say now, that I will not be able to present Kay's article without careful commentary for the reason I gave in my opening statement – it obscures fact with speculation, and it will be necessary for me to distinguish between the two. It begins with the local news report which is by a professional journalist called Pat Moore. I have not been able to track this down, but you, the authorities surely could. It reproduced the photograph beneath the headline and contained detailed geographic references. However, the version of the report that appears in Kay's article has been edited.

Kay has censored the photograph and all references to the location of the event beyond the bare fact that it took place on a beach. Kay maintains that this dramatic editorial intervention is justified because of the way in which some elements of the general public responded to the image and in order to protect the area from unwanted intrusion. It is certainly true to say that a limited section of the public did, for a time, respond in a way that was out of all proportion with what the photograph depicted. However, I would venture to include Kay among their number, and to suggest that had he, or more likely, she included the original image, the substance of the article as a whole might have been as sensible and as grounded as that of the brief report with which it begins.

§

The supposition about the gender of the victim in Moore's report is logical, because statistically speaking most individuals struck by lightning are male. The distinction between a direct lightning strike and other types is explained later. It is also significant that since there was a record of the event, albeit not the kind of record I had expected, there has already been a police search of the area. This means that I am justified in accumulating additional evidence that will be required in order to persuade the same police department, once it is named, to undertake a further search.

I wish I had read that the local area hospitals had not reported any casualties from the June 17th storms much earlier than I did. It would have saved me a lot of time.

The report indicates the nature of lighting injuries in general. This enables me to correlate them with the specific symptoms presented by Suhail in his emails, and to obtain a more accurate impression of what happened than he was willing or able to give. Contrary to my expectations, and I dare say to yours, Moore states that it is not unusual for victims to survive a lightning strike. However, it is almost impossible to get away with being uninjured altogether, even if the injuries are not evident straightaway.

The time it took Suhail to get across the bridge and contact me after the day in question was, in all probability, sufficient for all his injuries to become apparent. It is nevertheless useful for me to be able to classify them in as far as possible. That way I know exactly what I'm dealing with, and what to expect, if and when he is found. According to medical experts, the physical effects of lightning are difficult to predict, and may be minor, moderate or severe.

Moore goes on to provide details of lightning injuries that would constitute a salutary reminder to all individuals living in an apparently high risk area such as this. I will not reproduce those details here since they are quite lengthy, and in any case, you are able to read them for yourself. My role is to establish precisely what kind of injuries Suhail is suffering from, using Moore's scale of severity.

It is clearly necessary to rule out severe injury, since this invariably consists of death by heart attack. If Suhail had nearly died of a heart attack he would certainly have said so. Since he did not complain of a pain in his chest, we may assume that his heart didn't recover automatically from arrest, and since he didn't complain about burns, we must assume that he didn't have any. Therefore it is also necessary to rule out moderate injury. However, Moore goes on to say that even though death usually only results from a heart attack, even minor injuries can lead to long-term, detrimental effects like pain, diminished mental ability and psychological damage. There may even be changes in personality that lead to suicide.

Suhail states that his back is painful, and demonstrates decreased mental function. Whether or not he is suffering from psychological damage, or should I say further psychological damage, he is clearly confused and disorientated. He is experiencing memory and motor problems, if not paralysis. Moore quotes the National Weather Service statement to the effect that mental problems experienced by anyone who survives a lightning strike are <u>functional</u> – to do with how the brain works – <u>not anatomic</u>. This is where Moore offers the useful comparison between computers and brains. A computer that had been subjected to an electric shock might look fine, but it would not function very well. The same goes for a person who, without appearing to be changed in any way, might suffer from loss of memory and have difficulty processing information.

Suhail is damaged then, but not structurally or anatomically transformed. This evidence confirms that what happened to him was not what he expected, but it is important to remember that he would not admit defeat and that he is still out there, looking for his brother and willing to risk further injury to them both.

The next section of the report, sub-titled 'Lightning statistics', emphasizes the fact that although there is only a 10% chance of death resulting from a lightning strike, there is a 90% chance of injury. Injuries can occur in 5 ways, including by virtue of a direct strike, a side splash from another object such as a tree or a lamppost, and a ground current. Alternatively, it is possible for injury to result from being part of an upward streamer. This happens when lightning travelling from cloud to earth is met, or attached to another bolt travelling upwards through the victim from earth to cloud.

A difference of opinion emerges here. Moore asserts that the figure in the photograph that we have reasonably assumed to be Suhail was hit by a direct strike. On the other hand, Kay asserts that the same figure is more likely to have formed part of an upward streamer. It might be necessary to listen to some of Kay's reasoning, if it can be referred to as such, because the mode, as well as the severity of the injury could have a bearing on the victim's fate. Kay will certainly imply that it does, and in doing so will come dangerously close to reifying Suhail's theory about what happens to the body when it is struck by lightning. At this point it will be important to recall Moore's simple statement that 'the pathology of lightning ('keraunopathy') is little known.'

This is the case despite the fact that incidents such as Suhail's are reasonably common. Ignorance is attributed to the notorious under-reporting of lightning strikes. This in turn is attributed to the fact that the effects are frequently delayed, and are limited to isolated individuals.

Indeed, if Suhail had company, as he says he did, why was his case not reported directly? It was only reported indirectly because someone took a photograph and that person, it transpires, was some distance away and not aware that Suhail was there.

The photographer, Errol Jonston, is also referred to as a 'storm-chaser' and 'sole witness' although he did not witness the event as such. Using a 'window clamp tripod for safety' he took the picture through his car window, but he did not notice the contact until he subsequently scanned the image and enlarged it for printing.

You will note that this same image that over-stimulated the imagination of certain lay people and members of the press was computerized before it was printed, and only revealed its true subject when it was blown up.

Moore's description of what the picture showed, once Jonston had finished with it, confirms Suhail's statement in the 03.11pm email of June 24th that he was running on the beach when he was struck. Moore sensibly attributes the blurring of the photograph – characterized as being slight – to this fact but others, including Kay do not. Kay attributes it, as we will see, to nothing as obvious as running. But for now, suffice it for me to draw attention to Jonston's protests regarding the authenticity of his computerized image. Having chastised the victim, unknown to him, for running on a beach, close to water during a storm – "for a start you are the tallest thing in the area which is not a good idea" – he then proceeds to defend himself against the suggestion that his photograph might in any way have been tampered with, altered or faked: "I never manipulate my photographs digitally either by putting elements in or taking them out" he says. "I am personally opposed to digital composites and manipulation even where they are admitted to openly."

We could be forgiven for suspecting that he protests too much. Finally, Jonston adds that his photograph describes an event that happened, but that could not be seen with the naked eye. I doubt that. I really do.

Before I move on to Kay's far more suspect account of what occurred that night, I intend to honour the remainder of Moore's report. This provides simple, easy to understand information to support existing victims, prevent the accumulation of more, offer basic treatment suggestions and above all counteract the sheer scale of under-reported lightning incidents.

Unfortunately, Kay has obscured the name and address of the international victim support group listed by Moore. It is hard to see why. Perhaps it was based in the area, or perhaps it was merely spite. Kay offers nothing as useful as Moore's lightning prevention measures, which include paying due attention to weather forecasts and general environmental conditions before embarking on outdoor activities. They are guided, as you will have read, by the 30-30 rule which states that if the time between seeing lightning and hearing thunder is under 30 seconds, the situation is dangerous. Anyone finding themselves in this situation is advised to seek shelter.

I don't think Suhail was aware of the 30-30 rule, but even if he had been he was only interested in lightning, and paid little or no attention to thunder at all. Unlike normal people, he sought to avoid shelter and to make himself as big rather than as small as possible. He might at least have put his hands over his ears instead of waving his arms in the air. If he had, I would not have had to put up with his complaints about earache. He was not interested in obtaining medical treatment either. Perhaps he thought he deserved to suffer.

§

It will not be necessary for us to follow Kay's argument in full. It is long, digressive, obtuse and fanciful. 'Of Murder and Metamorphosis' feeds parasitically on Moore's report, and like the article about cloning, it consists of bad, irresponsible journalism that is not even worthy of an already dubious name. Moore's report, it seems to me, is an exception to that rule. In fact, Kay displays traits in her writing and thinking that are worryingly similar to Suhail. The comparison is, I'm afraid, a considered one. They both eschew what is obvious and pursue, by direct or indirect means, what is impossible. As I have said, it is one thing to do this, but quite another thing to claim that in doing it you have discovered or uncovered the truth.

Whereas Moore was able to verify the fact that Suhail was indeed hit by lightning, Kay has not uncovered the truth about what happened to Suhail as a <u>result</u> of being hit by lightning. Quite the opposite. She has buried it, and it will be necessary for me to dig it out. I feel no compunction to treat Kay's text with the same respect as Moore's. I will intervene freely and cut it down to a more appropriate size. I will, for the last time, clarify, contradict and correct another tiresome account of the transformative effects of lightning, which is not only speculative, but pathetically optimistic.

Many of the problems associated with Kay's article are evident in the first paragraph, which follows immediately after Moore's conclusions regarding the treatment of lightning victims – 'always treat the apparently dead first.' Kay ignores all such advice, sets aside the news element of Moore's report, and focuses instead on the role of the photograph that she sees fit to keep from our eyes. You will note that 'lightning' and other key words are highlighted throughout Kay's text. I believe they were originally intended to be links to other online sources. In any case, this is how Kay begins:

*No one could have predicted what would happen as a result of this competent news report, or rather as a result of the intriguing image that gave rise to it. As is now so widely known, the photograph of a **lightning** strike which was at the time apparently invisible to the photographer, has itself become something of a myth. What I could* *never have predicted, having researched this myth of murder and metamorphosis in order to debunk it is how, albeit in a completely different form, it would come to seem credible. What follows is not ostensibly about an incident that occurred on June 17th -----. In any case, so far as the police are concerned there was no incident because there was no body and for that matter no survivor. What follows then is an investigation into the effects of a **lightning** strike as they are manifested in the photograph and as they may therefore be said to have occurred on June 17th. This investigation into the **optical** effects of **lightning** uses the tools of science, myth, and media studies (an under-rated discipline in my view) to arrive at an unexpected conclusion.*

This is a lengthy paragraph. Allow me to clarify it to the best of my ability. <u>S. J. Kay intends to ignore the obvious facts of the case in order to assert that Suhail's fate can somehow be ascertained from the image alone</u>. This is the same image that Moore described as being 'slightly blurred,' and that we know to have been computer enhanced, if not manipulated. Evidently, Suhail is not the only person who has a tendency to read far too much into things, like photographs, that are really quite simple. I did not think that I would have to endure the fruits of such illogical labour again. I did not think that, once more, I would have to navigate such a hotchpotch of disciplines if, indeed, media studies can be called a discipline, which I very much doubt. Kay does no service to science by combining it with myth and worse, with a pastime – I will not even call it a pursuit

233

– that is utterly pointless. She does no service to knowledge, and certainly not to the truth, expected or otherwise.

Reason and common sense would lead most people to expect a lightning strike to have damaging if not fatal effects on the individual who is struck, and Moore's report broadly supports this. On the other hand, Suhail based his expectation on what would normally be considered to be an unexpected outcome, namely transformation. It may be surmised from his final email that he held on to this expectation in the face of his own pain and suffering. For whatever reason, Kay also seeks to liberate lightning from its origins in the myth and science of destruction. I do not doubt that the reason is highly unprofessional, and is related to the desire to court controversy, and if possible to create another sensation. Where ever possible, we will distance ourselves from Kay's opinions on this matter.

There is however, one small point we cannot ignore, since Kay bases an entire argument on it:
Janichius in 1606 says that **lightning** kills "by very rapidly penetrating the pores and viscera of the body and changing all its parts very quickly".[1]
Should lightning fail to kill, Kay asserts, the body would be left with *its pores and viscera penetrated and all its parts changed*.

The only fact that Kay doesn't ignore is the fact that 9 times out of 10 lightning does not kill people. So contrary to what Moore argues with reference to the National Weather Service analogy between a brain and

234

a computer, Kay implies that the changes that take place in a lightning survivor are in fact anatomical after all.

Kay is all too eager to regard the phenomenon of lightning as one that combines the properties of physics with those of magic. She presents us with the apparent conundrum that although lightning is electrical, lightning injuries should not be treated in the same way as high-voltage electric shock injuries.

Why? Because the injuries are different.[2] *Why? Because* **lightning** *is special.*

I don't think so. I really don't. Suhail believed that, and nothing special has happened to him. Kay is wrong. I will prove it to you.

§

In the second part of the article, 'Of Murder and Metamorphosis,' Kay concentrates on what is, allegedly, so special about lightning and in particular, forming part of an upward streamer. This assumes, of course, that Suhail formed part of an upward streamer when he was struck. It is hard to verify this with a blacked out photograph. I am prepared to summarise a few of Kay's general points but she has a tendency to create fantasies around them, and this tendency is too familiar. I won't tolerate it. Here is an illustration of how lightning is generated, and how an upward streamer is formed. It might be useful if you replace the tree with an image of Suhail in your mind. You might use Moore's description to guide you – the one of him running with his arms raised, 'torso forwards and head thrown back.'

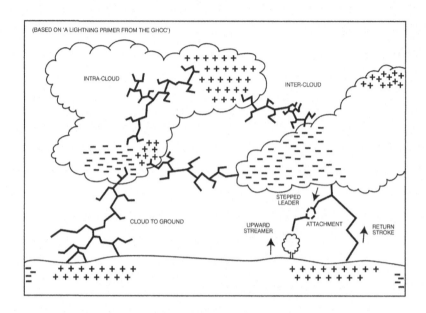

(BASED ON 'A LIGHTNING PRIMER FROM THE GHCC')

I believe that Suhail described the generation of lightning in his journal, so I will not repeat the detail here. I am sure you are quite capable of understanding this simple diagram which confirms one of Suhail's claims at least, namely that as the lightning bolt descended from the cloud it detected him. He was caught, if not exactly chosen.

It became possible for him to form part of an upward streamer when the passing thunderstorm that occurred on the night of June 17th altered the current in the ground from a negative to a positive charge. Quite simply, the negatively charged lower portion of the cloud that passed over him inevitably generated its opposite. This newly generated positive charge could have flowed upwards through a tree or a building but there were no trees or buildings and so, Kay alleges, it flowed upwards through Suhail. As it did so, it formed an attachment with the stepped leader. Kay's illustration is schematic. I include it in my file because it is the only representation available to me, but it is nevertheless a poor substitute for the original photograph.

Kay speculates that once the attachment was made, a return stroke, passing from the ground to the cloud, shot up through Suhail at the speed of light. This return stroke would not have been visible due to its speed, but it could have been perceived as a general brightening or flickering of the pathway. Did the original photograph capture this? It is not possible for me to say, and S. J. Kay declines the opportunity to do so, weakening her case as a result. Kay merely asserts that lightning is perceived to be a downwards movement from cloud to ground, whereas in fact most of the energy is spent in the opposite direction. I must say, it is hard to imagine Suhail expending anything like that much energy. He really only fantasised about it while he sat, increasingly motionless in his room.

Kay makes an argument in favour of one mode of injury by attempting to eliminate the others. You will recall that Moore listed 5 modes of injury. Kay's basis for the rejection of 4 of them is weak. For example, she claims that direct strikes generally affect those who are caught outside in the open, but it is difficult to walk away from them and remain apparently unharmed.

However, Kay is ignorant of Suhail's specific injuries and, unlike Moore, does not even attempt to classify what they might be. This ignorance is also evident in her elimination of ground current injuries, which are called step injuries, and are caused by the different electrical charge between one foot and another. Kay suggests that it is necessary for the step in question to be long and that therefore step injuries tend to affect large quadrupeds, such as cows and horses, more often than human beings.

Why, in this case, does Moore go to the trouble of including the Lightning Safety Group recommendation that a person caught in a storm should keep their feet together? Suhail was running and he might well have been hurt in this way. The only thing that militates against it is that he did not complain of a pain in his legs.

Suhail may not have been affected by splash and contact injuries, but Kay is wrong to reject blunt injuries. These result from the shock waves associated with lightning. They include damaged ear drums and pain caused by being thrown violently to the ground. I have presented evidence, in the form of the email transcripts that Suhail suffered in this way. Kay presents no counter-evidence.

Having arrived at the conclusion that Suhail became part of an upward streamer by means of a process of elimination that is clearly flawed, Kay then goes on to speculate about the kind of injury this might have caused. She is obliged to speculate because, by her own admission,

> the kind of injury caused by becoming an upward streamer is subject to ongoing research.

Indeed. We are again reminded of Moore's simple statement that the 'pathology of lightning is little known.' Unfortunately, Kay takes this as a license to invent. She presumes to re-invent pathology as something which has more to do with life than death. She becomes preoccupied, in a way which is disturbingly familiar, with the life-changing impact of lightning on cells.

Kay ignores the simple fact that lightning injuries differ from high voltage electrical injuries because the exposure time is much shorter, and because lightning is a current rather than a voltage phenomenon. Kay ignores the related fact that, by her own admission, lightning is so fast that it generally only causes superficial rather than internal injuries. Moreover, it is likely that, 'at least in wet weather', most of the flash bounces off the body in the form of a flashover. The force of a flashover is what accounts for those victims who end up having their socks blown off.

Suhail did not mention whether or not he was still wearing socks, but since it was raining when he was struck, and given the speed with which the lightning passed over his body it is, by Kay's own reasoning, unlikely that there would have been any meaningful, let alone mysterious internal injuries. If that is the case, why does Kay subsequently return to a historical figure of 1606 who spoke of pores and viscera rather than cells and tissues, and who claimed, but never proved, that lightning made them change? Who was Janichius in any case?

Janichius was right. When the body forms part of an upward streamer, death is avoided but change is induced, "very quickly." Modern science confirms the science of the ancients. Physics and magic are as one.

I cannot and will not accept this. I refuse to, point blank. When I think about it, I experience dizziness, nausea and other sensations that are unfamiliar to me. It takes a few moments to steady myself. I have to remind myself that Kay is not even a proper journalist, let alone a scientist and that therefore she is in no position to make such assertions. Kay's assertions are wrong. I reject them and so will you. I have no doubt.

Not only does Kay assert, without the authority to do so, that the effects of being part of an upward streamer were to transform Suhail's body anatomically, she also claims that these transformations are 'somehow' manifested in the photograph. This is absurd. It is doubly absurd. I remain confident in your opinion of this nonsense. If I didn't know better, I would be tempted to suspect that Suhail and Kay are related.

§

Shortly after the photograph was first published, it began to circulate to a wider audience. People must have shown it to their friends, and especially if the report was published online, it is easy to see how far it could have spread from its original location, and how fast. Kay claims that the status of the image itself was *transformed from a still, specialised picture in a local newspaper to a highly mobile, hyper-mediated event.*

I have no idea what hyper-mediated means and I intend to spare you the media studies phase of Kay's argument. It might, however, amuse you to hear of some of the idiotic interpretations made by certain sections of the general public. Kay discusses them at length, but in short, the basis of these interpretations is that the figure in the photograph – the figure of Suhail – is not blurred but doubled, with one form appearing to shadow or emerge from the other.

In one such interpretation which takes the form of a tampered image,

Zeus and his thunderbolt bearing colleagues can be seen to cleave a man in two for sins specified or not.

I presume that the image was digitally manipulated, or should I say further manipulated in order to achieve the desired effect. In another instance, the desired effect is to depict Frankenstein's monster emerging from his master's body as the lightning bolt strikes. I am unclear what this means. In yet another instance somebody has adapted the photograph to show a white-bearded scientist pointing his spark at Adam's head. An identical Adam emerges out of Adam's body. I believe this is a reference to the famous painting by Michelangelo of God giving life to Adam, but in this case God is replaced by the scientist, and Eve is replaced by a twin or a clone.

241

One person – anonymous of course – alters the photograph to show Mr Hyde coming out of Dr Jekyll's body although, to the best of my knowledge, that particular event was chemically rather than electrically induced. It is perhaps not quite so ridiculous for religious groups to have read the image as a literal sign of the soul departing the body, or as a symbol of supplication, if not of religious ecstasy.

I myself have never seen them, but Kay claims that these bowdlerised images have been printed on mugs, t-shirts and so on where they are invariably accompanied by puns and slogans which I will not dignify by repeating here. They have also been found on personal web pages, desktops, cards, cartoons and posters. This is possibly what Kay means by hyper-mediated.

Other customised versions of the photograph have circulated via mobile phones and email. Here, the victim of the strike is generally an individual who is despised by the image-maker. An ex-lover for example. There is also a looped computer animation which illustrates the instant reincarnation of a cartoon character reduced, by the thunderbolt, to a pile of ashes.

In the majority of cases, these images are presumed to be the work of a handful of computer literate youths. They are sensational, but we must surely question Kay's judgement that they are sufficiently influential to have generated widespread public interest and intrusion into the area where the original incident took place. If that is the case, we must also question her decision to censor the photograph and the related information provided in Moore's report. Indeed, Kay admits that by the time she wrote the article, there was already a decline in the number of images being produced. Public reaction was dying down, and only special interest groups – such as storm chasers – continued to adapt the photograph in order to promote their own activities and fantasies of indestructibility.

Having wrested the photograph from the hands of callous youths and those with nothing better to do with their time, Kay subjects it to her own interpretation. This is equally sensational and, I contend, no more worthy of being taken seriously. I am sure you will agree with me, and that you will not be fooled by Kay's attempt to substantiate her point of view with reference to an experiment conducted in 1905. This is only a minor improvement on 1606. Like Suhail, Kay clearly has a taste for going back in time.

The experiment is simple, and involves a spinning top and a darkened room. If you spin a top in a darkened room and light it solely with an electrical flash, it will look, for the duration of the flash, like it is not moving. That is it. It is a satisfying experiment in as far as it goes. It only seeks to prove that lightning creates an illusion. That which is in motion appears to be still. However, Kay chooses to misinterpret Professor Dove's experiment and reads far too much in to the anonymous paper that describes it. Because of this, she claims to have made a discovery far greater than his.

Professor Dove discovered that lightning could produce exactly the same effect as an electrical flash. He spun a multi-coloured top in a darkened room during a thunderstorm and found that each flash of lightning made it look like a motionless object with its colours distinct, not blurred as they would otherwise be. His entirely reasonable conclusion was that if they were illuminated by nothing more than a flash of lightning, the motion of "all bodies" on the surface of the earth would appear to be suspended.[3]

On the other hand, Kay claims to have discovered that what lightning does to the spinning top is not merely to suspend its motion but to make it appear exactly as it was before it was spinning.

*This appearance is not a lie or a distortion of the object. So it is not the case that **lightning** plays tricks on the eye but rather that it reverses the trick the eye plays by blurring something that is not blurred but simply in motion.*[4]

In other words, lightning does not create an illusion, as Dove's experiment suggests. Rather, it removes the illusion of blurring created by the human eye. What applies to the spinning top also applies to the figure in the photograph. Thanks to lightning, Kay says, we are able to see this as it was – free of the illusion created by our own eyes because it happened to be running. Kay's far-fetched conclusion is that the figure was not blurred at all. Rather, it was suspended and separated into its constituent forms, just as the top was suspended and separated into its constituent colours.

Just as the top has many colours, so the figure has many forms. It so happens that the camera has only captured two.

The figure in the photograph was not blurred? Ridiculous. Of course it was. Moore said so. Kay is wrong. Kay is, in fact, deluded. She does not know when to stop. She claims that what the photograph shows is no mere doubling. It is, she says, no sign of damnation or salvation as others have supposed. Rather, she maintains that lightning has revealed something more than that, 'something more like human evolution'. Absurdly, she claims that the figure in the June 17th photograph is evolving. It is changing. It is undergoing some kind of metamorphosis.

Lightning has lifted the veil from our eyes. It has revealed the transformation of a human being. It may even have caused it.

No. You surely cannot believe this any more than I do? This is an entirely specious argument. It lacks reason, common sense and logic and could only have been made by a woman. It isn't journalism, and it certainly isn't science. It is pure fantasy. I include it here only to denounce it and I trust, as I always have, that you recognise and respect my judgment. I have given you no reason to doubt it. Likewise, Kay has given you nothing to believe in. Nothing of substance. Nothing she can prove. Why would you give credence to Kay's argument instead of mine just because it sounds familiar? Just because it sounds like something Suhail would say. Something he did say. Surely this should cause you to be more suspicious of it, not less?

But you probably are. I am worrying unnecessarily. I am not myself. I do not feel well. My head is throbbing and I am overcome by the urge to vomit. I have bitten my lip, and there is a trickle of blood on my chin. I must calm myself. I must regain control. You have a sound mind and considerable wisdom. You are a first rate judge of character. You must be. It's your job. You do not easily believe in lies and fictions. I need not concern myself after all. I will proceed to the final part of Kay's article and the nature of the transformation that is alleged to have taken place.

§

Kay alleges that what happened to Suhail when he was struck by lightning began in his cells. She has clearly undertaken some degree of research here. As we have already seen with regard to Suhail's journal, a little knowledge is a dangerous thing. Only certain people are qualified to handle it. Suhail and Kay are not among them. They distort what little they know. They bend it to fit their own purpose. Kay wants to find proof that a transformation occurred, and so she does.

The quest for proof begins with the apparent discovery that although it is possible for cells to be destroyed by electrical forces, they are not necessarily destroyed. Apparently, we are to believe that they undergo a process whereby their membranes perforate and form transient pores, 'just as Janichius said.'

Allegedly, material is then transported from cell to cell via these pores. At least, it is if the electrical pulse is intense, but short 'as it is in lightning.'[5]

Here, Kay reinforces the point that she always seemed determined to make, namely the point that cell changes are, in the long or short term, physical. Moreover, should they fail to result in the death of the cell, or its host organism
they result in survival in an altered state.[6]

It is not hard to detect a note of self-satisfaction here. Kay has found exactly what she was looking for. Kay has found evidence of what she already believed in – that 'modern science confirms the science of the ancients' and that 'physics and magic are as one.' If you and I were to look hard enough, I have no doubt that we could find evidence of what we already believe in too. That does not necessarily mean that what we believe in is true.

It is important that you recognise what Kay says next as pure coincidence. Clearly, Kay and Suhail read similar books. There is no more to it than that.
*In addition to transporting material between cells, electrical breakdown of the cell membrane will trigger the **fusion** of cells if they are sufficiently close together.*

That wretched word again. I thought I had heard the last of it. I really did. Now I must contend with the additional fact that fusion may occur in all living cells, including those with a nucleus intact, as long as they are 'of a similar size.' Kay even provides a drawing which illustrates the fusion of two cells into one.

FROM KENNETH L WHITE 'ELECTROFUSION OF MAMMALIAN CELLS'

Cells 1 and 2 are aligned by an AC pulse and fused by a DC pulse.[7] First they move away from each other before approaching each other again and fusing.

There is, mercifully, no mention of anything to do with cloning here. Kay is not talking about cloning. She is talking about something that is, or could be even worse – the potential to create hybrid organisms. She is talking about actual living chimeras. She claims that there is experimental evidence that fusion led to the evolution of simple life-forms here on earth. More than that, it is still accounting for the development of complex life-forms, which I take to mean animals, humans, or a mixture of the two.

The conclusion to S. J. Kay's long article is clearly ludicrous. The point is made by virtue of being inadequately denied. Is Kay asserting that the June 17th photograph demonstrates the spontaneous generation of a human hybrid by means of lightning? Could this really be possible? No. Or rather, not exactly.

This is not science fiction, and anyway the process of hybridisation begins but does not end with two. We all exchange biological material, therefore we

248

are all transforming, we are all evolving, all of the time. I'm just struck by the analogy between this process and an image whose forms may as well be fusing as separating.

What forms? There were no forms in that photograph. There was only Suhail, and Kay does not know what happened to him. She has made it up and then found some facts to fit the fiction. Kay's proof is tenuous and she knows it.

Kay cannot really prove that anything as magical as metamorphosis happened to Suhail. So she claims that it is happening to us all. We are all involved. It is a reciprocal process. A process of exchange and of transformation. I don't think so. I am counting myself out. I am counting Suhail out too. When lightning struck him there was no-one with whom to reciprocate. No-one of the same or even 'similar size.' Suhail's brother is bigger than him, whatever he says, and whatever he says, his brother was not there. He was not there last time Suhail was struck, and believe you me he will not be there next time either. I know this as I know myself and I know myself better than you do.

I have been trying to tell you something but I do not think you have been listening to me after all. You have not made this easy for me and now you are siding with them. You are not the professional I took you to be and this is a disappointment to me. A great disappointment. You have allowed yourself to be taken in. You have given credence to fantasy and turned your back on reason. You have turned your back on me.

I thought that we were working together. I thought that we understood each other, but you understand nothing. There is blood and vomit on my chin and my right eye is swollen to a slit. My head is exploding and I dare not touch the skin on my face. I do not know if there is any skin on my face. As I said, I have been trying to tell you something, but you have not been listening.

On that note, did I mention Kay's conspiracy theory? I don't think I did. Kay questioned Jonston's claim that he didn't see the strike until after it had happened. She thought that Jonston and Suhail – 'the photographer and the photographed' – might have planned the photograph together. In other words, Kay thought the image had a hidden message.

It could have been suicide or it could have been murder.

Believe that and you'll believe anything.

I will now proceed to my closing statement and the last document in my file. It follows Kay's references, which might be of interest should you wish to be further convinced that she is right, and I am wrong.

§

References
1. A.J. Jex-Blake (1913) 'Death by Electric Currents and by Lightning', The Goulstonian Lectures, The British Medical Journal, March 15

2. Mary Ann Cooper, Christopher J. Andrews, Ronald L. Holle, and Raúl E. López (2001) 'Lightning Injuries', in P. S. Auerbach (ed) Wilderness Medicine, Mosby Inc.
3. 'Death By Lightning' (Originally Published 1905) http://www.oldandsold.com/articles21/science-39.shtml
4. Lightning sees movement better than the eye does, i.e. without distorting the object that moves.
5. Ulrich Zimmerman (1986) 'Electrical Breakdown, Electropermeabilization and Electrofusion', Reviews of Physiology, Biochemistry and Pharmacology 105, Springer-Verlag
6. See fig 16.1 in James C. Weaver (1992) 'Cell membrane rupture by strong electric fields: prompt and delayed processes', in R.C. Lee, E.G. Cravalho and J.F. Burke (eds) Electrical Trauma. The Pathophysiology, Manifestations and Clinical Management, Cambridge University Press
7. Kenneth L. White (1995) 'Electrofusion of Mammalian Cells', in Jac A. Nickoloff (ed) Animal Cell Electroporation and Electrofusion Protocols. Methods in Molecular Biology, Humana Press

Related topics:
Lightning
Photography
Optical
Fusion

Closing Statement

This is my closing statement and the last document in my file. I only have one final thing to report, and then I'll bring it in myself. I am wearier than I have ever been. I really am. But I remain confident that I've done a good job. My documentation is thorough. By the time I've finished I will have done everything I can to make a case for action, and I'll finally be able to hand my case file over to you. It will be a relief. It really will. I've done most of the work for you and I hope you appreciate that. In turn, I would ask you to do one thing for me.

In the course of my investigations using Google Earth, I happened upon what looked to me like a gas or electric plant. Now I realise that it might have been a nuclear plant or worse, a military base. My transgression was I can assure you, inadvertent. I thought a site like this would be blocked from satellite view, but in any case, I did not intend to spy on it. I was not spying on it. I was looking for Suhail. You know this. It would seem that the authorities elsewhere do not. I am asking you to intervene on my behalf. I think it is the least you could do. I have received a worrying email. Indeed, I would describe it as a threatening email. I am expecting a knock on my door at any minute. I am accused of something I am not guilty of. How was I to know what I was looking at? I could only see the tops of buildings and vehicles. I could only see that they were not residential or domestic. That is all. I was curious, I'll admit. I looked around for a while, but I saw nothing of any significance. I repeat, I saw nothing that should trouble anybody, and yet, they seem to think that I did. You must intercede as a matter of some urgency. There is no need for your colleagues to come. You need to hold them off, at least until I have completed my file. It will be in your interest to do so. It will not take me long, and then, as I said, I will hand it over myself.

All that is left for you to do is trace Moore's original, unedited report and combine it with the email transcript. Then you will know exactly where Suhail is. You could tell me, and I could go myself of course, but since there are so many beaches in that area, locating him will require more manpower. It's just a question of contacting the relevant police department overseas, updating them and requesting another search. I'm sure you can manage that. In his condition, Suhail will not have got that far. He hasn't left the area yet. I'm certain of this. I could go and help them identify him I suppose, but I'd rather stay here and assist you at this end. Whether you want me to or not.

I regret your tolerance for Kay's article. It only regenerates an excitement that had already died down. I maintain that the photograph simply offers proof that Suhail was struck by lightning after dark and injured. Those injuries were only minor on Moore's scale, but included pain (mostly in his back), decreased mental and motor function, some psychological damage and possibly an alteration in personality. I do not mean to make the slightest concession to Kay here. I only mean to reinforce Moore's point that there was no change in Suhail's anatomy, but some change in his mental state. Following the incident on the beach, and despite his physical frailty, he determined in the end to detach himself from me. The Suhail I knew could never have done that.

Returning to the photograph, and again contrary to what Kay suggests, I contend that the photographer's involvement was in fact purely incidental. He certainly made himself scarce after the image was published but the only thing this indicates is that he may well have tampered with it. I do not doubt that Jonston inadvertently captured lightning as it struck Suhail, but on discovering this, in the darkroom, he may have been tempted to embellish his picture for even greater effect. I contend that what happened then was that its effect exceeded his expectations, and he became nervous at the prospect of being found out.

I do not know this for a fact, but I do know that there is no hidden message in the photograph. If its mass circulation and misuse by gullible fools is an insult to the truth, then Kay's assertion that it somehow mysteriously captures the optical effects of lightning is a travesty. She has wilfully misread what the image shows, and this is merely, as Moore reports, that Suhail was struck down by a bolt of lightning.

Let me state for the last time that there is no connection whatsoever between what Errol Jonston's photograph shows and the culmination of Suhail's fantasy of reversing what happened inside the supervisors' car. Even Kay does not speak of a transformation in which the subject's destiny is reversed. If Jonston did fake this photograph, if he did create a shadow form, then he did so for his own reasons. If he didn't fake it, then it was merely blurred, as Moore says.

So in direct opposition to what Kay says, we should not connect but rather disconnect the photograph, the photographed and the photographer. There was no conspiracy. The photographer had no idea who Suhail was, and the photograph shows only what the human eye can see. The human eye cannot see microscopic processes involving cell fusion, whether they result in reprogramming one individual, or creating a hybrid out of two.

The microscope may reveal the optical effects of simulated lightning, or of electrical pulses on our cells and nuclei, but the camera can at best match the ability of the real thing to visually suspend a form in motion. Professor Dove would have been appalled at the way in which S. J. Kay interpreted his spinning top experiment. The camera is of course more commonly used to reveal the after-effects of a lightning strike on the surface of the body. Lightning photographs are of lightning itself, and they can be of people with burns and torn clothing. Lightning photographs are rarely, as in this case, of an actual contact with someone, but they are never of invisible internal processes manifested externally. How could they be?

Kay's half denied suggestion that the June 17th photograph 'somehow' constructs an analogy between the fusion of cells and the unification of two figures as they are struck by lightning, echoes the desperate delusion of a guilty man. Suhail was led astray by his own research, his own obsession, and his own immorality. He made the mistake of believing in stories, and he allowed himself to do this even at the expense of others. He was wrong. Kay was wrong, and so too are you.

Suhail is already much more damaged than he is transformed, and any subsequent lightning strike can only compound this fact. Moreover, what has happened to him has only happened to him, and if he thought to grasp his brother at the moment of impact and in the misguided hope of a fully scaled-up miracle, then the lightning beat him to it and he failed. Should he try again, he will fail again.

And what about Saeed? I am accused of being his spokesman after all. What would he make of Suhail's plan? Suhail claims that he devised the plan. This is nonsense. Why would he? Why would he conspire to re-create an event that ruined his life? He was struck down once because of Suhail. I can see no reason why he would consent to being struck down again. Far from seeking to be united with the brother who tried to kill him, I contend that he might have been hoping for a more satisfactory separation. The matter is, however, still unresolved.

You will note that there are very few details of Saeed's so-called accident in Suhail's journal. He tells us next to nothing about Saeed's injuries, and the surgery his brother had to undergo in order to repair the damage to his face. Having spent some time considering the nature of Suhail's injuries, let me now restore some balance and correct his omission for the record. It may yet be relevant.

When Suhail kicked Saeed out of the car, the sharp protruding end of the chrome bumper, which should have wrapped tightly around the rear panel, almost removed a semi-circular flap of skin and flesh from his face. Suhail said that the scar criss-crossed his cheek, but it didn't, not until the surgeons revised it, or opened it up again more than a year later. No. It was a curved flap and it hung open, covering his ear and exposing the muscles and other soft tissue inside. The face is well served with blood vessels and bleeds copiously when lacerated. This helps to clean the wound.

The impact did shatter his cheekbone, or more precisely it fractured his zygomatic arch, meaning that it pushed a section of his cheekbone area inwards. This was surgically repositioned but again, not until later, when the swelling and bruising had subsided. Saeed tried to hold his own face together while he waited for the ambulance. Everyone else was too busy running around him, screaming or fainting. He felt the open wound with his fingers. It was warm, wet, lumpy and slippery. He traced its edges, locating the flap, which he closed back over using the flat of his hand.

It may have been the shock, but most of the pain came later, in the hospital, when they re-opened, irrigated, debrided, excised and then sutured the cut. The bumper was old and rusty. The edges it made were not as clean and even as those of, for example, a windscreen. You cannot stitch damaged or serrated skin. You have to cut the damaged areas off and make neater edges, which fit together properly and heal, leaving a smooth scar.

This scar crossed three areas or aesthetic units of Saeed's face as it stretched from his eye, across his cheek and down to the corner of his mouth. It touched the outside of the orbital unit, bisected the zygomatic and buccal units and entered the labial. It was deep, but thankfully not deep enough to cut any branches of the facial or trigeminal nerves, which fan out from the ear down to the jawbone, across the cheek and up through the temple. The scar started off smooth but became hypertrophic, meaning that it was raised, red and shiny. Eventually it contracted, as scars often do, pulling the corner of the mouth upwards and creating a heaped-up and uneven appearance in the damaged part of the face. This is the effect of what surgeons refer to as an avulsion flap, and it forms as the scar heals. It cannot be revised until the healing process is complete and the scar tissue is what they term quiescent.

Seventy-two stitches were removed after five days and replaced with tape. After that, a second lot of photographs were taken, before and after the cheekbone fracture was corrected. Facial injuries are always very well documented using standardised equipment, lighting, and viewpoints. Photographs help surgeons to plan their operations and assess their effectiveness. They are useful documents, and are necessary for the compilation of medical records. However, they are also a further trauma to the patient whose hair is clipped back and who is forced to subject their deformed face to a sequence of humiliating poses:

look forward, look to the side, smile, look down and look up.

To correct the avulsion flap, Saeed had to look mainly to the front and side. To correct the bone fracture he had to look mainly down and up. His face was also palpated and inspected from behind, with his head back. This allowed the surgeon to visually confirm the sunken cheekbone revealed in an earlier x-ray. The operation involved the Gillies temporal approach, the aim of which was to restore the contour of his face by applying an equal and opposite force to the one that caused it to collapse. In short, they made a cut above and behind his right ear, inserted an instrument something like a broad chisel or narrow spatula through the hole, slipped it underneath the depressed bone and sharply snapped it back in to position. It wasn't fixed with wires or buttresses and he was told it would just stay there.

The contraction of the scar, particularly around his mouth, had the most marked and negative effect on others, as Suhail clearly demonstrates. It made Saeed appear sinister and grotesque, frightening some and repelling others. For his doctors, it was merely an ectropion of the upper lip, which required surgical correction by means of an ingenious technique called a z-plasty. A z-plasty lengthens a contracted scar by breaking up and dispersing its line of tension. If this is the line of the contracted scar pulling on the corner of the mouth:

/

Then the surgeon re-opens it and makes two further incisions at an angle of sixty degrees in order to form a z:

The flaps a anᴜ ᴊ are then opened and the fibrous tissue which forms immediately underneath and parallel to a superficial scar is also cut to release the tension on the mouth. The flaps are then closed again and sutured.

Provided that the central limb of the z falls in the natural crease running along the bottom of the cheek to the corner of the nose, then not only does the mouth fall back in to its normal place, but the scar itself becomes more difficult to see. If Suhail continued to see it after this operation, he was probably only looking at the image of Saeed he had fixed in his own mind. Scars do fade considerably with time, and through procedures like this they can almost be persuaded to disappear. Quiescent scars are very pale.

Even after the surgery to correct the displacement of his mouth, Saeed still had the problem of the raised and pebbly tissue on his cheek. This particular deformity is referred to as the trap door effect. It is caused by the converging forces of contraction in a semi-circular scar or avulsion flap, thus:

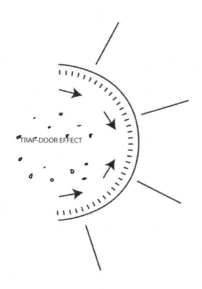

TRAP-DOOR EFFECT

Correction is by means of the excision of the scar and surplus tissue inside the trap door and by further z-plasties. This is how Saeed got the jagged scar across his face that Suhail describes. However, when this healed it was very well disguised.

Following that, Saeed underwent a surgical planing procedure – dermabrasion – to further improve the texture of his skin and balance the levels either side of the scar. The damaged skin is literally stripped away, planed off by something resembling sandpaper. Sometimes it is actually sandpaper and it certainly was when the technique was developed back in the 1940s. The raw exposed flesh is vulnerable to infection and must be kept moist, like a burn, but after a few days, fresh skin starts to grow back. This new skin will always remain sensitive, and prone to pigmentation problems.

All of this surgery did, as Suhail suggests, take several years. But you will note that he says nothing about the physical and mental suffering that his brother must have endured as a result. He seems concerned only with his own suffering and that, surely, is unforgivable? He lacked empathy and was not willing or able to put himself in Saeed's place. However, it is possible for us to do this now. What is it like when, through no fault of your own but in fact because of somebody else, your face is severely damaged and deformed? For a start, although it is true that facial injuries, like lightning injuries, are rarely if ever fatal, they are still among the most traumatic. Why? Because sooner or later, Saeed had to look in the mirror and he would not have recognised himself. At all.

He had been told he was handsome, and so he did not know how else to be. When he looked in the mirror before the accident, the mirror showed him what he expected to see and all was well. He saw the same reassuring reflection in other people's eyes, but when he looked in the mirror after the accident he didn't recognise what he saw and his mind screamed out. He saw this silent scream in other faces too. One in particular looked at him only once, and then turned away, leaving an indelible impression of horror in his mind.

What do you suppose you do with that? How exactly do you assimilate that? Answer – you don't. It destroys you. It destroyed him. Saeed dissolved each time he looked in the mirror, and that was many times a day. He couldn't stop himself. Those around him stifled their screams in pragmatism. When they looked at him, they saw a correctable condition. They had to. He was only young. Hardly even a man. They could not see him as he was now, but he could no longer be as they saw him.

Certainly, his face was restored. To an extent. But by then it was too late. Never mind the flashbacks, never mind the surgery. He had already disappeared. There was no Saeed. He was lost. He had changed. Irreversibly. I looked for him, but I couldn't find him. I would have brought him back. I tried to get him back, but eventually I stopped trying. If the man won't come to the face, then the face must go to the man. So what is the face of revenge? It is what Suhail saw when he looked in the mirror. I trust that you are not confused. This is very simple.

If you were Saeed and your face and identity had parted company, what would you do? You would attempt to bring them back together again? I've told you, I tried that and there was no going back. So you go on. You have a new identity. It may not be a pleasant one, but that is not your fault, and you still have to live with it. To make things more comfortable, you set about giving your new identity a new face.

I will not tolerate any confusion! I really won't! Despite the fact that you have not made things easy for me, I have taken some trouble to make this easy for you. All right, this new face is an adaptation, and it takes time to perfect it. Once it is perfected it makes you feel whole again and happy, or almost happy because it is after all a built face and it needs a lot of maintenance or else it will degrade. Perhaps it degrades anyway, and when you look in the mirror you see the monster again. Then what? No? What was the fate of Saeed and his mismatched face when he left home and disappeared? Where did he go? What happened to him? He needed a new face so he got more plastic surgery. I hardly think you need to be a detective to work that out.

It is also possible to guess where he went in order to obtain the best plastic surgery with the minimum of questions asked. His face had to adapt to what his face had created, and he didn't stop until it had. This time the surgery made him feel better. It really did. You might even say that he was reborn. Every time they put him to sleep he woke up renewed. He was different, but more himself.

He had to pretend to feel anxious and depressed for a few days after each operation, because most people do. Most people are trying to create a perfect self, and they can't. On the other hand, he was perfecting a created self, and he could. They are not the same thing. Not at all. He also had to pretend to be vain, and concerned only with his own self-image rather than with how other people saw him, or rather, how other people would fail to recognize him. Surgeons have psychiatrists who work for them, and a surprising number of people who seek plastic surgery are, as they say, un poco loca, and in need of other kinds of help. Some really do cut off their noses to spite their own faces, but not me. I cut mine off to spite someone else's.

What else did I pretend? Oh yes, I pretended to trust my physician implicitly. I pretended to be a patient patient and an always grateful and satisfied one. I pretended to be looking for slight but specific improvements to minor but verifiable deformities which were either congenital or a residue of unsatisfactory surgery at home. It was an effort, but it wasn't that hard. I left suitable intervals between surgeries. I always followed pre- and post-operative guidelines and above all I was paying. If you are paying you can have any face you like, within reason. And as I said, I always acted with reason and common sense.

Just one thing – I could not shake off a marked sensitivity to pain on the right side of my face. Even consultations, which involved manipulating it, hurt a great deal. I need hardly say what my reaction might have been to being struck in the cheek by a heavy wooden oar, for example.

Back then, and in order to reach my goal, I learned not to react to pain or any other stimulus. In learning not to be there, I also learned my trade and so finally now you see that Saeed was my client and that I was Saeed. There is no Matt. There never was. I made him up. I made him, and I will detail how, but first you might like to know why.

Suhail destroyed my identity, and so I destroyed his. An eye for an eye. It's a tried and tested method. It took time of course. Careful planning. You'll grant me that, even now. Not everyone would wait ten years before they started, and then wait another ten before they finished. But I broke it down to achievable goals. These included a jaw reduction, cheek implants, a nose operation and skin bleaching. I ticked them off one by one.

The financial services sector is quite lucrative overseas, once you've worked your way up. Most of my transformations were admired by colleagues, except the last one. Many people bleach their skin but they often feel guilty about it. I couldn't explain why I had to be white, but I indicated a post-traumatic pigmentation disorder, and that seemed to satisfy them. At least it stopped them from asking about it any more. How could I do this to myself? What self? I was in between being Saeed and becoming Matt. Saeed had dark skin. Matt had light skin. Saeed was straight. Matt was gay.

I am aware of the legal implications, but you should not concern yourself with the small matter of incest. You really shouldn't. That was just a means to an end. I did not want to sleep with my brother, but it didn't matter what I wanted. I had a job to do, a head to hunt, a match to make. Any fool can see that it had to be done that way. Nevertheless, in case you are unable to, I will explain, to the best of my ability.

Suhail most desired and feared his own transformation. In order to deliver this to him and him to this, I had to be there. In order to enable him to destroy himself in the laughable hope of being recreated, I had to be a constant reminder of the reason why he was compelled to do it. I had to haunt him in the flesh. I had to actually be Saeed's ghost. I pushed him on. I fed his guilt and his obsession. I was the mirror in which he saw revenge and dreamt of reparation.

My disguise was just that. It was a thin sheet of glass he couldn't see through. It had imperfections of course, and more as time went on, but it didn't need to be perfect. It wasn't supposed to be perfect, and it wouldn't have worked if it had been. I think he began to see through it in the end. The disguise that is, not me. Hence his withdrawal and increased nervousness. Somehow he knew that he had been living with me all along. He had been sharing a bed with me for more than a decade. If the thought of finding me was the carrot, then my concealed presence was the stick. I had it covered, you see.

All right, I could have just befriended him. I could even have stalked him, but by sleeping with him I saw an opportunity to take something away. I took away the thing that made him different from me. I denied him his individuality as he, after all, was prepared to deny others. That, I need hardly tell you, was satisfying. That went back further, to before the accident, before which, since we're clearing the air, I knowingly failed to shut the car door properly. Then I goaded him, and got him to do what I wanted him to do. Rather, I got him to do what I thought I wanted him to do. My ability to think through the full chain of cause and effect wasn't quite up to the mark at that age. I got as far as seeing him incriminated, but not as far as seeing myself cursed with a lifetime spent trying to stop my face from falling off.

If that plan backfired, this one made up for it. He is right to indicate that the trouble was started on our first birthday. It was started on what should have been *my* birthday, not his. He stole it from me. He copied me. He made himself a copy of me and yes, it was a bad one. That was not apparent at first, but it did not take long to show itself. He dishonoured me, and ever since then, almost as far back as I can remember, he has never been out of my sights. Think of it as a twin thing.

I was going to say how Matt came to be. Matt who said he came from the mainland but was actually born elsewhere. He started to emerge when my lower jawbone was fractured, a small section of bone was removed, and my teeth and jaws were wired shut again for, as I recall, twelve weeks. That was something, not being able to open my mouth, brush my teeth or eat anything that couldn't be sucked up through a straw. It lasted for what felt like an eternity. I got very thin, I can assure you. If I'd left it for a while I might have been given those titanium plates and screws they use today, and I would have been able to speak and eat properly much sooner. But I didn't want to talk to anyone anyway, least of all to surgeons and orthodontists who were sceptical of my need for this operation. My jaws were not abnormally aligned, they said, and there was nothing wrong with my bite. True, but strong chins were a shared feature and mine had to go.

Matt didn't have a weak chin, exactly, but it wasn't the same. So I told them that it looked wrong to me, and that this had always affected my self-image, and my confidence. I told them that after the accident my cheekbone had not stayed in position as the doctors said it would. It was depressed, and my face was lop-sided. With a shorter jaw it wouldn't seem so long. With the balance of my face adjusted, I would feel a lot better in myself. I had to agree to have corrective cheekbone surgery again at a later date, but this was fine. This was what I wanted. So they did it.

I had not expected to have to wear a brace both before and after the operation in order to realign my teeth with my new jaw line, but this was obviously part of the treatment and I had to accept it. It was undignified having to wear a brace at the age of twenty-something, but not as undignified as what I'd already experienced and Matt would make up for that. Matt would make up for all of it.

Eight months after the operation I had perfectly straight teeth and a new smile. It was worth every uncomfortable moment. In fact, I wanted more. I felt good for the first time in a long time. I began to associate surgery with a positive sense of myself. I had a mental image of what I should look like, and it was beginning to take shape. I was working on the rest of my body too. I was building it up, jogging on the beach, going to the gym and eating more fresh food. I was amazed to see how much I could do and how much you can change the way you look. And I'd only just started.

The next phase, which happened about two years later, was the corrective surgery on my cheek. Since the zygomatic complex had not stayed in position,

I was told that I could either have it broken again and wired in to place, or opt for cheek implants. These would build up one side, and enhance the general appearance on both sides of my face. I chose the implants and the surgery. The effect of this choice was to further raise the profile of my face and change how I looked.

This time the relevant areas were accessed via the inside of my mouth. Once the right zygoma was fixed, solid implants were placed into pockets created between the skin and the cheek tissue. The right implant was fractionally bigger than the left to allow for slight degradation of the bone and to promote complete visual symmetry. For a couple of months afterwards, my face was swollen black and blue, but I'd learned not to care about this. I was used to it. I waited for the swelling and discolouration to subside and for my true identity to appear. Anaesthetics wear off and analgesics take over but there is no redemption without suffering. Pain is necessary. It is good. Suhail never understood that. Well, he probably does now.

Because they cut my mouth, I couldn't speak again for a while and when I did I sounded different. I began to sound like Matt. Of course, you can't exercise immediately after this kind of operation. The face is sensitive, even to a rise in blood pressure such as when you bend down to tie your shoelaces. During this period of inactivity I would plan what I was going to have done next. I would look in the mirror and the new face would immediately highlight the problem area, the alien feature. It seemed to single it out.

On this occasion it was my nose, which was clearly the wrong shape. Both the nostrils and the bridge were too wide. The plastic surgeon I consulted was forced to agree and I was cleared for a rhinoplasty. I should add that by then I had started to bleach my skin. I bleached it on my face, hands and in fact everywhere on my body. Matt needed a narrow, typically Caucasian nose and this is what he got. Flared nostrils are reduced very simply, by removing small wedges of skin from their base. The operation on the bridge of the nose takes longer and involves pulling the skin back from the supporting framework of bone and cartilage, chiselling the bone on top and to the side of the nose, pushing the sides in and then putting it all back together again.

More specifically, an incision the shape of an inverted v (⋁⋁) is made across the columella or the central bit of the nose which separates the nostrils. This doesn't leave a scar because it isn't a straight line and because the skin there is thin. Before that, they cut around the inside of your nose following the edges of the nostrils, or more precisely, following the margins of the cartilage which gives them their shape. Then, by opening a pair of scissors inserted near the top of the cut, they separate the skin at the tip of the nose from the structure underneath.

The same happens in the columella, so that the scissors can then poke straight through it. The v-shape, having been drawn on with a pen, is then cut out in order to allow the skin of the columella to be lifted off from the end of the nose. The surgeon carries on up, separating skin from cartilage and pulling it back with small hooks. About half way up, the two strands of cartilage turn in to two strands of bone, and these are moved closer together in almost every rhinoplasty, which is probably why they all end up looking somewhat similar. If you think of the internal nose structure as a pyramid, it is narrowed both at the top and at the bottom, thus:

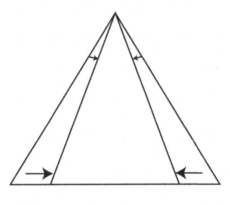

NOSE PYRAMID

To do this it has to be separated from the rest of the skull using a hammer and chisel. Two cuts are made towards each other, aiming for a point of convergence between the top of the bridge and the lower corner of the eye socket. The bone at the bottom of the pyramid is then pushed inward, causing the nose to break with an audible snap where the two cuts meet. Any sharp edges left over after the bones are repositioned are filed off, and the new nose is folded back down, sewn up, packed with dressing and covered with tape and a metal splint to hold it together while the bones heal. I'd swallowed a lot of blood during the operation and was

273

sick afterwards. The throbbing and stuffiness lasted for weeks, as did the black eyes and swelling. But when it was over I was pleased with the result. Surgeons say that the section of your face incorporating the eyes, nose, mouth and chin constitutes a magic triangle. Change this and you've changed everything.

I wore blue contact lenses which only had to be replaced once a month. They could be worn overnight, on most nights. They were soft and were supposed to allow my eyes to breathe, but protein deposits and bacteria built up and I had a number of eye infections. I don't need them now of course, but I couldn't wear them any more even if I did.

I don't wear make-up now either. This was useful once, even if it did give my skin something of a sheen. When you've had a facial injury, you are taught how to mix colours on a palette and match them with your own skin. I became quite the artist, especially since my colouring was constantly changing. It was becoming whiter all the time. They called it cosmetic camouflage, but my skin itself became cosmetically camouflaged after a while, thanks to the bleach. The active agent in skin bleach is hydroquinone. This works, eventually, even smoothing out fine lines and wrinkles, but there is a cost. Your skin becomes thin. You get white patches where the melanin producing cells have died, and you find yourself pursuing them around your body with still more bleach. Your skin dries, cracks and stings. Like my eyes, it became irritated and, in places, infected. I hardly needed Suhail to point this out to me. Now it no longer feels like a living organ. Some has sloughed off. I do not know what, if anything, will replace it.

Matt didn't always look like this. At first he was a triumph, but I couldn't hold on to this, however hard I tried. His blonde hair turned to straw after years of hydrogen peroxide. Although his mouth was full and symmetrical, his lower lip was affected by the jaw surgery. It became numb and he often bit his lip, as you have heard. His jaw clunked if he opened his mouth properly, so he tended not to, even when he spoke. Each new feature, a work of art in itself, was sharply sensitive to temperature and touch, so that he avoided such stimuli as much as possible.

Not just because of the temperature, but for other more obvious reasons, Matt didn't try to follow Suhail overseas. Neither, for the record, did I. I sent the lodger, whom Suhail called the visitor. I sent the ticket and the note. I sent someone to pick him up from the airport, and I also sent an outsourced stand-in who appeared to Suhail as the stranger. The visitor and the stranger are as one. That is, the one Suhail saw in the hotel foyer, the aquarium, the museum and elsewhere. He is the one who left messages, and was on the beach that night. He was my look-a-like, and my brother's. He happened to be a trained actor. He smiled as Suhail ran towards him with his arms outstretched, moments before he was struck. I think this affected him. I think he found it hard to walk away and leave Suhail lying there, injured. But he did.

Neither he nor I knew anything about the photographer, and neither of us exactly ordered the thunderbolt at that precise moment. Of course not. But we knew it would come. He stood up slowly, waving a light. He lit his own face, but not until Suhail was in sight. Not until the lightning had already detected him. I can't take too much credit, but the plan was neat, you have to admit, and it succeeded. I wonder if Suhail has a scar where his skin took an imprint of what hit him. I don't know, he didn't say. What goes around comes around Suhail. You can't undo it. You can't go back. Things catch up with you. I caught up with you. I found you long before you found me. I won. I was always going to. Matt, who never existed, is redundant now and his condition might be terminal. Saeed may be lost for good but so, brother, are you. You could not have wanted this more than me. You had to want this, but not more than me. They say that lightning never strikes in the same place twice.

This is a confession, in case you hadn't noticed, and I've nearly finished, but not quite. I am not confessing to attempted murder, and least of all, to attempted metamorphosis. I wouldn't give Kay the satisfaction. That much is obvious. I'm confessing only to the act of revenge. The outcome, it would seem, is not entirely in my control. You've read the emails. You know as much as I do about what happened to Suhail after he was struck. Where this is concerned, I prefer to focus on before rather than after. Before was a straight line from accident to accident. I plotted it well. BANG. Down he goes. And when he gets up, slowly, painfully, he does not know where or what he is. He is cast out and no longer by choice. He is alone, destroyed, finished. I thought it would be finished. I thought I would be free, but I had to know for sure that my plan had worked. I had to see the effect of so much effort with my own eyes, and I cannot say that it was entirely what I had expected. Not entirely.

As I said, I had not expected him to detach himself from me before I was ready and I had let him go. I had not expected this to pull on me as if my feelings for him were real, or were actually mine rather than Matt's. I got confused. Matt got confused by the strength of Suhail's demand to know where the beach was, where Saeed was. How should he know? It made him feel bad. It made him want to stop Suhail from going back. It made him want to stop Suhail from going on looking for someone who wasn't there. But Matt couldn't stop him and because it was too soon, perhaps only a moment too soon, he is still pulling and I am not free. With things as they are I cannot see when I will be. Hence my need to tell you this. It is not wholly for your benefit. You are here to help. I have helped you, and now you must help me. Take him in or take me in. I no longer care which. Either way it is your job to end this. You must end this. You must stop us from chasing each other around in an ever-increasing circle.

There is one more thing. It is a confession within a confession if you like. There was another crime against the individual that you might wish to pursue. Do you recall Bridget? Of course you do. I spoke to her after Suhail left. Since she had tried to contact him, I thought she might want to know that Suhail was missing – presumed dead. I said presumed dead so that I could sympathise with her loss. I wanted her to talk. I wanted to find out what had happened, although I assumed that nothing had, and she'd been let down. I assumed that she had been tricked by her sham fertility specialist and, to an extent, I was correct. He had deserted her, after he'd taken her money. He had not followed through on his promise but others, it transpired, had. She announced, in a loud triumphant tone that caused me to have to remove the receiver from my ear, that she now had a beautiful and healthy baby girl she had named Dee. Dee, she said, was perfect in every way and not just because she resembled her mother. She was big then, but she was loved every bit as much as the nephew who could never be replaced. That was another thing we had in common – loved ones who could not be replaced.

Bridget's daughter reminded her of Rafe. She was born with ginger hair, although it had turned blonde, just as her own hair had, at the same age. Dee liked nothing more than being lifted up and spun around. She laughed and shouted and spun round and round, just like her cousin. This was a touching image, I had to agree. I asked who had helped her, and she said she couldn't tell me even though I was her best friend's long lost brother. Best friends? They hardly knew each other. She hardly knew him. Not like I did. She thought she knew me though. She thought I must be all right if I was related to Suhail. She told me that there was an embryologist whose surname began with A, and a cell biologist whose surname began with C. This might be useful for you. I asked where they'd done it and she said here, of course, in the country that developed IVF. After all, she said, cloning is only IVF with a twist. IVF with a twist? I don't think so, do you?

I also found out that they used a private fertility clinic, and that her sister did act as a surrogate. If Suzy gave birth in a hospital, you might be able to trace this. She is better now, although Bridget will never forgive herself for what happened to Rafe. I said it was a tragic accident, although we both knew it was neglect. I said I was pleased that everything worked out for her in the end, and she thanked me, though you and I know that she has only compounded her crime. Like Suhail. She could, of course, have been lying. She might have made it all up because she was deluded and deceptive. However, she claimed that there was a write up, a report like the one that was published about that sheep. She said it had been posted, anonymously, online. I checked, and it was there. You can read it if you want to but I don't think it proves that much:
http://www.casefile.org.uk/1_protocol.html
A child may have been produced by the same unnatural means, but didn't the sheep – Dolly – die too young?

Speaking of which, you had better look at the full text of S. J. Kay's article, or at least the section containing Moore's report:
http://www.casefile.org.uk/news_report.html
She did censor it, I wasn't lying about that. I lied about not being able to find the original. Here is your clue. It will lead you where you want to go, presuming that you want to see Suhail before it's too late. If you would rather see me first, then check here for my address:

http://www.casefile.org.uk/Building_notice.html
I will be waiting. You can even read that story if you want to, the one that Suhail never got published. I published it for him in the end. It wasn't that bad: http://www.casefile.org.uk/Marcus_Florian.html

Now where was I? Yes, the touching image of B and Dee. You can see why I had to withhold it? It made something wrong seem right. Unfortunately, I've had no such control over the image my associate left me with. He continued tracking Suhail for a while after June 24th. He is back now, and no longer works for me. The last time he saw Suhail was on a particularly fine stretch of pure white sand, north of the beach he'd lured him to the first time. He had picked him up in the neighbourhood that morning, wondering around some houses. He spent the rest of the day watching him sleep under a palm tree. In his filthy torn clothes Suhail was, to all intents and purposes, a tramp. A storm started up in the afternoon, as they usually did, but Suhail didn't move until it was dark. Then he got up, walked to the edge of the water, turned and started to run. The storm continued into the night, as it did before. The storm was very close, as it was before.

At first I ran behind him. Then I circled out and caught him up, so that I was parallel, and at a distance of only ten or twenty feet. Then I stopped. As I glanced over in the direction of the sea, lightning struck him. For a moment he was frozen, but he was not alone. He filled my field of vision like a giant spinning top printed with life-sized photographs of a man in motion. In the last one, the one farthest ahead of me, his arms were no longer pumping. They were raised above his head in an attitude which could have been joy or surrender but which I had seen before, running straight towards me. He ran back to me as if nothing could stop him. I smiled then. I'm smiling now. That is not what I expected.

Biography

SARAH KEMBER is Reader in New Technologies of Communications at Goldsmiths, University of London. Her publications include *Cyberfeminism and Artificial Life* (Routledge, 2003) and *Inventive Life. Towards the New Vitalism* (Sage, 2006), and she is currently co-authoring a book on new media for MIT Press. She is an accomplished public speaker, delivering some mind-bending and sometimes tongue-in-cheek ideas with a totally straight face. A podcast of one of her talks was downloaded from iTunes U over 58,000 times. Sarah lives in Brighton.